For Charlotte

1

If the ugly man with the beard and the bacon sandwich had looked where he was going, Emily wouldn't have been trying on a white shirt in Ruffles Department Store, wouldn't have trodden on a sleepy spring wasp and wouldn't have run out of her cubicle wearing only a pair of pink knickers, straight into the arms of Sam Finch.

Sam had been looking for a birthday present for his sister. When Emily suddenly joined him, he took a heavy step backwards and closed his arms around her, a skirt in one hand, and for a few seconds he held her there, hot breath against his chest. He looked down at her bare shoulders and at the golden brown head tucked half inside his coat and knew he should give her up again, any longer and she'd think she'd thrown herself at the wrong sort of man.

'I'm sorry. There's a wasp in the changing room,' she told him, keeping her arms tight around his waist.

'It won't buy anything. They never have any money.'

'I'm not joking. It stung me. It hurts.'

'I'm sorry.'

'Hurts a lot.'

'I'm *really* sorry. Shall I find you some ice?' Ice? What was he thinking of? Where was he going to find ice?

She shook her head and let go of him and made a

quick dive back towards her cubicle, but as she opened the door the wasp flew out at her and she had to duck away towards the open shop floor.

The wasp went too, hovering in wait as she slipped behind a rail of coats, then zooming in on her the instant she re-emerged. It was like watching film from a police helicopter of a stolen car, Sam thought, one that bumped across ploughed fields, forged across rivers, demolished gates but was never going to get away.

Still holding the skirt, he went after her, followed at a trot by a fat, breathless sales assistant and a few grinning shoppers. Pinned against a range of tartan shirts, Emily was keeping one hand across her front and swiping wildly at the wasp with the other.

'Help me,' she hissed at the sales girl, who rifled hurriedly through the shirts, selected one, held it out to Emily and leapt back quickly.

'No, I meant kill it, stamp on it!' Emily cried. 'Stamp on it!'

As Emily pulled the shirt against her Sam stepped in, slapped the wasp against the wall behind her with his hand and then ground it into the floor with his boot.

The sales assistant glowed at him admiringly and smoothed back her hair.

Emily gave him a shy smile. 'Thank you. Again.' She turned quickly away and pulled the shirt over her head, stopped, hair tumbled around her face, and looked back at him.

'I thought so,' she said. 'It's even worse! I *know* you . . . It's Sam!'

He smiled. 'Hello, Emily.'

They looked at each other, neither knowing quite what else to say.

'This season, I shall mostly be wearing pink pants,' Emily said.

He laughed, thinking how those pants were going to be etched upon his brain for evermore.

'You can wear this if you want to.' He held out the skirt and she looked at it dubiously.

'Do you still want ice? There'll be a cafe somewhere. Or I could find a first-aid box?'

'I think I'd better go and get dressed. I'm going to be late for an interview.'

'For a job?'

'Yes, sort of. I hope so. I've a feeling it's more of a chat.'

'Then don't go. Come and have a coffee with me instead.'

She thought about it for half a second. 'I'd love to but I can't. It's the first chance I've had for ages.' She shifted restlessly from bare foot to bare foot and glared back at her still-fascinated audience of shoppers. 'I can't stand it. Talking out here like this. I have to go and get dressed.'

He nodded.

'But thanks so much, Sam. You were fantastic.'

She was back in control, wanting to be dressed, thinking about the interview, turning away from him, moving smoothly out of his life. But Sam still had the feeling of her in his arms. He desperately tried to think of something to make her stop, to keep her next to him for just a few moments more.

And then she did stop and turned back to him.

'Do you ever hear from Oliver?' she asked.

Not what he wanted her to say. He saw the interest in her face and felt old, familiar frustration rising inside him.

Sam nodded. 'Did you hear he's back from the States? For good this time, he says.' Why had he told her that? 'That's why I'm here. I came up from Cornwall to see him.'

'He's come back early?' She sounded thrown by the news.

Sam shook his head. 'No, he's done the year. Like he planned.'

'But it's gone so fast.' She still couldn't take it in.

'Well. Time flies. He's back again.'

'I had no idea. I can't believe it. And if I hadn't been stung, I'd never have come out. And then I'd never have seen you.'

And it's a good trade-off, is it? Sam thought sourly. A wasp sting in exchange for some news of Oliver.

She came back to him and touched the skirt bunched up in his hand.

'Say hi to him for me.' He shrugged and nodded, sure he wouldn't. 'And Sam – ' she was looking curiously at the skirt – 'tell him that I left my job.'

He gritted his teeth. 'OK.'

'And Sam – ' now she was smiling again as she tugged the skirt out of his hand – 'satin. Mmm.' She held it up in front of her. 'And with pleats too!'

'I could have got it in green and white, but then I thought the brown and yellow—' He saw the look on her face. 'But you don't like it, do you?' he groaned. 'It's horrible, isn't it?'

'Who are you buying it for?'

'My sister. For her birthday.'

He waited and Emily shook her head.

'Damn. Give me some advice, then.'

'Go across the road to Jigsaw. It'll be open now.'

'But I'm sure I could find something here. If you helped me.'

'There is nothing nice here. Trust me.'

'But you're here . . .' Sam said, unable to stop himself, cringing even as he said it.

She smiled up at him. 'I'm here because this was the only shop that opened at nine.'

Sam lost. Emily left him, running back to the safety of her cubicle. He put the rejected skirt back on a nearby rail and slowly looked around. Where before sales assistants had been thin on the ground, now it seemed as if they were all around him with dewy eyes and soft smiles of appreciation, watching the brave wasp assassin and his beautiful girl.

Sorry to spoil your enjoyment, he wanted to tell them, but we are not talking *Brief Encounter* here. Didn't you hear? She doesn't like my skirt and I don't think she likes me much either. But, until he'd seen her again, Sam had forgotten how it felt to have her glance at him, to be, for just a few seconds, the object of her complete attention. He looked across the floor to where she had gone and thought how lovely she was and how she looked no different to when she was sixteen, when he'd first met her, in Cornwall with Oliver.

He eyed her cubicle, thinking, this is too good a chance. I don't have to give up so easily. I am not going to give up so easily. Not again. He slowly circled the shop, wanting to put some distance between himself and the sales assistants, then strode over to the cubicle and put his head close to the door.

'You have got to help me,' he insisted. 'If you don't, it'll be my sister who pays the price.'

There was a pause, then a quiet 'OK'.

'I'll wait for you at the door.'

He turned away, delighted. But then an unfamiliar voice asked, 'Has she been taken hostage?'

'Oh, God.' He laughed, knifed with disappointment. 'Wrong changing room.'

When had she left? How could he not have noticed?

He moved away, aiming for the door, but even before he'd reached it he could see that it was too late. The streets outside were empty. She had gone.

In ten more minutes she'd be late. Twenty and they'd wonder if she was showing up. Thirty and they'd have their answer. It wasn't ideal but the wasp sting had been the final straw, that and running around the shop in her knickers – she who hated coming out of the changing room with new clothes *on* – and admitting to herself that she was wasting her time going to the interview anyway. And seeing Sam again. And hearing Oliver was home.

Emily stood on the street looking for a taxi but when one pulled up she mouthed an apology. She wasn't in a rush any more. She could walk to work in fifteen minutes and be at her desk for nine thirty. No excuses necessary.

She walked, thinking the same thing over and over again. *Oliver's home. I don't believe it, Oliver's back.* Every step she took he was with her, jostling her, making it impossible to think about anything else. And at first it wasn't the Oliver who had left England a year ago who was there at her shoulder, but the Oliver of eight years earlier. Oliver as she'd first met him, one late afternoon on a wide, empty, sun-streaked beach in Cornwall. She'd seen his shadow first, had watched it moving across the flat hard sand towards hers until it had taken over and become hers, and she had looked up, her heart already beating with anticipation. It was a vivid enough memory to make her falter and then stop in the middle of the street.

She imagined what he would say if he was standing in front of her now, his surprise and outrage when he realized where she was heading. *So you told Sam a lie! You haven't left your job at all! And you promised me you'd leave. How can you still be there when you promised me you would leave a year ago?*

Because I am too much of a wimp to leave without something to go to, Emily would tell him. And bloody hell, I didn't realize you were about to turn up again, did I? I didn't realize I'd run out of time. Because, you see, the longer I survive there, the more I have to make all those miserable days count for something. Yes, I want to throw up every time I see the front door, but I fought off hundreds of other people for that job and I'd be crazy to walk away from it just because of *her*.

And yet hearing that Oliver was home again threw everything into the air. There was no ignoring the fact that one whole year had gone by since she'd joined Carrie Piper's theatrical agency. When Oliver had left for the States she'd only just started. She remembered Oliver arriving to take her out one lunchtime in her first week, how he had shuddered at the cold, stagnant atmosphere, had listened to how miserable she was and had angrily sworn to send the boys around if only she gave the word. But she hadn't and those awful minutes and hours and days and weeks and months had now clocked up to a whole massive year, and nothing at all had changed apart from her, each day a little more dented and knocked and miserable than the one before.

She walked faster down the grey streets, stamping down on the pavement in her long leather boots, pulling her coat tightly around her, head down, teeth clenched, clamping down on the flashes of panic and frustration, consumed with the need to put things right. It was as if that wasp had stung her awake at last.

For the first few weeks working with Carrie Piper, her boss, she'd still managed to believe it would get better, that once Carrie Piper got to know her, she would drop the hostility, that the two of them would get on. When, instead, the hostility had got worse, Emily had spent the next few months sure that something new was just a week away. That she was about to be tipped off about a great new job in another agency, or she'd see one advertised, something that she would only have a chance of landing if she were applying from inside the business. But as the months went by and nothing came to save her, her optimism inevitably dimmed. She'd gradually stopped following up every contact she'd ever made because, despite all the effort, nothing ever materialized. But now Oliver was home again and suddenly it was as if a little light of determination had been re-fired.

I am handing in my notice, she decided. Today. And as she thought about it, she realized there would be nothing she missed. That she didn't care if she never read another script or screenplay in her life, didn't care if she never saw another play. She was getting out. And that was why she'd told Sam a lie, a little lie that was so white it was almost true. She was leaving because on measured, mature consideration she could see that a year was long enough. Absolutely nothing to do with the fact that she'd been taken by surprise and didn't want Oliver to think badly of her.

Perhaps she was wrong, she told herself, and a year on Oliver wouldn't care anyway. Perhaps he'd be confused when Sam passed on her news. *Emily? Do I know an Emily?* But of course it wasn't so. She knew that even if they hadn't ever met again after Cornwall, Oliver wouldn't have forgotten her. As it was, they *had* met again years later, working together at a production company called Black Box, when they'd been brought together on the same production. It had been a surprise to see him again, an even greater surprise to realize she would be working with him, every day, breakfast, lunch and tea, for at least three months. But then, no surprise at all to hear that in the intervening years he'd not only built himself a dazzling career but also of course found himself a dazzling live-in girlfriend.

By now she'd walked far enough for the streets to have become decidedly downmarket. Gone were the pretty flower shops, the delis and boutiques and in their place were the cheap burger bars, two second-hand office furniture shops, a pawnbrokers and a launderette that took up the first fifty yards of Robbins Road. As she turned the corner an empty Budweiser can rolled towards her in welcome.

She thought about how it would feel at last to tell Carrie Piper that she was leaving. The wonderful satisfaction as her carefully selected words of resignation, honed and sharpened for so many months, were finally released. How the relief would feel, how it would get to work inside her, unfreezing her brain, lifting the weight off her shoulders, allowing all the new ideas to unfold and shake themselves out, excitement like soft warm rain, giving life to plans that she'd long given up on.

She wanted to walk around for a bit; rehearse her words one final time. But it was too late. She knew she would already have been seen from the upstairs windows.

Emily stopped outside the front door and searched her bag for her keys. A dead pigeon was lying in the doorway of the launderette next door, a frail little pigeon. She concentrated on what she was doing but in the corner of her eye its downy breast kept moving, blown first one way then another by the wind.

She found her keys and took them out of her bag, imagining herself walking in, the door slamming behind her, picking up the post and placing it on the stairs for Carrie Piper to take up with her, then going into the dark cave that was her office, sitting down at her desk. But she didn't move.

Why did you leave my post on the wrong stair? Carrie Piper, with fiery red hair and livid electric rage, trembling yet elated, relishing the confrontation. Carrie Piper, whose anger bent coffee spoons, burned holes in mouse mats, fused lights and shattered glass.

I'm not going to go in, Emily decided.

Why did you do that? What are you trying to tell me?

She would stand behind Emily's chair, waiting for Emily to turn to look at her.

Emily, I need to understand why you hate me.

Slowly Emily looked up to the first-floor window. She was there, staring down at Emily, hunched over the window sill.

Emily looked down at her keys, hating the weight of them in her hand, and then she pushed them, one at a time, through the brass letter box, feeling the heavy springs bite greedily at her fingers each time she pulled them clear.

Chubb first, Banham second. One after the other, her keys hit the cold stone floor on the other side of the door and at the sound Emily felt a wonderful exuberance lift her up and spin her away. She turned, looked up one last time and waved a quick, cheeky goodbye before she was off down the street, so light-footed she was nearly dancing. She paused for a cat, tickled him quickly under the chin and then she was gone. Leaving the squalid, rubbish-strewn, infested, dirty street for ever, she turned to the bus stop and the number 29 and freedom.

2

It was a celebration cake for Emily, and it looked great for about thirty seconds until Holly tried to get it out of the cake tin and only half of it came away.

'This is good,' Holly told her friend Caitlin, trying to shake and scrape at the same time. 'It proves it's home-made.'

'Which counts for so much more,' said Caitlin, taking the knife from her, sliding it around the inside of the tin and loosening the cake expertly. 'Now Emily will know who is her kindest, most talented, most *caring* friend.'

'Stop it!' Holly cried. 'And wait until you see what I've got for her birthday!'

'Given it's Emily, I doubt that it's a blow-up Robert Downey Jr.'

There was a familiar edge to Caitlin's voice. Holly heard it and stopped shaking the cake tin and stopped smiling, on the brink of warning Caitlin that as she was gatecrashing Emily's evening, she should watch her step.

They'd met a couple of hours earlier at Holly's front door, Holly just off the tube and weighed down with food, Caitlin fresh from an afternoon buying a new pair of boots and sleeping through a facial. Caitlin had walked into the kitchen with a bag of Holly's shopping swinging from a finger and had then jumped onto one of the high silver bar stools where she had stayed for the next hour, swinging her feet and admiring her new brown pony-skin boots, while Holly made her some toast and poured her a glass of wine, cleared the table of newspapers and dead flowers, emptied the dishwasher, hung up her coat, whipped cream, marinated prawns and tossed a salad. And yet, as always, Caitlin was so funny, so disarmingly rude about her terrible boyfriends and everyone else, that Holly didn't mind. Not until she began on Emily.

Holly gripped the tin hard so that Caitlin could again run the knife around the inside, and they watched as, at last, the rest of the cake slowly gave up the struggle and fell out.

'There,' Caitlin said, watching Holly shove it all together, 'you clever thing. It looks perfect.' She picked up a stray crumb and dropped it into her mouth. 'Tastes perfect too.'

Caitlin slid off her stool and went over to Holly's huge stainless-steel fridge, opened it and peered inside. Then she held up another bottle of wine. 'Do you mind?'

In answer Holly flung the corkscrew to her, a bit too quickly, and Caitlin gave her a glance of alarm. Hands on hips, Holly watched while Caitlin twisted it in.

'What?' Caitlin asked, looking up, the wine bottle between her knees. 'I only said I liked your cake.'

'Please don't give Emily a hard time tonight,' Holly begged. 'She's left her job. Let's concentrate on that.'

'She can handle me. Anyway, I'll be nice!'

'But she upsets you. And you always let it show and I don't want you to.'

'She doesn't upset me, condescending person. She confuses me,' Caitlin said. 'And I'm not the only one.'

Without replying, Holly carried the last of the dirty bowls over to the sink and squirted an arc of washing-up liquid over them. Behind her, Caitlin waited for a few seconds more, then stalked out of the room, flicking off the light switch and leaving Holly in darkness.

Holly washed up by the light thrown in from the hall. Caitlin's walking out of the room made her smile because Caitlin was the most self-assured, opinionated person she knew and yet Emily got to her, made her tongue-tied and awkward like no one else could.

She dried and put away the last of the bowls and then looked around for the bottle of wine, guessing that it had probably left with Caitlin. She went over to the fridge and took out another one, jumped up onto a stool and poured out a glass, knowing that Caitlin would soon be back.

Free of all the usual clutter, her kitchen looked and felt as it had when it had first been fitted, all stainless steel and chrome and spare clean lines, with a reinforced glass floor, pale lilac walls and wonderful hand-painted tiles. Holly loved it. And she loved it best as it was now, immaculate, expectant, ready for a party, bowls of food taking up every spare inch of the fridge, the floor swept, the dishwasher empty. Around the house she knew she'd made some bad mistakes but she was confident that she'd got her kitchen right.

Behind her, Caitlin shuffled back in apologetically, pulled out another stool and sat down next to her. 'Sorry.'

Holly looked over at her.

'Very, very sorry,' Caitlin pleaded. 'Please don't expel me. Please let me stay.'

Holly laughed. 'Of course you can stay.'

'I can't believe Emily stayed at that office so long,' Caitlin said in a normal voice, hands gripping the sides of her stool. 'That she found it so hard to admit she'd made a mistake.'

Holly shrugged.

'Sad that she'd rather spend a whole year being miserable than admit to it? Don't you think so?'

'Yes. And she'd be the first to agree that she's wasted her time. She can't believe she took so long to go.' Holly glanced across at her. 'Why does that irritate you so much?'

'It doesn't irritate me. It troubles me. It makes me think. Perhaps she should ask herself if she's right about other things, too. Whether there are other parts of her life that are making her unhappy, attitudes that she won't let go of.'

There was a mutinous silence from Holly.

'Holly, I like her!' Caitlin insisted. 'I do. I just don't want her to say in ten years' time, "*Oh, my God! Made a huge mistake about that too!*"'

'She's not making a mistake. And I don't think it's any business of yours if she is.'

'Oh, why can't I ever talk about her to you?' Caitlin pleaded. 'Why do we all have to step around her so carefully? Why is her love life such a taboo subject? We talk about everybody else's! Why do you always have to shut me up about Emily? You don't even know what I'm going to say.'

'I don't need to know what you're going to say. I know what you want to do. You want to get me to agree with you that Emily's got it wrong. That she's making another *huge mistake*. And I won't.'

Caitlin shook her head. 'I hope you're this protective about me.'

'No one needs to be this protective about you.'

Holly slipped off her stool and turned the lights on, then went to the fridge, opened the door and brought out the bowl of whipped cream, moved to the cutlery drawer and found a knife and a spoon and pulled the cake towards her. Next to her, Caitlin dipped a finger in the bowl of whipped cream and licked it.

'Self-denial is not a virtue,' she said quietly. 'Emily is wrong about that.'

'She might move to Cornwall,' Holly said, ignoring her. 'Go and live near her brother and open a shop.'

'Then that'll be the end of her. She'll never meet anyone. Mr Wrong or Mr Right.'

Holly lifted out a spoonful of whipped cream and flicked it at the top of the cake. 'She'd call her shop "Saltwater". I think it's a great idea. You know she'd be brilliant at it. She's not in love with the theatre any more and she's certainly not in love with London. She was thinking of paintings and sculptures and things to do with the sea.'

'Emily left university with a first,' Caitlin said, full of

frustration. 'Why would she want to go and work in some shop in Cornwall? Why is she so determined to miss out on everything? And I'm saying that because I do like her.'

Holly smeared the whipped cream all over the cake and then reached for a punnet of raspberries. 'You've got her so wrong. You're presuming she's unhappy, living as she is, but she's not. She knows what she wants, she knows what she's aiming for. She's happier than any of us is.'

'You should have got her a cherry,' Caitlin said flippantly, pinching one of the raspberries between her finger and thumb before biting it in half.

Emily walked up the flight of old York stone steps, knocked gently with the polished knocker and waited. Every time she arrived on Holly's doorstep, she thought the same thing. She would look up at the glossy black front door and think how incredible it was that Holly was going to open it. That Holly could possibly own such a house, a house that must be worth millions. Big enough for huge families to get lost in, let alone one twenty-five-year-old woman.

It was on Richmond Hill, a take-your-breath-away Georgian house, leaning out towards the water meadows. Holly had been the only grandchild of an extremely rich grandmother who had left her the house, figuring rightly that her only child, Holly's mother, didn't need it. In the basement was a two-bedroom, self-contained flat that Holly rented out, using the income to pay for the running of the rest of the house. Grand, flamboyant, extravagant things had happened to Holly ever since Emily had first met her at university. The house was merely the best and most extravagant.

Hearing Emily's knock, Holly opened the door, exclaiming at the blast of freezing night air that greeted her. She shut the door firmly against the cold and led Emily in, whispering that she hoped Emily wouldn't mind but that Caitlin was in the drawing room.

'Why should I mind?' Emily asked, less interested in Caitlin's presence in the drawing room than in a new painting taking up most of one wall in the hallway.

She handed Holly a bottle of wine and went over to look at it. 'Tell me this wasn't here last time I came.'

'No, it wasn't.'

Holly came and stood beside her.

'What's it called?'

'It's called *Naked lady blowing bubbles*,' Holly said, a look of wonderment on her face. 'What do you think? Do you like it?'

Emily nodded and grinned. 'Indescribable.'

'Fuck off, Emily!' Holly protested. 'You clearly know nothing.'

'When did you get it?'

'In the summer. I saw it in this fantastic exhibition in Piccadilly.'

'Not the Royal Academy?'

'No, on the street! It carried on all the way down the road from Green Park. All the way down.'

Given how the hall had already suffered at Holly's hands, Emily mused that perhaps it was no bad thing that a joyous, fleshy lady and a cloud of iridescent bubbles now covered most of it. Painted an inoffensive cream when Holly had moved in, the hall had been one of the first areas she had tackled, choosing a purple and gold shiny striped wallpaper that went all the way up the stairs, from the ground to the cathedral-high ceiling, and clashed badly with the old black and white checked floor that fortunately was listed and therefore safe from Holly's unpredictable taste.

'But I don't want to talk about my picture,' Holly said, turning to her and giving her a great beaming smile. 'I want to talk about you. Brilliant to walk out like that. Fantastic. I'm so proud of you!'

'I pity my replacement,' Emily said, taking off her coat. 'I'm going to have to write and warn her. But thank you for saying so and thank you for organizing this. You're very sweet.'

Holly took Emily's coat and hung it up on a rail beside the front door. 'It's only the five of us: you, me, Rachel and Jo-Jo, and now Caitlin. It's not as if I've made a huge effort.'

'It's lovely of you.' Emily lowered her voice. 'I'm surprised Caitlin wanted to stay. She must be spoiling for a fight.'

'Don't say that,' Holly protested. 'It's not like that. She was really upset when she realized that this was happening and that I hadn't invited her.'

'Oh, great,' said Emily sarcastically. She nodded towards the drawing-room door. 'She's probably selecting her spell as we speak.'

'No! She's realized that we're getting together, wanting

to celebrate what you've finally done – ' Holly squeezed Emily's arm – 'and she wanted to celebrate too.' Holly raised her eyebrows. 'So, how does is it feel to be gone? To be free at last? Actually, I don't know why I'm asking. It must be fantastic. You're free! You must be so happy.'

But Emily shook her head. 'No, it was wonderful for about the first ten minutes but since then it's not felt so good . . . It's not felt good at all.'

Holly stopped, one arm already stretched to open the drawing-room door, knowing that if she did, that would be the end of the conversation. In all the years of knowing Emily, Holly had never been so taken aback. Emily didn't say things like that, had never admitted to anything being less than good before.

'I left because I had no choice. But that doesn't mean I'm not scared of tomorrow, scared of the next day. I knew I'd feel like this, too. It was what kept me there so long. At least I had something to do when I worked for Carrie Piper, somewhere to go to, even if it was grim when I got there. Now, I have a dump of a flat that needs the rent paying on it but no money. I don't think I want to go to another theatrical agency but I don't know what else to do. I have a vague idea that I might set up a shop in Cornwall, because I don't think I want to live in London any more, but I don't know if I want to do that, and nobody would want to come and buy anything anyway. I have two parents but I haven't spoken to either of them for eleven months—'

'Don't say that.' It was such a shock to hear Emily speaking like this. Holly had to stop her. 'You haven't got used to the change, that's all. You need time to adjust. Have a holiday. I am – I'm having a couple of weeks here in London, and then I'm going skiing.'

Emily laughed. 'Good for you. But how do I pay the rent?'

'By spending a few of the thousands of pounds that I know you have stashed away in the Alliance & Leicester. Don't pretend you're so broke.'

Emily shook her head. 'I'm not pretending.'

Holly went on, 'You only left the place *yesterday*. Please give yourself a break. And don't, please don't, go straight into the first job you're offered or it will be another disaster. Don't do that!'

'What about Saltwater? Do you think I should go for it?'

'If you have to.'

'Glad you think it's such a good idea.'

'Don't you think Saltwater comes up when you don't know what else to do?'

'But I need to do something . . .'

'Emily,' Holly insisted, coming back to her, squeezing her shoulder affectionately, 'you don't have to have your life all organized by tomorrow. Why don't you have a holiday? I could ask Jo-Jo to come and Rachel. We can ask them tonight. It would be fun. Don't even think about Saltwater just yet. And please don't go and live in Cornwall,' she beseeched her. 'Have holidays with your brother there, but don't go and live there. We'd all miss you too much.'

Emily smiled. 'I'm sorry. And thank you. Believe it or not I was in quite a good mood when I walked in just now. I don't know what happened. Why I did I tell you all that?'

Holly had been more taken aback by Emily's outburst than she was going to let on.

'We'll talk about it later. We shouldn't leave Caitlin on her own for too long. She'll be wondering what's wrong and you don't want to get her involved. But tell me quickly. Might you come skiing? In two weeks' time.'

'Thank you, of course I will. I'd love to come. I've got a couple of interviews lined up. I rang around a few recruitment agencies this afternoon. Nothing very exciting. But I can't believe any of them would want me to start before Easter.' For a second Emily let herself lean in against Holly. 'I know, what am I doing? Have a break, take my time, you're right, but it's hard. I need to know where I'm going next.'

Holly thought how this was the girl who'd always seemed to know where she was going, far better than any of her other friends did. Who'd always seemed so strong, so sure of what she believed in and, as a result, invincible. And she kicked herself for ever thinking it could be so simple. And she wondered how much more was going on, wondered if she could have missed danger signals over the past few months, thought how the departure from Carrie Piper wouldn't alone have provoked such a wobble. Had Emily been less buoyant and optimistic for a while now? Had Holly not noticed? And Holly kicked herself for not knowing the answer, for not thinking about it until now.

As she opened the door to the drawing room she pushed Emily inside. 'Talk to her while I check the food.'

But I don't want to talk to Caitlin, Emily thought, walking reluctantly in. She looked across the room. As far away as was possible, Caitlin was waiting for her, sitting in the corner of a lime green velvet sofa, the size of a double bed, with her knees up. She was dressed in black, which seemed to emphasize how tiny she was, and the contrast between the green sofa, the black clothes and the striking silvery blonde of her curly hair was dramatic. Emily caught her eye and smiled and thought how Caitlin looked like a little pixie, untrustworthy and enchanting, and she felt a familiar wariness prickle down her spine.

'Hi!' Caitlin pushed herself off the sofa and came across the long, purple-painted wooden floor to Emily, to greet her and kiss her lightly on each cheek, and Emily breathed in the warm scent of orange blossom, just as Holly popped her head around the door. 'I'm going upstairs to change.'

'No, please. We love you as you are!' Caitlin called after her. And Emily imagined that what she was really calling was, *Please, don't leave me alone with her*.

She guessed it was a deliberate ploy on Holly's part. A ploy to give her and Caitlin a chance to talk, break the ice before the others arrived. But Holly had missed the point that Caitlin didn't want to be left alone with her, hadn't taken it in that in eight years – three years of university and five years in London – Caitlin and Emily only had conversations when somebody else arranged them.

Emily had guessed right. From the beginning, Caitlin had told herself and anyone else who'd listen that Emily's looks and style disguised a personality that was too good to be true and, as a result, had never got close enough to get to know her. Yet, in most respects, Emily was exactly the sort of person Caitlin loved to have as a friend. She looked great, had a glamorous job (until that morning anyway) and was witty and fun. But having a conversation with her always left Caitlin calling out for a drink. Emily made her feel as if she shouldn't even mention rock and roll, let alone the sex and the drugs.

Occasionally Holly or one of the others might be coerced into acknowledging that Emily was a bit of a control freak, and, yes, perhaps a bit unworldly, but that was as far as it would ever go. The others loved Emily and wanted to look after her. Emily made them laugh, held their attention and enjoyed their respect in a way Caitlin never could. And in return they could tease Emily about her lifestyle and attitudes with a lightness of touch that Caitlin knew she'd never be able to achieve herself.

Having kissed her hello, Caitlin went over to the window, pulled aside a heavy curtain and stood for a few moments, staring out into the street. To Emily it was obvious that Caitlin was looking out for Jo-Jo and Rachel, clearly hoping that they might already be approaching the front door. Then Caitlin dropped the curtain, turned back to the sofa and sat down.

Emily followed her across the room and felt Caitlin start as she sat down beside her.

'You haven't got any wine,' Caitlin said, immediately jumping up.

But Emily got up too and walked away in front of her, leading the way to the kitchen.

'I was in Ruffles in Hammersmith yesterday morning,' Emily said, attempting to kick-start the conversation.

'What were you doing there?' Caitlin lived in Hammersmith and passed Ruffles almost every day.

'Do you mean in Hammersmith, or what was I doing in Ruffles?' Emily fetched herself a glass and handed it to Caitlin who refilled her own and poured some wine for Emily.

'In Ruffles. It's where all the old ladies get their twinsets and their trouser suits. It's ten per cent off on a Monday.'

'I was running around in my knickers actually,' Emily said.

'Are you joking?'

'No, you should try it. I find it's a great way of meeting new people.' She took her glass from Caitlin and turned towards the door, back to the drawing room. 'Come in here. I'll tell you about it.'

Emily told her.

'But *Emily*! Wait!' Caitlin said melodramatically, putting a concerned hand on hers. 'I cannot believe that you came out without any clothes on. Not *you*!'

'I can't believe I did either.' Emily flinched from Caitlin's hand. 'But you have no idea how much that wasp hurt. I wasn't exactly thinking about what I was wearing. You'd have done the same.'

Caitlin sat down on the sofa and this time patted for

Emily to join her. 'Let's face it, Emily. I'm out of my clothes rather more often than you are. For *you* to do that . . . you must have been so embarrassed.'

'I didn't look that bad,' Emily insisted, deliberately misunderstanding her. 'It was no worse than being on the beach. I don't think anyone saw me properly, anyway.'

'Don't tell me you go topless on the beach.'

'Sometimes I do,' Emily retorted, wanting to slap Caitlin's incredulous face. 'If it's a hot day and my dad isn't around.'

'Oh, my God! I would never have had you down for topless sunbathing.'

'Why do you have me down for anything at all?'

Caitlin didn't know what to say to that. Looking up into Emily's cool, clear eyes, she went quiet, feeling out of her depth, floundering, kicking feebly in some vast ocean as she searched in vain for a way to save herself. How was it Emily always managed to do this to her?

'It's only a turn of phrase,' Caitlin said, standing up again, now pacing the room so her heels rapped out hard on the wooden floor. 'I don't . . . have you down for anything.'

She could feel herself blushing, which was all the more humiliating, and she lowered her eyes and found herself staring awkwardly at Emily's thighs in their faded button-flyed jeans. Little Mother Superior, she thought, turning longingly towards the door, towards the distant stairs. Come back Holly . . . R. E. S. C. U. E. M. E. Tell me what one says to a virgin. What to talk about? Seashells? Puppies? Alice bands? Apple blossom?

27

There was a pale blue leather armchair at a right angle to Caitlin's sofa and Emily moved across to it, sat on its soft squashy arm and leaned towards Caitlin.

'You mustn't worry so much about me,' she said quietly. 'I was covered up in no time.'

Caitlin nodded, scrabbling for an excuse to leave Emily alone in the room or at least for something to say, something that would change the subject fast and for sure. And she managed to come up with something sufficiently bizarre that also happened to be true.

'You know I have a boyfriend called Leon?'

Emily nodded.

'He took me out for tea with a chimp last week.' Caitlin made it sound rather casual, as if it was the sort of thing that could happen any time.

'Fantastic!' Emily laughed in appreciation and Caitlin surprised herself by cautiously smiling back.

'He was called Bert and apparently he's especially popular with the under-fives, which, I suppose, says rather a lot about me.'

'I'd like to have done that too,' Emily reassured her.

'I didn't think I would. But I fell in love with him,' Caitlin smiled again. 'He was gorgeous. And as Leon said to Holly, what do you give the girl who will dissolve if she has another spa treatment? After tea I washed his face and he cleaned his teeth . . . And then I put him to bed.'

'And he was good, was he? Good in bed?' Emily asked, remembering suddenly that she'd been supposed to follow up a call about another job at seven thirty and she'd forgotten all about it. She looked at her watch, wondering whether it was too late to call now.

'He was so good. And once you've had a chimp . . .'

But Emily had leapt up and was out of the door before Caitlin had finished the sentence.

Typical bloody Emily, Caitlin thought, left alone in the room. Let down your guard for just a second, think you're getting on, think she's fun, that she has a sense of humour after all. Then you say something you shouldn't and immediately she's stomping out of the room in disgust. Nervously she wondered what Holly would do when she found out. But then, seconds later, Emily came back. She stood in the doorway, pressing buttons on her mobile, not even looking at Caitlin, then held the phone up to her ear. Caitlin saw a look of frustration flash across her face and then Emily put the phone down on a bookshelf and sat back down.

'Sorry.'

'No problem.' Caitlin shrugged.

Emily beamed at her

'Why did you run out of the room?'

'I was meant to have called someone about a job. I forgot about it. I forget everything all the time. But I can ring him in the morning. Please tell me more about Bert.'

Caitlin nodded slowly, looked back at her. 'If your memory's that bad,' she said, 'perhaps you *have* slept with someone after all, and forgotten about it?' *Don't let me have said that out loud.*

'Oh God! That's true!' Emily laughed. 'Perhaps I've had sex loads of times.'

Had sex? It sounded so wrong when Emily said it. 'I thought you'd left the room in disgust. I was wondering how I'd explain it to Holly.'

'Why would I do that?'

Caitlin shook her head. 'No reason at all. I just thought . . .' She picked up her glass of wine and took a huge swallow.

'We've often got it wrong, haven't we?' Emily said gently. 'You and me.'

Caitlin nodded.

'I don't think there is anything you could say that would make me leave a room.'

'And I wouldn't want to.' Caitlin got up and walked over to the doorway, looking up the stairs for Holly.

No, she thought stubbornly, not willing after so many years to admit she'd misjudged her. *You and I* don't get it wrong, *you* get it wrong. I'm not the weirdo, you are. Everyone else can think you're on to something, that you're a happy, harmless twenty-first-century hippy, but I don't. 'Where is that girl?' she exploded instead.

'Don't hurry her,' Emily said, 'she'll be down soon. We can manage without her.'

Caitlin turned back to her.

'What do you think of *Naked lady blowing bubbles*?' Emily asked.

'That she shouldn't be allowed.'

'Did you tell Holly?'

'I told her she has less taste than chamomile tea. What did *you* say to Holly?'

'That I liked it. I didn't want to hurt her feelings.'

'How come?' Caitlin asked, still standing in the doorway. 'I thought you believed in honesty, in being true to yourself, standing by your principles?'

'How about you change the habit of a lifetime and give me a break?' Emily retorted. 'For this one evening, how about you try to forget that I haven't ever had sex?'

Had sex. She'd said it again.

They both heard the creak of footsteps on the stairs, and then Holly was walking across the hall towards them, coming through the open doorway, joining Caitlin, and although they both smiled at her, they couldn't disguise the tension still crackling in the air.

'She started it!' Caitlin insisted, finally starting to laugh.

Holly shook her head in despair. 'I'm going back upstairs.'

'Don't, don't,' Emily reassured her. 'Everything's fine. Caitlin was saying how much she liked your new haircut.'

Holly combed her fingers through her hair and looked at Emily uncertainly. 'Why don't I believe you?'

'I agree,' Caitlin insisted. 'It looks great.'

Holly's hair was the outcome of a reckless trip to the hairdressers at the end of the road that had, against the odds, worked brilliantly well. It was cut short, sliced back behind her ears, and dyed a dark fox red which looked great against her wonderful creamy skin.

'It's perfect,' Emily said again, meaning it. Long hair

hadn't flattered Holly, disguising the angle of her jaw line, making her face look heavy and round, whereas the new cut seemed to lift weight away, and emphasize her cheekbones and huge brown eyes.

'And we were just wondering where those other two tarts could have got to.' Again Caitlin walked over to the window and checked the street outside.

'OK?' Holly asked Emily, keeping her voice low.

Caitlin heard her and turned. 'Stop fussing.'

Ignoring her, Holly went over to the other side of the room to put on some music and Caitlin kicked off her shoes and sat down on the floor beside Emily's chair.

'Did anyone tell you how she ran around Ruffles stark naked?' Caitlin asked Holly.

'Caitlin's very worried about the damage it's done to my reputation,' said Emily.

'I heard,' Holly replied, still searching through CDs.

'And she ran slap bang into Sam Finch!' Caitlin went on. 'Do you remember him?'

'We met him once with Oliver Mills, didn't we?' Holly asked.

'That's right,' said Caitlin. 'And he always fancied you, Emily. He must have thought today was his lucky day.'

Emily opened her mouth to deny it, but decided there was no point and closed it again.

'So how did he react when you threw yourself at him?' Caitlin asked Emily. 'Did he offer to suck out the sting?'

'No, of course not. He shielded me. From the wasp and from all the nosy people standing around watching me.'

'How nice.'

'He was . . . surprisingly nice.' Emily remembered Sam wrapping her up in his coat. 'And so relaxed about it too. He acted like it happened all the time.'

'Surprisingly nice because you thought it would be nasty but actually it was nice?' Caitlin asked. 'Or surprisingly nice because nothing like that had happened to you before?'

'No,' said Emily. 'Surprisingly nice because he was surprising and nice.'

'But what was he doing in Ruffles?' Caitlin persisted. 'I thought he lived in Cornwall?'

'He does. But when I saw him he was buying a present for his sister.'

There's so much more I want to know. All those things she's never going to tell me, thought Caitlin. She sat back on the sofa and studied Emily. What had it felt like to be Emily then, she wondered, standing naked and close up against a man perhaps for the very first time? How had it been to feel his heartbeat, the warmth of his body against her bare skin? How much had she liked it? Had it tempted her at all? Made her want to do it again? Do some more? But Caitlin couldn't ask, and Holly wouldn't ask, so Caitlin could only guess that of course Emily had liked it. Of course she had been tempted.

'So did you buy the white shirt?' Caitlin asked instead.

Emily shook her head. 'I should have done. But I was late and I wanted to get away.' Emily stopped, remembering the sense of futility that had hit her outside the shop. 'Anyway, I didn't make it to the interview, so I'm glad I saved the money.'

'What happened? Why didn't you go?' Caitlin demanded. 'I don't understand.'

'Because I knew I was wasting my time. There was no job there anyway.'

'And then you chucked it in at Carrie Piper's! Why?'

Emily pulled her top lip between her teeth, not sure what to say. She was sure that she shouldn't be confiding in Caitlin about anything, long used to hiding any vulnerability from her, and yet at the same time she felt certain that it couldn't do any harm. And, more than that, she wanted to tell them both, to say his name aloud again.

'Because Oliver Mills has come home,' she said.

3

Rachel Croft and Jo-Jo Beecher met in the dark at the pedestrian crossing at the bottom of Richmond Hill. Rachel had been walking fast, her eyes stinging from the bitter cold, her chin tucked deep inside her coat. When she'd caught sight of Jo-Jo moving through a knot of people fifty yards ahead she had pushed on even faster, but as she'd found herself getting close something – shyness – made her slow down, held her back from making contact. She'd followed Jo-Jo, watching the way she strode through the crowd, head up, shoulders thrown back, seemingly oblivious to the cold. She was wearing a bottle-green corduroy coat with the belt tied tightly around her narrow waist, and her shiny, slippery-looking hair was lifted up off her long neck and spilling out of a clip on the back of her head. The only concession to the cold was a long stripy scarf.

Then Rachel had felt like a stalker and she'd broken into a run, ducking and diving between people, reaching Jo-Jo as she went to cross at the lights, grabbing hold of her arm just as the man went green.

'Hi there!' she said breathlessly. 'Are you on your way to Holly's?'

'Sure am,' Jo-Jo said, turning to Rachel and giving her a big, wide smile. Her teeth were very white and slightly

crooked at the front, Rachel noticed. In the street lights
and icy cold air, everything about Jo-Jo seemed to sparkle
and shine. 'It's celebration time for Emily, isn't it? She said
you were coming. Great to see you again!'

'You too!'

Now Rachel felt rather awkward, and wished that she
hadn't caught Jo-Jo up, that she was still walking alone,
without the pressure of having to think up things to say.

'I'm so pleased for Emily,' she began tentatively, as
they strode up the hill. 'I mean I know she's got nothing
else lined up, but so what? I'm sure she'll walk into a new
job.' Jo-Jo didn't answer. Rachel went on, 'And did you
hear about her last day?'

'Holly called me at work and told me – asked me
around tonight to celebrate.'

Rachel pictured Jo-Jo at work, colleagues all around
her, everyone vying for her attention. 'She was fantastic,
wasn't she?'

Jo-Jo nodded non-committally.

'Don't you think?'

'Depends how ambitious Emily is. It was a good job on
paper.'

At twenty-eight Jo-Jo had already proved how
ambitious she was. She had worked as a second assistant
director on two major television dramas and was currently
in pre-production on her first feature film, for which in a
couple of months she'd be off for eighteen weeks' shooting
in Tuscany and North Africa. It would be very hard work,
she insisted, exhausting seven-day weeks, late nights and
crack-of-dawn starts to catch the early Tuscan light . . . Her

friends heaved great sighs of pity on her behalf. Jo-Jo would make a show of denying any such thing but there was no doubt that she was on the fast track.

Jo-Jo had met Emily on a low-budget television drama when they had both been runners. But Emily had not been quite as quick to leap up the career ladder, which was exactly why Carrie Piper's job had seemed such a golden opportunity: a chance to stay in the world of television – and theatre – but come at it from a different angle, with no secretarial work and the long-term chance to develop her own list of clients. When Emily got down to the last four applicants, it was Jo-Jo who'd primed her and pumped her with information, worked out what she was going to be asked, made sure she had the answers ready.

Neither of them knew then that the tiny Carrie Piper Agency was on its knees, or that within six months of Emily's arrival the one surviving co-director would leave, taking the last of the five major-earning clients with him.

Rachel, on the other hand, had first met Emily at school and, although they'd lost touch soon after they left, some years later they had found themselves living one above the other in a rented house in Clapham. Supper once every few months had developed into time out together every week. But despite the fact that Jo-Jo and her both counted Emily as one of their closest friends, they hadn't got to know each other. Rachel, shy and insecure, found that being with Jo-Jo always tied her tongue up in knots, while Jo-Jo was unaware of the effect she had and didn't think much about Rachel at all.

'When I spoke to Emily,' Rachel told Jo-Jo now, her breath coming faster with the effort of matching strides with her, 'she told me how she'd stood outside her office yesterday morning, knowing she couldn't face another day of work, and so she posted her keys through the letter box and ran for it! Didn't bother with saying goodbye or the fact that she should have given three months' notice.'

But Jo-Jo didn't react as she was meant to. 'It's a shame she let it get to her. It was a great break for Emily.'

'Oh, come on, it was terrible! You have to be pleased she's gone.'

Jo-Jo let out a long sigh, then laughed. 'You're right, of course. Why am I doubting whether she was right to leave? Of course she was! Emily always knows what she's doing.' She smiled again to show there was no malice in her words. 'Emily knows exactly what's best for her. Knows what she wants better than anyone. If it's time to leave she's not bothered about some silly little convention like handing in her notice first.'

'Wasn't that great?' Rachel agreed. 'Whereas if it had been me, I'd have stuck my keys through the letter box and then realized I'd left my handbag inside and I'd have to ring the bell and be let in.'

Jo-Jo laughed. 'Absolutely,' she said. 'Me too.'

'Oh, no. I don't think so.' Glancing across to Jo-Jo, seeing the grin on her face, Rachel felt warm bubbles of pleasure popping inside her. She'd never made Jo-Jo laugh before, never had a conversation that flowed so easily. 'And yet the strange thing is, I still feel far more protective of her than I would of you or Caitlin or Holly,' she went on, and glanced again across at Jo-Jo, expecting another nod of agreement. It wasn't there. 'I'm not feeling protective of her,' she backtracked instantly. 'Not really. And not protective of you or Caitlin either.' Now there was definite disagreement on Jo-Jo's face. 'I'd say I was *concerned* about Emily, that's all. You said it yourself,' Rachel reminded Jo-Jo hastily. 'She hasn't seemed so happy recently.'

'Do you think Emily needs your concern?'

Rachel tried to laugh it off. 'Of course she does, everyone needs my concern.'

'Why?'

'Because she's so funny.'

'You think Emily's funny?'

'No! Yes. Funny and odd and all sorts of other things too. Unconventional, courageous, stubborn, wonderful . . .' Rachel searched. 'And also fragile. I think she's more vulnerable than the rest of us, because of the way she's chosen to live her life. And that makes me want to look out for her in a way I don't for other people. That time when her boss refused to speak to her for four days, I wanted to kill that woman. I wouldn't have felt like that if it was you or Holly. I'd think, "Put up with it." But with Emily . . .' Rachel searched again for the right words. 'And now I'm worried it's actually about something else altogether. And I'm looking out for her all over again.'

'You make it sound like we're all protected against something that Emily's not. Like she's missed an important vaccination. '

In a way that was what she meant, but Rachel couldn't think how to explain herself, wished that a few precise, insightful words might fall – just for once – from her lips.

'You know, it bothers me that even you – someone who's been her friend since school – can't seem to put it aside,' Jo-Jo challenged her. 'It's as if every time you think about her you see this big *handle with care* sign flashing above her head.'

'Oh, no,' Rachel exclaimed. 'Is that how it seems? That's not how it is at all.'

'Tell me how it is, then.'

But Rachel couldn't go on. Why, when she needed to think on her feet, did her brain always grind immediately to a halt? Why, when she had a perfectly good point to make, did she always lose it somewhere in mid sentence and then say something she hadn't been meaning to say at all? It didn't happen with her close friends. With Emily, whom she'd known so long, she knew she could be quite funny but with Jo-Jo and Caitlin it was a nightmare, like she was being controlled by a ventriloquist, hell-bent on getting her to speak the most clumsy, embarrassing lines.

'Emily does not need us to look after her,' Jo-Jo said more gently, seeing her troubled face. 'Emily has not got a problem. She has not got a disorder.'

'I know that. I don't mean that she has.' All Rachel wanted now was to shut up, but Jo-Jo was still pressing her to explain. She took a breath and thought about what she wanted to say. 'It's not just seeing the men trying it on all the time, thinking Emily's this wonderful challenge, or the bitchy comments she has to put up with, or people thinking she's a bit freaky, because we're used to that. It's wanting to make sure Emily is happy, that she's not lonely, that she's not beginning to shut herself away.'

'You think there's a danger of that? I don't. I don't think it's like that at all. Emily's not struggling to keep hold of this big idea. It isn't an ideal that Emily's holding on to. It's just happened that way: she's an accidental virgin, not a deliberate one.'

'I don't know how you can say that!'

'She's come this far, she's damn well going to make sure it happens with someone worthwhile. If I was in Emily's position I'm sure I'd feel exactly the same.'

Rachel had never heard anyone talk like this about Emily before and couldn't imagine how Jo-Jo had got it so wrong. She believed Emily's virginity was absolutely deliberate, that Emily was a pillar of conviction and wisdom, not the accidental virgin at all but the victorious virgin, the triumphant virgin, holding out against a culture that glorified cheap thrills and instant gratification. Someone she thought was absolutely wonderful. Now Rachel felt terrible because Emily deserved her to stand up and defend her and explain how it really was, but she couldn't do it. I'm twenty-five years old, Rachel thought. But this person makes me feel about ten.

'Don't worry about Emily, worry about us,' Jo-Jo argued. 'We're the ones getting into trouble all the time. Getting hurt. Getting dumped. If Emily's looking to us to show her the way, I can see why she's still waiting.'

When were you ever hurt or dumped? Rachel wondered, looking at Jo-Jo striding up the hill as she talked, shining with confidence.

'We sit there panicking that some guy hasn't called or miserable because we got drunk and had some grim one-night stand or because we've been dumped for some personal fitness coach,' Jo-Jo went on.

'Don't pretend any of that stuff has ever happened to you.' Jo-Jo turned to her, surprised. 'I know what you're talking about, but I don't think *you* do.'

'You'd be surprised.'

'Yes,' Rachel agreed. 'I would.'

Five more houses and they'd be at Holly's.

'The problem for Emily,' Jo-Jo said, changing the subject, 'is that she has tuned men out of her world. She doesn't smell, see, hear, taste them, and she certainly doesn't touch. Otherwise, surely, somewhere along the way, there'd have been a starry night and an attractive guy and she'd have ended up going for it. But there hasn't been anyone, and I can't see how it will ever change. Unless she lets herself go a little, it never will happen, with Mr Right or Mr Wrong or anybody else.'

'You're so unromantic.'

Jo-Jo ran lightly up the steps and banged on the knocker and then turned and grinned back at Rachel, a hand resting on one of the two white pillars that flanked the front door. 'And you think her prince is out there somewhere, do you? Hacking down the forest. You think someone will manage to wake her up?'

Jo-Jo could hear Holly coming to the front door and she turned away from Rachel and slowly unwound her scarf from around her long, elegant neck. It was striped in pinks, turquoises and a soft oatmeal brown, a scarf Rachel would have walked past in a shop without a second thought but which looked beautiful on Jo-Jo.

'One day I want you to tell me what Emily was like at school,' Jo-Jo said, folding the scarf over in her hand. 'Was she head-girl? I bet she was.'

'She's just the same as she was then,' Rachel said slowly, thinking about it and not liking what she was saying. 'Exactly the same. She hasn't changed at all.'

Holly's conservatory was a golden spotlight in the pitch dark of her garden and beyond her garden wall lay the huge presence of Richmond Park. Somewhere close by the house a fox barked and there was an answering crackle in the bracken as sleeping deer shifted warily in response.

Inside, the small, warm conservatory was smothered in luscious plants, so well fed and watered that they looked ready to burst. Sweet-smelling stephanotis twined with winter jasmine and tiny butter yellow orchids. And in each of the four corners of the conservatory, a little orange tree grew in a beautiful pale terracotta pot, their scented, waxy flowers pinpricks of white among dark green oval glossy leaves. It wasn't down to Holly that they flourished so beautifully but thanks to a housekeeper she had inherited with the house from her grandmother, who, for over twenty years, had watered and pruned and cherished, so that the conservatory was as lush and well established as a mini rainforest.

'Sautéed in lemon and garlic and chilli oil, wrapped in petals of rocket and watercress ... It's just a simple supper,' Caitlin teased Holly as she came down the two shallow steps that linked the conservatory to the kitchen and joined them at the round oak table. Holly leaned over Caitlin and placed a large blue terracotta bowl in the middle. Thirty or forty tiger prawns hid between leaves of salad.

'Who said anything about simple?' Holly replied. 'This took me hours.'

Across the table, Emily leapt to Holly's defence. 'They look delicious,' she said, wishing Caitlin could be drugged and locked in a faraway bedroom until the rest of them were ready to go home.

Jo-Jo leaned across to Caitlin and touched her arm. 'How is Leon, by the way? Still being sued?'

'Don't joke about Leon.'

'Why, what's he done now?'

'Nothing.' Caitlin lifted her glass of wine to her lips. 'And Leon is very thoughtful, very kind . . .'

Jo-Jo nodded seriously.

'And he gave me tea with a chimp for my birthday!'

'That's downright weird.' Jo-Jo stabbed together a fork-ful of salad and then skewered her last prawn on the end of it. 'You should watch out.'

Caitlin stood up and reached across the table for the breadboard. 'Why don't you like Leon?'

And she cared, Emily realized, surprised. She really cared.

'I like him,' said Holly unexpectedly. 'I think he's good for you, Caitlin, he's softening you up.'

'And I don't *not* like him,' Jo-Jo insisted. 'I've hardly even met him.'

Caitlin nodded. 'He's a good guy.' Then she turned purposefully to Emily and Emily felt herself stiffen in response. 'Now, I want to know something.' She paused, knowing she'd got everyone's attention. 'And I hope you won't mind me asking. But how come we spend a year telling you to get out of that job, and you take no notice whatsoever, but Oliver doesn't even need to make an appearance, you just hear mention of his name, and you leave the place immediately?'

Emily hadn't known what she might say and for a moment she sat still, looking up at Caitlin, thinking about it. 'You're right to ask,' she agreed eventually, tipping back her chair. 'The fact is, I'd stopped noticing how long I'd been there. I needed a jump-start, a reason to get myself back in gear. And Oliver was it.'

'Do you mean Oliver Mills?' Jo-Jo interrupted. 'Beautiful Oliver from *Breaking Free*? Oliver who snogged you in the sand dunes when you were sixteen? Oliver who highlights his hair?'

'That's not true.' Emily laughed. 'Yes, he's back from New York.'

Breaking Free was the film that Jo-Jo and Emily had worked on together – where they'd met each other, and where, a couple of months after they had started, Oliver had joined them. Hearing a lot about him before he'd arrived, Emily had guessed it would be the same Oliver Mills she'd known in Cornwall so many years ago and anticipation and hope had sent her heart knocking against her ribs at the thought of seeing him again. And then the hope had flickered and died within an hour of meeting him, because while Oliver was as big and golden and attractive as ever, and was so pleased to see her again – instantly regaling the whole cast and crew with the story of how they'd snogged in the sand dunes within half an hour of meeting each other – he also told them all about his girlfriend, Nessa O'Neill. Not deliberately, in a warning-Emily-off kind of way, but casually, so that she slipped into all his conversations in such a way that everyone, but especially Emily, couldn't fail to understand that she was the only woman in his life; he adored her. There was so clearly no chance of anything more happening between them, no point in falling for him, that all Emily could do was switch her excitement off again, her pride intact, and do it so successfully that she hardly ever remembered that she'd wished for something else. She managed it. She might still have felt the occasional flutter in the stomach when he came too close, but it was so feather light she could easily ignore it. And when he pulled her into a hug, and told her how adorable she was, she didn't let herself relax in his arms or remember how it had felt to kiss him.

She and Oliver worked together only once more, on a short film where they had crossed over for just two weeks, but they still saw each other most months, often with others – Holly, Jo-Jo and Nessa especially – but sometimes out on their own. The last occasion was when she had promised him she would leave her job.

'I saw Oliver at the weekend.' Holly surprised them all. She walked out of the conservatory still speaking. 'He had a party. Sam Finch was there too . . . He'd come up from Cornwall.'

'Oliver had a party!' Jo-Jo cried, 'and he didn't ask me or Emily?'

'He wanted to,' Holly comforted her. 'He couldn't get hold of either of you.'

'But we were around. He can't have made much effort,' Jo-Jo grumbled.

'He only called me on Saturday. It was a last-minute party. He told me to bring you both but neither of you was around.'

'You only know Oliver because of me and Emily!' Jo-Jo was used to being the party queen. 'Who else was there? Was Nessa there?'

'No.' Holly took a breath, poised to explain, and in that split second Caitlin glanced across at Emily and so happened to catch the look of wide-eyed disbelief that crossed her face when Holly said again, No. Explained that Nessa had stayed in New York. Nessa and Oliver had split up a few weeks before he came home.

'She always said she'd done her bit in England,' Holly went on, unaware of the effect she'd just had on Emily, 'that if she and Oliver were going to last, it was going to be in New York.'

'But they were perfect for each other. I can't believe it,' Jo-Jo exclaimed. 'Oliver must be devastated.'

'I don't think so. He was having a great time at the party.'

Caitlin quickly looked around at the others but nobody else had noticed Emily's reaction. She turned back to Emily and saw shock, alarm and hope all still battling it out in her face.

Then Emily pulled herself together. 'I should see him sometime,' she said light-heartedly. 'Maybe he can find me a job. Oh, I didn't tell you all,' she went on, and Caitlin thought how chattery and strained she sounded. 'I might have found something. I'm having an interview next Thursday with the Williams Office, in Bloomsbury. They called me this afternoon.'

Caitlin had heard and seen enough. She watched as Emily regained her composure, as the faint flush in her cheeks subsided. She took in how she even managed to laugh at herself for finding the interviews so quickly. And Caitlin carefully clicked together all the facts and impressions, the frustrations and presumptions, everything she'd ever known about Emily over the years, and realized at last what she'd got. That in Emily and Oliver's case, one and one made a perfect two. That here was the man who could refresh the parts the other guys couldn't reach. It wasn't Sam, Caitlin saw in sudden absolute clarity. It wasn't Sam Finch she was interested in. She was completely in love with Oliver.

All of a sudden, Emily was restless and keen to go home. Refusing to acknowledge why, she told herself she was fed up with them all: with Jo-Jo always having to be the girl everyone wanted or wanted to be; with Caitlin's sniping and her horrible boyfriends, Leon being just the latest in a pinstriped, slimy snail-trail of others; with Rachel's gushy clumsiness; and with their collective fascination with Oliver Mills and Sam Finch. But truly she knew it wasn't her friends who were the problem. She loved them all, had even enjoyed sparring with Caitlin and listening to her talk about the horrible boyfriends. If she felt as if they were all suddenly rasping away at her good humour, it was because something else had got to her.

She would go home, Emily decided, as soon as she could. She would eat a slice of her raspberry cake, wait for a pause in the conversation and slip away. She picked up a piece, stuffed it into her dry mouth and found she couldn't swallow. She took a sip of coffee and burned the roof of her mouth, so she coughed and spluttered and had to wipe away tears. She knew that when she opened her eyes again Holly would be watching her, wise brown eyes full of concern, Holly, from whom she could never hide anything. And when she did and looked around the table she saw that they were all looking at her.

'What?' She made herself laugh.

'Emily, you sounded as if you were dying,' Holly told her. Emily shrugged and determinedly swallowed the mouthful of cake.

When she did finally push back her chair and stand up to go, Rachel leapt up to join her.

'I'm sorry we're breaking things up,' she said, going over to Holly and kissing her goodbye.

Jo-Jo yawned and stretched back her arms. 'I'm coming too. I've got to be up again at four.'

At the front door, Emily turned to Holly and hugged her. 'Thank you,' she whispered, 'it was great. I'm sorry I'm leaving so early.'

'Did something happen? Something I missed?'

Emily shook her head. 'Of course not. I'm tired. You know I'm always the first to go home.'

'Call me tomorrow?'

Emily nodded and went through the doorway, down the steps and out onto the street, wanting to put a bit of distance between herself and the rest of them. Then she waited for Rachel to join her.

4

Holly, Jo-Jo and Caitlin stood in the doorway and watched Emily and Rachel walk away down the street.

'I should be off too,' Jo-Jo said, breaking the silence. She picked her coat and scarf off the rack by the front door and slid her coat around her shoulders, then turned back to Holly. 'Was Emily OK?'

Caitlin pounced, taking hold of her arm. 'I'm so glad you noticed.'

'What are *you* talking about?' Jo-Jo asked.

'I'll tell you. It's nothing awful, don't worry,' Caitlin reassured them both, noticing Holly's sudden look of panic. 'But there is something the matter with Emily. And I think I know what.'

Caitlin said nothing while Jo-Jo took off her coat again and then led her and Holly into the drawing room, still waiting while Jo-Jo and Holly sat together on the sofa. Then she dimmed the main light, switched on a couple of lamps, then turned to face them both. And Holly was struck by the thought that it was as if the three of them were on a stage at the start of a play, that there was Caitlin – hero or villain? – preparing to win them over with her words.

'What is it,' she said, worried. 'I knew something was wrong. Poor Emily.'

'There's nothing wrong.' Caitlin prepared the ground

in her mind, aware that she was deliberately softening her voice, switching on all her persuasive charm. 'There's an idea I have about Emily,' she said. 'It's something I've known for a long time, but tonight it was so obvious it kind of jumped at me. And I want you to forget it's me telling you this, because I know you think I have a problem with her. And maybe I do, but it's got nothing to do with what I'm going to say.'

'Wait,' Holly said, 'I need a drink.' She leapt off the sofa, and ran out of the room, returning at lightning speed with three glasses and another bottle of wine. 'Now talk,' she said, pulling the cork.

Caitlin smiled, liking the way they both leaned in towards her.

'You know Oliver's come home without Nessa?'

'Yes,' they both replied at the same time.

'Did you see what hearing that news did to Emily? She didn't know.'

'Yes, she knew. That's why she left her job,' Holly cried, impatient with Caitlin.

'That's not what I meant.'

'Then what did you mean?' Jo-Jo asked suspiciously. 'What are you trying to suggest about Emily?'

Off we go again, thought Caitlin. Attack of the giant mother hens.

'He's come home *without Nessa*. Don't you see that changes everything for Emily? Oliver's free. He could get together with Emily now.'

There was a pause. Then Holly asked incredulously, 'Are you suggesting we try to set her up?'

'Don't be ridiculous.' Jo-Jo laughed at the thought. 'Why would Oliver fancy Emily?'

'Why not?' Caitlin challenged.

'Because there's no point in fancying Emily!'

'No point! Of course there's a point. I can think of three, four, ten men who would tell you just what the point is. And Oliver too. Oliver's not oblivious to her charms. Think about how she met him. It couldn't have been more romantic. Hot sun, swimming in the sea, snogging in the sand dunes. All that wonderful long hair and those amazing legs. Sweet sixteen and probably never been kissed. He probably wishes he'd got in there and finished the job when he had the chance.'

'It wasn't like that,' Holly insisted, putting down the wine bottle and throwing herself back into the sofa. 'It really wasn't. Emily would have told me. They barely kissed and they didn't even keep in touch afterwards. When Oliver walked into *Breaking Free* it was the first time Emily had seen him for over five years.'

'Maybe,' Caitlin said quietly. 'But you didn't see her face when she heard Nessa's not come back. Emily's in love with Oliver and she has been ever since she first met him. After that holiday she never forgot him. Sixteen, seventeen, eighteen, nineteen, twenty . . . I know she had a few boyfriends, but none of them came close to those memories of Oliver. No one else ever made her feel like he did. All the things you do in those vital years, going out with guys for the first time, losing your virginity, falling in love – letting all the most important, life-changing things happen to you – Emily didn't do any of them. And it's because of Oliver. And look what happened. Look where she is now.'

'What happened to her?' Holly said, but half-heartedly, because neither she nor Jo-Jo was fighting now and Caitlin could tell from the silence that she had them listening, that they understood, that they were halfway to agreeing with her.

She bent to the floor and poured more wine to give them a moment to think about it. 'Maybe that brief time with Oliver wouldn't have mattered. Emily would probably have met someone else, eventually. But then she leaves university, she gets her first job and who walks onto the set of *Breaking Free* and back into her life again? It was the worst thing that could have happened to her because this time, right from the start, he was with Nessa. You tell us all the time about how intense it gets on location,' Caitlin reminded Jo-Jo, 'how you get to know a crew better in twelve weeks than other people in twelve years. Breakfast, lunch, evenings, early mornings, every second he's there, reminding her how there really is nobody else as perfect as him. And he is perfect. Big, strong, sexy, scruffy, charming when he wants to be, bolshie enough to be interesting, fantastic at his job. God, we *all* fell in love with him, didn't we?' She went on before the others could agree or disagree. 'But he's got Nessa. And so there's no way Emily can take it further. No need to put herself on the line, no chance of being rejected. She can love him from afar, she doesn't have to deal with any realities.' Caitlin hadn't thought about it like this before, but the more she talked the more she was sure that she was getting it right, because it all made such sense, explained so much about Emily.

'And do you see how Oliver is never going to get the chance to let her down? He's never going to mess up – he'll never get pissed with the lads or shag some other girl, or call his friends on his mobile from the bus to tell them what she's like in bed.'

'But Oliver wouldn't do that anyway, would he? Because he's a lovely guy,' said Holly, hopelessly sentimental, and her eyes filled with tears. She blinked, stretched her arm down for the glass on the floor and automatically gulped down the wine. 'Has she really been waiting for him all this time?'

Caitlin nodded. 'I think she has.'

'I always wondered at the way she could turn everyone down,' Jo-Jo admitted. 'I sometimes wondered why it wasn't more difficult for her.'

Caitlin nodded. 'I've wondered too. And believe it or not, I've been there too. I know what I'm talking about,' she went on, turning away from them and walking across the room to the windows.

'*You* were never a virgin!' Jo-Jo asked, mockingly.

'I know how it feels to be Emily,' Caitlin insisted. 'Getting into work at seven thirty because he does, convincing yourself it's your *job* you love, not *him*. And I remember how I felt and I multiply it maybe one hundred times for Emily, because for Emily there's never been anyone else!'

'But does she realize? Has she admitted to herself how she feels?' Holly asked.

'I don't think so.' Caitlin said. 'She's never acknowl-edged he's the reason why.'

'Why what?'

'Why she's still an Extra Strong Mint, not a Polo. But, yes, I think she must know she fancies him. And now that he's free again, she'll crucify herself about what to do about him and end up doing nothing at all. She'll be paralysed with fear. Poor Emily. Holding out for Mr Right might be wonderful in theory, but in practice it must be a nightmare. Don't you think she's having a far harder time *not* having sex than we are having it?' She challenged Holly and Jo-Jo.

'Don't look at me,' Holly countered. 'I haven't had sex for so long I wonder if I am a virgin again.'

Caitlin grinned. 'What I think I'm trying to say is that we're happy. Aren't we? Generally happy?' She looked at them both. 'But Emily is *miserable*. Even I can see it and I hardly know her. And don't think protecting her, not challenging her, not making her talk about whether she's doing the right thing is being a good friend to her. You may believe you're supporting a good cause, but you're not. You think I don't like her, but I do,' Caitlin said quietly as if reading Holly's mind. 'It's just all the time I've known her I've wanted to shake her, because she's missing out on so much. But now it's different. We can't let her go through the next ten years waiting for some fairy-tale ending that's never going to happen.

'We have an opportunity that we didn't have before,' Caitlin continued. 'We have a chance to get involved here and now. Oliver is available for action.' She pulled apart the curtains and looked out through the glass. 'He is two miles away! Either he's the one or he's not, but it's time Emily found out. And she's not going to find out if we don't help her.' Caitlin turned back to them, waiting for a reply.

'Yes, Emily admits that Oliver is her perfect man. She's told me as much already,' Jo-Jo said, clearly treading carefully. 'And, yes, I can see that Oliver's pedestal can't be knocked over unless she gets much closer to him, and that meanwhile Emily is getting older and older and it's becoming a bigger and bigger issue that she's not sleeping with anyone. She's almost *famous*. She's a phenomenon. It's ridiculous! Other people, people she doesn't even know, discuss her sex life around the supper table and they have no idea what she's really like. And I can see that if she was forced to confront Oliver and even if it all went wrong, then still his spell would be broken . . .'

'So you agree that I'm right?' Caitlin asked, coming back eagerly, sitting down again. 'Do you agree that we should try to do something to help her?'

Jo-Jo glanced quickly to Holly but Holly had her eyes to the floor. 'Yes, I think I do,' she admitted. 'I think you're right. If we can find a way to do it. I think we should step in.'

Caitlin hurried on. 'All I'm suggesting is that we set up some dates for the two of them. Make sure they get some chances to be alone together over the next few months, that's all. The rest we leave up to them. Or we leave it to Emily to decide what she really wants to do. I don't think it's likely that Oliver would turn her down.'

Then, just when she thought she had them both, Holly interrupted. 'It makes great sense,' she said, 'as long as we forget we're talking about Emily. You know her – ' she turned to Jo-Jo – 'you've listened to her, you've been won over just like I have, and Rachel has too. How can you now agree that everything she has said and done – or not done – is simply the result of an infatuation with Oliver? Aren't you belittling her? And is that, perhaps, because you don't want to believe in what she says? Maybe we're talking about our own motives, not Emily's, because she makes us judge ourselves as well as her and maybe it's making us uncomfortable.' She turned her attention to Caitlin. 'Forgive me, but I wonder if you're envious. Maybe you wish you could wipe the slate clean of some of your encounters and whenever you see Emily she reminds you of them.'

'Oh, no.' Caitlin laughed to soften her words. 'Don't start on me. I'm not the issue here. And I'm not wanting to trick her into anything. I'm not even trying to get her to admit that, yes, she's living in the nineteen fifties. And, if we leave her alone, yes, maybe she will eventually run around a few cornfields holding hands with some suitably patient man, get married, finally have sex and live happily ever after. But before that can happen, she needs to get Oliver out of her system. And if it is him, if it turns out that he *is* the one, the one and only Mr Right, then she may as well find out now.' Then she added, challenging them for an answer, 'Either way, tell me the harm in putting the two of them together?'

'Perhaps we should ask her about it?' Holly said instead.

'Completely pointless. If you do that,' said Caitlin, 'she'll deny it. Firstly, because she's absolutely terrified of the idea of getting close to Oliver, so she'll probably hare off to Cornwall, to her brother's to hide, and secondly because she has had her radar trained on all of us for years. She knows we'd love to fix her up with someone. It's why she never tells us anything. We cannot let her know we have any interest whatsoever in her and Oliver.'

Holly nodded and sighed. She thought how surprising it was to hear Caitlin, of all her friends, talking and thinking about Emily in this way.

'And we thought all you ever cared about was sex and shopping.' Jo-Jo laughed, echoing Holly's thoughts.

Caitlin smiled back. 'I think you'll find this is all about sex, Jo-Jo, don't you think? It was the expression on her face when she heard Nessa had stayed in the States. It was so sweet and sad. I liked seeing her like that. It was good to see that she's not so completely in control of herself after all.'

'I've known Emily for so long,' Jo-Jo said, 'and I can't believe I've never thought about Oliver like this before. Surely we'd have picked it up if she was in love with him. Wouldn't we have noticed something?'

'No, because Emily is a queen of deception,' Caitlin said. 'She's even deceived herself.'

'But if you put them together and Oliver doesn't fancy Emily . . . What happens then?' Jo-Jo asked.

'I know she won't die. She won't throw herself off a bridge or under a bus. If Oliver doesn't fancy her, tough. It's happened to all of us. We survive.'

Caitlin got up and walked away, circling the room, and again Holly was reminded of an actor on stage, trying to win over her partners in crime. Caitlin turned to her. 'Don't you think it's important to get hurt, to *feel* things and take risks with our emotions, even if it sometimes means getting kicked in the teeth by some bastard? Of course it's horrible at the time but you get over it. It's what makes us who we are. Emily needs to know those feelings,' Caitlin went on, into her stride, certain now. 'She is not happy living her bland, uneventful life. She's searching around for something more. So she chucks in her job, talks of going to live in Cornwall, but we all know it's not that. She's frustrated! She's lonely! She's worried she's never going to have sex, she's starved herself of physical contact of any sort. When was the last time we heard about Emily kissing someone, let alone sleeping with them?'

'Come and sit down,' Holly insisted. 'Stop throwing yourself around the room and tell us what to do.'

Caitlin sat back down. 'Get them together before he meets someone else.'

The thought that Oliver might meet someone else galvanized Holly and Jo-Jo.

'We need candlelight and log fires and soft feather beds,' Jo-Jo started enthusiastically.

Caitlin nodded. 'I'll start. I'll invite her to supper in the next few days and I'll have Oliver there, waiting for her, all very casual, very last minute.'

'And I'll invite everyone to the chalet,' Holly said generously. 'I've already asked Emily.'

'Oh, darlings, do let's all go to Holly's chalet,' Jo-Jo teased. 'Holly, I always forget you're from a different planet.'

'I know, I'm sorry.' Holly looked embarrassed. 'Feel free to take advantage of me.'

'We do!' Caitlin grinned. 'That's a great idea. Take Emily out of her natural environment. Nothing matters so much when you're on holiday. Skiing would loosen her up, help her forget her inhibitions ... Skiing would be perfect.'

'If we can persuade Oliver to come,' Holly said doubtfully. 'Will he come? He might know Emily and Jo-Jo, but he hardly knows me!'

'Of course he'll come. What are you worried about? That he'll be a bit shy? Ask a friend for him if you're worried. Get Sam Finch along.'

'And anyone else? Who else can we think of?' Holly asked, and because this was how she always was, keen to fill her house, or houses, with friends, Jo-Jo and Caitlin took her at her word.

'How about Leon?' Caitlin said.

'I thought you were getting rid of him.'

She shook her head. 'I can't. And I think it would be good if he came, not just for me but because he's fun and he's someone we all know and because I think we'd be more likely to persuade Oliver if he thought he had a few allies, if he didn't think he was coming along with just a bunch of girls.'

'Really? Isn't that just the sort of holiday Oliver loves?' said Holly.

'Sam would be great,' Caitlin went on. 'But if we can't persuade him we need Leon as a back-up, because we can be certain that he'll come.'

'Sure, of course, ask Leon.' Holly turned to Jo-Jo's groan. 'I know, I know. Tell me I didn't just say that.'

'No, I'm groaning because I can't come. Not over Easter. I'll be in Siena. I leave next week. Damn!'

'But if you're not there, how do we persuade Oliver?' Holly started to panic. 'He hardly knows us.'

'I think sex with a virgin is an extremely good offer.' Caitlin grinned. 'Get Emily to ask him.'

'Find him a friend and he'll come,' Jo-Jo said confidently. 'It's a fantastic offer. Of course he'll want to.'

'And we have to invite Rachel, too,' Holly insisted. 'I'd feel terrible if we left her out.'

'Don't feel terrible,' Caitlin said. She had no time for Rachel. 'If she wasn't such a tired little mouse, she wouldn't have gone home, she could have been part of this. But she did and she's not. I don't trust her. She's Emily's self-styled protector of high morals. She certainly doesn't have her worst interests at heart, like we do.'

Much later, when Caitlin finally did up the buttons of her coat in readiness to leave, she turned to Holly one last time. 'What are we hoping to achieve here?' she asked. There was no challenge in her question but genuine concern. 'What do you see in six months' time? I hope it's not a church and Emily in a big white dress and a long aisle with Oliver waiting at the end of it. You know we're not about to make a Disney film?'

Holly shook her head.

'It's not happy-ever-after we're aiming for, is it? Or happy-later-on. It's happy-now, isn't it? She needs to have some fun. She's miserable and lonely. You can see that, can't you?'

'Virginity can fuck you up, can't it.'

'Exactly.' Caitlin smiled. 'And I'm pleased we can admit that now. Before tonight we all had opinions about Emily but we kept quiet about them . . . She's missed out on too much for too long, don't you think? And I'm not just talking about her love life. I'm talking about talking, about how we didn't feel we could get involved.'

'She talks to her brother.'

Caitlin nodded. 'I'm glad she has *someone*.'

'I know we're doing the right thing for her,' Holly said. 'I'm sure that we are. But I'm scared stiff that she'll sleep with him.'

Caitlin shrugged. 'And I'm scared stiff that she won't.'

5

Having two distracted strangers for parents – a couple who had never got to grips with the fact that they had children – Emily was forever thankful that she'd also been given a brother like Arthur and her default setting was to turn to him whenever she felt under pressure or wanted good advice. Endlessly interested, and utterly adoring of Emily, he was her suit of armour, her shield against the harsher realities of life in London, against the assaults of the Carrie Pipers and the skirmishes with the Caitlins. Whenever she needed him, she didn't have to ask herself whether he would be there for her. He was always there for her, and not just in spirit – because Arthur hardly ever left St Brides, the little town in Cornwall where he had found the friends and environment that suited him best, where he could look out of his office window at the sea and could surf all weekend if he wanted to. He lived alone – girls were always falling for him but he hadn't met the one he wanted to pick up and hang onto – and so, whenever Emily wanted, she could go to St Brides and slot straight back into Arthur's life.

Emily knew that when talking about him to her friends she'd probably made Arthur sound a bit eccentric, exaggerated him even, telling them how he lived alone in Cornwall, in a converted coastguard station, on a spit of land called Dodger Point, and had a social life that revolved around the Hen's Tooth pub in St Brides, how he hardly ever travelled and was happy to spend the weekend surfing or walking the cliffs, alone but for his dog Clara. The decidedly strange parents, and the rather unconventional sister, probably only added to his oddball credentials.

But then, one by one, Emily had brought Holly, Jo-Jo and Rachel down to stay at Dodger Point and watched their preconceptions crumble. A day at Dodger Point and even Jo-Jo, the ultimate city chick, was wondering aloud if you could hear the sound of the sea from Arthur's bedroom, was standing on the cliffs, staring out at a soft pink sea fading in the evening light, and talking about falling in love.

Dodger Point had to be one of the most ruggedly beautiful places on earth and Arthur's home one of the most perfectly romantic. It sat small and squat and secure on a rocky peninsula a couple of hundred feet above the sea, with a little windswept garden leading up to the front door and rough steps carved into the rocks winding down to the tiny beach below. And it had a tower, so that it was possible to climb up a spiral staircase to look out at the sea. A couple of years after he had bought it, Arthur had put on an extension to the back, adding two more small bedrooms and another bathroom to the single bedroom in the main house.

Having brought her to St Brides, Emily had watched Jo-Jo fall, like others before her, just a little in love with Arthur as well as with his house, but despite Emily's blatant matchmaking Arthur never obliged. He flirted enough to be flattering and was always charming and kind but never took it further, displaying an evasiveness that was never unfriendly and certainly not calculated and only served to make him all the more attractive. And when this detachment made him distant, as it sometimes did, this only served to remind Jo-Jo and the others of Emily, and then they would recall Emily and Arthur's parents, who had emigrated to New Zealand six weeks after Emily had left school. Neither Emily nor Arthur had seen them since.

Whenever Arthur made a trip to London, Emily spent most of her time fussing around him, convinced he or Clara were about to be run over or mugged or abducted. Of course she knew he could look after himself. It was only because she loved him so much, because he was all she had, that she became so neurotic. When she failed to prevent Caitlin from finally meeting Arthur – Emily had done her best to keep the two of them apart – and Caitlin immediately arranged to take him clubbing the following evening, Emily had nearly exploded with outrage. Whereupon Arthur had held her firmly by the shoulders and reminded her that he'd lived in Tooting for five years and could well cope with the pressure of ordering a round of drinks. Emily had wanted to tell him that Caitlin wasn't anything like the girls in Tooting, that she was a vampire who would sink her teeth into him and suck him dry, but Caitlin was standing there at his shoulder and even Emily didn't dare.

And now here she was thinking about joining him in

St Brides for good. She wondered whether Arthur might not want his sister to move to his town but deep down was sure he wouldn't mind. Arthur had moved to St Brides because of a good job and because of the sea, not because he was wanting to escape anything. Far from feeling she would cramp his style, Emily got the impression he would love to have her living nearby.

If anything, it wouldn't be Arthur's refuge she might be destroying but her own, because surely it was the stark contrast with London that made St Brides so idyllic. She needed the enclosed London streets in order to appreciate the vastness of the sea, needed to breathe in the city fug to appreciate the salty clean air, needed to open her bedroom window to row upon row of cramped and scrubby back gardens in order to appreciate the cliffs of Dodger Point.

And yet, Emily was filled with a terrible restlessness. It was time to do something seriously different, something bigger than merely walking out of her job. Something that would jolt her and make her feel alive again. She had been marking time for too long.

The next morning, her second day of unemployment, and even before she was fully awake, Emily stretched out an arm for the telephone and called Arthur. The longer his mobile rang the wider awake she became. Finally he picked up.

'Can I come and stay?' she demanded immediately.

'Hello, Arthur. How are you? Oh, hi there, Emily. Good to hear from you. I'm very well, thanks.'

'Hello, Arthur,' she said smiling. 'Where've you been? Why did you take so long to answer the phone?'

'None of your business.'

'I wanted to come and see you.' When he didn't say anything she went on more tentatively, 'Tonight. Is that OK? If I get in at about seven.' Surely it was OK? It was always OK.

There was a pause. 'Come for supper at the Pelican?'

'What? No fish and chips in front of the telly?'

'No, you can come out for dinner.' Emily could hear there was something else coming. She pushed herself up against her pillows. Lying down was suddenly making her feel vulnerable.

'Come and meet my girlfriend,' he said.

There was another pause.

'A desperately-in-love-with-her girlfriend or an only-just-met-her girlfriend?'

'Perhaps both.'

She could hear in his voice that he meant it too. *Why the bloody hell do you have to find a new girlfriend now?* And she couldn't think what else to say. Her mind was leaping ahead: *What if she wants to move into Dodger Point? What if you get married? How can I come and stay then? Where will I go?*

'What's her name?'

'It's Jennifer.'

Jennifer. What kind of a person was a Jennifer? Not a Jenny or a Jen but a Jennifer. A Jennifer filled her with foreboding. She saw someone tall and serious, with long straight black hair and a pale, unsmiling face.

'When did you meet her? And where? Does she live in St Brides?'

'Only a week ago. On the beach. And yes, she does. She was looking for shells and we kind of bumped into each other.'

'That sounds so unlikely.' *Damn Jennifer.*

Arthur laughed. 'Don't be so suspicious. Weren't you looking for shells when someone bumped into you?'

'Yes, but I was sixteen and, anyway, he didn't bump.'

'She did.'

'So she has little milk-bottle-bottom glasses, does she?'

'Emily!'

'Or someone jostled her? The beach was packed full of people?'

'It was empty.'

'Then she didn't bump, did she?' Emily challenged. 'It was a cunning plan to get talking to you.'

'I hope so. She's beautiful . . .'

Emily laughed warily. 'OK. You're keen. I'm going to have to like her.'

'But if you don't?'

'Then I'll behave really badly, let you down.'

Arthur sighed theatrically. 'I think we're going to have to find someone else to come to supper. Someone to dilute you.'

'Do you have someone in mind? Some sad work colleague who never gets out?'

'Actually, I do know someone. Someone who happened to wander into my office yesterday morning. Do you remember Sam Finch?'

'I know Sam. What was he doing in your office?'

'Do you like him? Would you like him to come?' Arthur waited but Emily didn't say anything. 'We were talking and then he asked me if I had a sister called Emily and I said yes, I had, and he said he remembered meeting me years ago. He said it was with you, here one summer. And how he'd seen you again just this week.' Arthur wasn't about to tell Emily how it had taken Sam perhaps twenty seconds to bring the conversation around to Emily, nor how obvious it was that she was really the only reason why Sam was there in his office. 'He's just come back to live in Cornwall.'

'I don't need setting up just because you've got Jennifer.'

'It wouldn't be like that.'

'I met him through Oliver. Oliver Mills? Do you remember him? I worked with him on *Breaking Free*. He's just come back from New York.'

'You snogged him in the sand dunes. I remember Oliver. He could water-ski with bare feet.'

'That's the one.'

Emily, with time to think about it, liked the idea of Sam joining them and she didn't really mind Arthur knowing but she wanted to move the conversation on from Oliver. 'Call Sam,' she encouraged Arthur. 'Don't let him say no.' She was nervous about meeting Jennifer and it would be good to have an ally.

Afterwards she put down the telephone and lay back against the pillows. Her bed was at a right angle to the window and she lay there with her eyes closed, feeling the air from the half-open window cold on her face. She ran back over the conversation with Arthur, hearing his words again, the reverential *she's beautiful*, and in her mind Jennifer transformed into someone laughing and bewitchingly pretty, an undefined version of Jennifer Aniston. Emily saw Jennifer and Arthur striding away from her across the beach at Dodger Point, Clara at their heels, their arms round each other, a criss-cross of unity on their backs. Great that he'd found someone, she told herself bouncing up again in bed in agitation. She meant it too. She loved him. She was thrilled for him, she really was – or she knew she would be when she had got herself sorted out.

But right now the effect of Arthur's news was to make her feel distanced from him, turned and twisted and wrenched away. Not surprising that the loneliness that had been creeping around for the past few days was suddenly there, full on, harsh and unrelenting. While some might picture hordes of men beating on her bedroom door only to be turned away by a virginal Emily in a long white nightdress, the reality was that there had been no one for Emily to turn down for nearly a year. Nobody to test, nobody to miss, nobody to think about, and now, with Arthur in love and Oliver back home Nessa-less, it felt as if she had been left more alone than ever, while around her everything had turned upside down, so that all those things that had been impossible before were possible now and she found herself hating the change.

She got up and opened the curtains. She looked out of her third-floor window and down to the twelve tiny gardens below, a messy, irregular patchwork of dilapi-dated garden fences dividing one set of weeds and rusty bicycles from another. In one garden hung a row of red-coloured washing, surely frozen to the line it had been there so long and hung there so still.

She shut the window and sat down on her bed again, then rose once more and left her bedroom, made her way down the short hall to her kitchen, fed a slice of bread into the toaster and filled the kettle, pulled out a chair and sat at the small square wooden table. Then decided to go running.

Before the kettle had boiled or the bread toasted she was back in her bedroom. She didn't want breakfast. She couldn't sit down. She didn't want to eat. She imagined herself sprinting effortlessly though dark woods, twigs snapping under her feet, up and down hills, like Clarice Starling in *The Silence of the Lambs*. She wanted to do what she knew other people did when they were so worked up they couldn't stop themselves prowling around their flats. She would go for a run in Richmond Park.

She dug in a drawer for a pair of socks and then burrowed deep in her cupboard and found a pair of trainers rolled up in some Lycra running shorts and a fluorescent vest. She straightened up, holding them in her hands, and for a brief moment she could hear the blood roaring in her ears and the sound of her gasping, rasping breathing, could look down at her thighs, mottled orange and purple with cold, spattered with mud. She pushed the memory away. Running was a good idea. This would be a fun run, she would take it gently. She would walk as soon as she wanted.

The park was less than half an hour away, but if Holly hadn't taken her there for a picnic soon after she'd moved into the house in Richmond, Emily doubted she'd ever have thought to go. Now she knew it would be the place she missed most if she ever did get around to leaving London.

She parked at Sheen Gate. It was a cold, bright morning and there was hardly anybody about – only a few committed dog walkers, sitting in their cars with the doors open, pulling on wellingtons and buttoning up oilskins, or opening the boots of hatchback cars to let out eager, bouncing dogs.

Emily locked her car, re-tied her trainers, stuffed her keys and phone into her belt-bag and went to touch her toes, but quickly changed her mind. She walked at first, instantly soothed by the silent magic of the woods. There was a fallen tree ahead of her and, seeing it, she started to jog, measured it up, then leapt lightly over the trunk, only to land with a noisy splash in a puddle on the other side.

I think that's enough running a loud, persuasive voice in her head said then. *Stop now, before it gets nasty.* But she couldn't, she told the voice, not yet, not when she'd hardly begun, when she'd managed to run little more than twenty feet.

Determined to keep going, she left the woods and made herself run on into the park, her feet squelching in her now soggy trainers. Keeping the boundary wall on her right, she found that she was running easier, even able to let her mind wander a little, to think how the wall kept out so much more than it kept in, how it embraced the park and held it safe from all the concrete and glass and exhaust fumes that were crowding up behind it. Inside, the sun rested warm on her back, the sky pure and blue.

She ran along the edge of the woods, sending squirrels leaping for the safety of the oaks, and thought how Charles I hunted deer there, had maybe galloped along the very path she was running on now. How wonderful it was that the park and the deer had survived so unchanged, to be here still, centuries later.

And then the path turned and she saw her first hill. She dug deep and started to climb and immediately any ideas of this being an enjoyable experience disappeared completely. Within a few strides the hill became an assault course and benign King Charles faded away, replaced by a vicious red devil who jabbed her in the ribs with his pointed trident.

She heard herself hissing through clenched teeth. Why had she done it again? Why hadn't she remembered how much she hated running, had always hated it? She'd done this so many times before. She remembered thundering along a lane in Cornwall after Arthur, in the same trainers, shorts and vest she was wearing now, blood roaring in her ears, convinced she was about to die.

She made it to the top of the hill and left the path like a shipwreck survivor staggering from the sea. There was a bench ahead of her, bracken all around it, too tempting to ignore. She sat down and with trembling hands managed to take off her wet trainers and feebly wring out her socks. And then she lay down with her knees bent, clammy cold feet resting on the slats of the bench while her breathing slowly calmed and eventually she could see clearly again.

She pushed herself upright, keeping her knees bunched up against her chest, and looked around.

Now everywhere looked beautiful. Around her bench, baby green shoots of new bracken were just starting to uncurl, bursting through the earth at her feet, above a kestrel circled idly in the perfect blue sky. Tipping back her head she found that the sun felt warm on her face. And she wondered why she was thinking of moving to St Brides when all this was on her doorstep. She could move three miles rather than three hundred and rent a flat in Richmond if she wanted open spaces. She hadn't acknowledged before that it wasn't London she wanted to escape from. That moving away wasn't necessarily going to make her any happier.

And then she stared more closely at the branch sticking up out of a patch of bracken a gentle toss of a stone away from her bench, and realized, belatedly, that the branch was one of a pair and that where there were two branches, there were maybe a hundred others rising out of the bracken all around her. And how had she not noticed the Bambi-brown eyes staring at her from all around? Not even taken in the two huge stags facing each other aggressively less than fifty feet away?

As if they had been waiting for her attention, the two stags dropped their heads, clashed antlers and roared at each other and Emily picked up her socks and shoes and sprinted, head down and without a glance behind her, back to the path.

When she thought she had put a safe distance between her and the deer, she stopped and put her trainers back on and looked back. Maybe they hadn't bothered to chase her, but she wasn't going to tempt them a second time, which meant a wide loop around them before she could return to her car.

The path led her downhill now and her wobbly legs began to run away with themselves even as she tried to walk and with each bump and jolt another wave of self-pity rose within her until she found she was almost willing herself to trip over, wanting to hit the ground with a smack, wanting the shoot of pain from a twisted ankle to take her attention instead and allow her to burst into tears. But her feet kept her upright instinctively, balancing and springing her deftly off the tussocks of grass and sharp rocks that littered the path.

As far as self-diagnosis went, it was pretty obvious something was shifting inside her. Was it simply a recognition that she was lonely? It felt as if she was missing someone, but perhaps someone she'd never even known. She'd arrived home after supper with Holly and the others and had lain down on her little patchwork sofa, her knees pulled up almost to her chin, and it had felt as if she was waiting for someone, someone she could almost touch, smell, whose smile she could almost see. Six months ago –

even six weeks ago – it hadn't been like that. Work had been miserable, but once home she'd been able to forget about work. Having Rachel downstairs and Holly down the street and her brother on the end of the phone had been all that she'd needed, but not any more.

Oliver was home again and Nessa had been left behind. Emily finally allowed herself to confront it, to face the niggling, nagging, sleep-destroying fact that had been tormenting her ever since she'd first heard. Oliver was free. What did that mean for her?

Another great hill loomed up ahead of her. Her legs were hurting, her lungs heaving for air, in her head she was screaming every expletive she'd ever known, in her head only because she hadn't the breath to say them aloud.

She came to a second exhausted halt and stared down at her mud-spattered legs, looking so distressed that an old lady walking a West Highland terrier stopped to offer her a piece of chocolate.

She looked up at the high ornate gates open just ahead of her and saw that she'd got as far as Richmond. She was only a few hundred yards from Holly's house. And Holly was taking a few days off, she remembered, and so she might possibly be in.

Emily walked out through the gates and down Richmond Hill in her Lycra shorts and soaked vest, sweat pouring down her flaming cheeks, oblivious to all the smart boutiques and shoppers to match, thinking about being strong and following a path she had carved out for herself years ago and was not about to give up on, however much the dazzle of Oliver might tempt her. Oliver. Again, her mind skidded away from the challenge of him, ignoring the opportunity that was presenting itself – the fact that she could, right now, go after him with the same single-minded determination that she'd seen other girls use on other men.

A hundred yards from Holly's front door, her mobile rang and she turned away from the noise of the street to answer it.

'Emily. Hi, it's Caitlin.'

Sounding unusually friendly, Emily thought, instantly suspicious.

'I've left a message on your answerphone, but then I thought why not try your mobile?' Emily waited. 'I wondered if you were free for supper on Saturday night. Probably not,' Caitlin added without pausing for breath. 'I know it's not much notice, but it would be so good to see you.'

'Saturday? This Saturday?' Emily cupped her hand around her ear trying to block out the sound of the street, convinced she wasn't hearing right.

'Yes. But I can hear you don't want to. You're trying to think of a way out, aren't you?'

'No, I'm not! I'm out of breath. I've been running,' Emily protested, even as she was trying to think of an excuse. 'That would be great. I'm off to see Arthur. Catching a train in about an hour.' An hour! What was she doing in Richmond? 'But I can come back on Saturday.'

'Fantastic.'

'Caitlin,' Emily said, 'why do you want me?' She knew

she sounded confrontational but she had to ask, knew it would be bugging her all the time she was in Cornwall if she didn't.

Caitlin paused. 'Does there have to be a reason?' And from the way she said it, Emily knew there was of course a reason. Then Caitlin sighed, acknowledging what they both knew already. 'OK. You're right! There is.'

'Why?'

'I want you because . . . you're such good company.'

'Rubbish.' Emily laughed. 'Try again.'

'No, you are! I should have got you round years ago.'

Emily shook her head. 'That's not the reason.'

'No,' Caitlin admitted. She started again, 'Half because I was horrid last night and I want to apologize. Really, that's the truth . . . and also because I've got Oliver coming and I want someone I know he likes to join us.'

Oliver was coming. 'Anyone else?' Emily asked, carefully avoiding mentioning his name.

'Only Leon.'

'I'd love to come. Thank you.' *Caitlin and Oliver?* Was that the reason Caitlin wanted Oliver to come for supper? Because Caitlin was after him? The thought made Emily want to punch her. Leon being there wouldn't stop her. Probably it would make it more exciting for her. 'Caitlin, I've got to go,' she said, walking up the steps to Holly's house and leaning on the bell. She wanted to ask Holly if she was right, not talk to Caitlin any more, and so she said a hasty goodbye and put away her phone.

Holly opened the door and gave her a startled look. 'Tell me you haven't run here all the way from Clapham.'

Emily rolled her eyes at the terrible thought and didn't reply. She walked past Holly and went into the kitchen in search of a glass of orange juice.

In Holly's shower, she closed her eyes and lifted her chin to the water, letting it beat down blissfully onto her forehead. She would get to Arthur's for supper. She would meet Jennifer. She would persuade Arthur to take tomorrow morning off, and would ask him to drive her along the coast, looking out for suitable places to open Saltwater. Back to London on Saturday morning. Saturday evening, supper at Caitlin's, where she would somehow have to fix it that Oliver didn't fall for Caitlin. Caitlin. How she was going to stop him she wasn't quite sure.

'Why do you think Caitlin wants me there?' she asked Holly, sitting in the kitchen afterwards in a pair of Holly's jeans and one of her T-shirts. 'Is it because I am the most unthreatening single woman around?'

Holly put a croissant and a cup of coffee down in front of her. 'There are other single women who are far less threatening than you. No. I think Caitlin genuinely wants to begin again with you.'

Emily shook her head. She hoped Holly was right, but she knew Caitlin well enough to give it less than a ten per cent chance of being true.

'You'll find out on Saturday,' said Holly. 'It's not long to wait.'

'How did you know it was Saturday? I didn't tell you? Has Caitlin already told you about it?' Emily caught the troubled look on Holly's face. 'She has! Why? What's going on? Holly, what have you been saying about me?'

'Don't be so suspicious,' Holly said smoothly. 'Caitlin called me about half an hour ago. It must have been just a few minutes before she called you and she mentioned it then.' Which was true. The fact that Holly had already known Emily was going to be asked for supper was beside the point. 'That's how I know. And do you know something? I've booked the skiing today.'

'Don't change the subject!' Emily's eyes bore into Holly's. 'Is there anything else I might like to know?'

'Caitlin mentioned that she was asking you around on Saturday night.'

'But why would she do that? I think it's because she fancies Oliver. And do you know – ' Emily groaned – 'I couldn't stand it if that's the reason. I cannot think of anything worse than sitting in Caitlin's flat watching her moving in on him.'

Holly took in the groan and the misery on Emily's face and was pleased by what she saw. 'Go and have a good time,' she insisted. 'Don't think about Caitlin. Think about seeing Oliver again. Don't try to outguess what might happen.'

And then, later, she drove Emily back to her car, leaving enough time for Emily to get back to her flat, change and pick up her bag to catch the early afternoon train to St Brides.

6

Emily saw Arthur from her window on the train, standing in a fisherman's jersey and dark cords, tall and thin among the huddle of people waiting in the neon lights and the cold.

He let her walk right up to him before he made a move, then suddenly opened wide his arms and let a great grin break across his face. Then he caught her in a hug and she knew she'd done the right thing, that she'd come to stay with the world's best person. She took his arm and let him lead her down the steep steps of St Brides station.

'Jennifer?' she said tentatively as they reached his car, raising her eyebrows at him. 'I'm so looking forward to meeting her.'

'And she's so looking forward to meeting you.'

Emily was momentarily taken aback. Then it dawned on her that of course Arthur and Jennifer would have talked about her, she should have expected it. Even so, it was a new feeling. She wanted to know what Arthur's description would have included and what he would have left out. She had a sudden image of Jennifer, lovely eyes crinkling with surprise, Jennifer laughing, her hand over her mouth. *A virgin? You're joking! How sweet!* And she hoped she was right to trust that Arthur wouldn't have told Jennifer that. Wouldn't have revealed something so personal.

Emily opened the passenger door of Arthur's car, slid into her seat and waited for him to join her, and behind her Arthur opened a back door and swung her bag onto the seat.

'I've booked a table for eight thirty,' he told her as he started the engine. 'Sam and Jennifer are going to meet us there.' He paused. 'So you've got time to change if you want to.'

'That sounds like I need to.'

'Not at all.'

She did need to. She wanted to dress to kill. She wanted to dispel the image of the soft, gentle innocent that Arthur had perhaps planted in Jennifer's mind. The irritating thing was that soft and gentle was exactly the image she'd packed for that evening: jeans and a pale pink cotton shirt printed with roses and a minty-green angora tank top. She'd have to find something else, she thought. She'd have to adapt it.

In companionable silence they drove away from the station and followed the main road, through the austere grey-stone town of St Brides, then along the coast road which in a few months' time would be clogged with holidaymakers but now, in the early evening dusk, was tranquil and empty. And then they picked up speed and left the town behind, the road still hugging the coastline but climbing and twisting all the way. Emily knew it all so well. It felt like coming home.

They were soon at the bend in the road from where they could see the lights of Dodger Point even though it would be another ten minutes before they arrived. She told herself not to be so excited about being here again, reminded herself that it wasn't her home.

They drove on, both aware that the other had more to say, neither of them fooled by the catching-up conversations that they continued to persist with. Emily timed Arthur's change of subject almost to the second, noticing how his lips started to move before he spoke, as if he was trying out the words before he spoke them out loud.

'I'm terrified at the thought of you meeting her,' he admitted, glancing at her.

She was struck by the vulnerability showing on his face. 'You mustn't be. And watch the road.'

'You're the only person whose opinion I care about.'

'Of course I'll like her.'

He nodded.

'And I'll be diluted, remember.' She smiled. 'It'll be fine. I like Sam. We'll have a great time.'

She described to Arthur how she'd literally run into Sam the other day, and he decided not to admit that he'd already heard it all from Sam.

They turned another corner and they were running along the coast again. Emily wound down her window, closed her eyes and breathed in the sea-scented air.

'Can you still smell the salt or have you become immune?'

Arthur didn't answer. She closed up her window again because it was freezing cold, turned back to him and touched his hand holding the steering wheel.

'I'm pleased for you. Now, can you fix it for me too, please?'

He squeezed her hand back. 'You want that?'

'Of course I do!'

'Then thank God I suggested getting him along! I'm so pleased you want to give him a chance.'

'Not Sam! I don't mean fix it for me with Sam!'

'Oh, I wasn't talking about *Sam*.' Arthur backtracked. 'Whatever made you think I was talking about Sam? I meant to say *her*. I meant give *her* a big chance. I was talking about Jennifer.'

'You big liar.' She looked across at him and slowly shook her head. 'Let us be clear about this: I am not interested in Sam.'

'Who *are* you interested in, then?' he said, obviously disappointed. 'Who is it who's turned you so prickly?'

She smiled. 'Picky or prickly?'

'Both.'

'Nobody. It's how I am.'

'And you're getting worse.'

'No, I'm not. I'm the same as I've always been. Tell me more about Jennifer,' she said, looking out of the window again. 'Have you shown her Dodger Point?'

'Yes.'

'And did she like it?'

'She did. Who is he, Emily?'

They drove on, both watching the road in the car's headlights, until Emily said, 'She was with you when I rang this morning, wasn't she?'

'Why do you say that?'

'There was something in your voice.'

'Yes, she was.'

'So, I suppose you were in the middle of showing her your bedroom, were you?'

Arthur was tempted to tell Emily the truth. To say no, they hadn't bothered going up to his bedroom because they'd just had icy-cold, fantastic sex in the sand dunes instead.

'Let's talk about you,' he said instead. 'Who do you want to be fixed up with? I can't help if I don't know who it is.'

Emily said nothing. 'OK, we'll talk about something else,' he said, looking at her with concern. 'But we're going to come back to it again and again and again until you tell me. So,' he added brightly, 'have you had any interviews?'

'I've fixed up a few. Everyone's telling me to have a break.'

'What about revenge? How about dropping a scorpion through Carrie Piper's letter box?'

'She'd probably eat it alive.' Emily took a deep breath. 'I was thinking about moving here, Arthur. Would you mind?'

'You know I'd love you to do that.'

'I'm wondering about Saltwater again.' Arthur nodded. 'And I thought perhaps you and I could do some shop hunting tomorrow. I wondered whether you might be able to take a bit of time off work to show me around.'

'I could.'

'Thank you.' She smiled gratefully.

'You know I think Saltwater is a terrific idea.'

'You don't think I'd be running away?'

'Would you be?' He waited five seconds, then tried again. 'From who? Tell me who he is?'

She shook her head again. 'It's no one!' Then she sighed. 'Nothing is wrong, at least not in a big, dramatic kind of a way. But I suppose something has changed and I don't know what to do about it . . .' She shrugged. 'And it's probably making me twitchy. Distracted. Prickly, whatever.'

'Try telling me.'

But just as they'd reached the moment where Emily might have opened up to Arthur, they turned into the short bumpy drive that led to Dodger Point. Arthur pulled up beside the house, turned off the engine and waited in the moonlit darkness for her to say some more.

She heaved a giant sigh. 'I suppose we're talking about sex,' she said.

'Or no sex?'

She laughed bitterly. 'You know me.'

'And someone in particular is making it an issue?'

'No. But I wish he would!' She gave him a flicker of a smile before her face fell again. 'For the first time, I'm seriously asking myself what I'll do if I meet someone I really care about. What I'll do if he won't wait for me. I'm amazed it's never happened to me before, but it hasn't. It's always been me ending relationships, not them. And the guys I've been out with, so far they've been happy to wait, happy for us to do other things . . . It hasn't been a problem. And it's been easy for me to say if they won't wait for me, then they're not worth sleeping with.' She stopped but Arthur knew better than to interrupt her flow. 'Now I'm wondering whether I should have thrown myself at some man years ago. Got it all over and done with, stopped it becoming an issue, like everyone else did.'

'But you didn't and you can't change that.'

'But I still could, couldn't I? It doesn't take much.'

'Someone is making you talk like this. Do I know him?'

'Yes, you do,' she said simply. 'It's Oliver.'

'Oliver Mills.' And from the way he said it, she knew it was no great surprise.

Her admission made, she felt cold. She wrapped her arms around herself and pulled up her knees, lifting her feet onto the dashboard. Now that she'd said it out loud it was as if she was freed up to think about Oliver in a way she hadn't allowed herself to for years. Admit how much she liked him. How much she'd like more of those entrancing moments that she'd been given so many years earlier, but had had to forget.

Then she swore out loud with the certain knowledge that while she fretted and did nothing he would quickly find somebody else, had probably found her already.

'He's back and he's single,' Emily said. 'But I know he won't turn to me . . . And for the first time he's making me question something I've always been so sure about. And it's making me angry . . . It's making me think if I wasn't so realistic, perhaps I could have jumped into bed with lots of guys. It's only because I know they're not going to last that I don't. I never saw the point in sleeping with the wrong guy. By wrong I mean someone I knew it wasn't going to last with. But other people don't think like me, other people throw themselves into their relationships, they're optimistic about them, they don't think realistically about the future. Why do I have to?'

'Is it possible – ' Arthur chose his words carefully – 'that the reasons you had for making that promise to yourself don't hold true any more? Might it be the promise to yourself that's keeping you back, more than the reasons behind the promise? And if that's the case, you mustn't think of a promise to yourself in the same way as a promise to someone else. If you're changing your mind now, that's not wrong. What would be wrong would be to deny it or run away from it. I've sat up for too many evenings with you not to know you've thought it all through. You have more courage than anyone else I know. But you're more stubborn, too. It would be hard for you to admit to yourself that it's time to change your mind.'

'You're right, and if that was all there was to it I'd agree with you, but it's not.'

'Tell me.'

Emily swallowed, trying to gather together the right words in her mind. How to explain a certainty that had grown and taken root over so many years.

He looked at her, full of kindness and concern. 'I'm Emily and I'm a virgin because . . .' he suggested helpfully.

'Stop it.' She laughed. 'This is serious.' And it was and yet it wasn't too, because while she could give lots of good reasons for why she'd stayed a virgin, the simple truth was that nobody had made it a difficult choice, until now.

'Lots of girls – and men too – have slept with people

because they felt they should, because they wanted to be part of the crowd. Not because they really wanted to.'

'That's true,' Arthur agreed. 'And if you sleep with Oliver for the wrong reasons, you'll be more angry with yourself than if you lose him over it.'

'But the years are flying by and I'm still alone. I never thought it would take so long!' she cried. 'Dammit, I sound completely sex-starved. Do you think that's what all this is about? Is it finally getting to me?'

'No.' Arthur laughed.

'You don't think I'm mad to be holding out?'

'As I've said, it depends what you're holding out for.'

'Holding out for more than a quick shag. Holding out for someone I really love, who really loves me. Holding out because I don't have a problem with waiting.'

'And there's nothing wrong with that.'

'Isn't there? Because I wonder sometimes if I'm making it impossible for me ever to get to know anyone. Perhaps waiting went out of fashion because it was such a bad idea?'

'All you've ever said is that you don't want to have sex with someone until you know your relationship will last; that you don't see the point in sleeping with a series of Mr Wrongs, men you know are going to slip out of your life and disappear. You want to wait. You believe that sex is something that should happen between two people who really love each other and you want to wait until you've found that.'

She nodded. 'And I can't help thinking what a lovely

thing it would be, *for me*,' she interrupted him, 'to give my virginity to the right man.'

Arthur said, 'And for those reasons I don't think it's mad, or terribly old-fashioned, or pointless. I think it's great. It's a wonderful ideal to have. And I wonder why it should be so hard. Why you're not surrounded by people thinking the same way.'

'But you didn't wait,' Emily reminded him. 'I don't suppose you and Jennifer have waited.'

'No.'

'What would you have done if she'd wanted to?'

'Dumped her instantly.'

'Seriously!'

'I'd have respected her! I'd have waited for as long as she wanted too, and I've have hoped it wouldn't be too long. As it was, it was about a day and most of a night.'

'Arthur! You shouldn't have told me that.'

'She wouldn't mind.'

'And won't you be crucified now if it all goes wrong? Won't it be far worse for you than if you hadn't slept together?'

He shook his head. 'I don't think of it like that. Better to have loved and lost, perhaps. And I'm eternally optimistic too. The truth is that until *you* get into a relationship, you won't know how you want to take it further. You have to get close, you have to let yourself fall for someone before you can know where it's going next. And you've never done that, have you?' He turned to Emily, waiting for her to respond, and she gave a small nod of agreement. 'It's only then that you'll fully appreciate what it is you've been holding on to, and whether it's right to let it go. Right now, you're saying that to be in lust isn't enough, that you want to be sure of a lifelong commitment. But how do you know? You've never been there! Wait, yes. Waiting is good. But be brave, too. Don't be so wary or you will never get involved.'

'I do understand how it can be,' said Emily. 'I know it often sounds like I don't. And I want to tell you something else about Oliver Mills,' she went on. 'I am not in love with him. But I could be. I want the chance to fall in love with him and what's driving me crazy is the thought that I'm not going to get it because he won't wait around for me. In fact, he won't come near me, let alone hang around, because for Oliver, my being a virgin will mean I'm off-limits. He will never see me as anything other than a friend, or perhaps a little sister.'

'How do you know? He didn't think of you like that when you were sixteen. You don't know Oliver won't want you just as you are.'

'I do.'

'Then stop being off-limits,' Arthur encouraged. 'Let him know you fancy him.'

'I don't think I can.'

'You've done it before, with other boyfriends,' Arthur urged.

'I know I have. It's just with him I feel paralysed. Completely hopeless.'

'You can't say that. Get a grip, girl. Take hold of your destiny. And now we have to get a move on,' he told her, opening his door, 'or we will be late for Jennifer and Sam.'

Emily left Arthur in the kitchen and, although they were running out of time, she climbed the spiral staircase to the tiny round room in the tower. She'd decorated this room for Arthur, painted it with a sea green oil glaze right up to the high round ceiling, somehow carrying a chair up the spiral staircase to do the highest bits. She'd hunted through antique shops for furniture and had eventually found an old oak curved bench with an arm at each end that must have once been made for a round table and now fitted perfectly into the curve of the tower. Arthur had had to chop off the legs to get it up to the room, then glue them on again afterwards. She'd added deep velvet-covered cushions in red and burnt sienna and green to match the walls and had polished the grey stone floor and left it bare. Now one could sit back, comfortable and secure, against the cushions and look out of the large rectangular windows down to the sea below.

She sat there, warm inside her coat, looking down at the midnight blue water, at the cliffs and the dark sky ... and wondered what to wear to meet Jennifer.

She was looking forward to the evening now, she felt rejuvenated. The conversation in the car with Arthur had changed her mood, filled her with anticipation. She was glad now that they were going out, that there was a chance to dress up and to see Sam again and to meet Jennifer.

It was a calm night and the sea was flat and reflective

like oil. To the west, Emily could see the lights of St Brides. She thought how much fun it would be to look around there tomorrow with Arthur, because of all the nearby towns St Brides was the place she was most familiar with and the place she could best imagine opening her shop.

She stretched out her fingers and touched the china animals that had been hers as a child and had found their way to St Brides, to this window sill. She picked up a galloping horse, pricking her fingertips on its spiky china mane and then tracing the line of its delicate thoroughbred legs. The horse had come with a foal, but her mother, knowing how much her daughter adored it, had given it to one of Emily's school friends, one of the times when she had stopped being just vague and had seemed deliberately cruel. Why did she have to remember that now? Emily put the horse down. Next to it was a bronze bell, green with age and without its knocker, and beside that a purple velvet gonk. She picked up the gonk and turned him so that his big, lopsided, grinning face could look out of the window.

When she'd dressed she made her way back down to the kitchen. Arthur was filleting mackerel, Clara had her head between her paws, watching him intently. He stopped when he saw her in the doorway and stared at her. 'Very nice.'

'Thanks!'

Emily pulled out a chair. 'Is that our breakfast?'

He nodded. 'I bought them on the way to the station

just after they'd been caught. I thought I'd finish preparing them before we go out.'

In the summer Arthur would have caught them himself. He had a little motor boat that he'd take out after work, dragging a line of hooks behind him.

'Do *I* look all right?' he asked her then, turning around so that she could see him properly.

She smiled at the question because she didn't think she'd ever seen him look any other way. Did he own a loud shirt, or a jumper that wasn't olive green or navy blue, or trousers that weren't denim or cord? She wondered what plans Jennifer might have for him, whether next time Arthur might be waiting for her at the station in flip-flops and a sarong.

'You look very handsome.' She walked over to him and stretched up and kissed his freshly shaved cheek. 'Holly and Jo-Jo are going to be very disappointed when they hear about Jennifer.'

Like most tourist towns, St Brides survived on its summers. For the past three years visitor numbers had been boosted by the presence of the Pelican, a seafood restaurant situated in a spectacular setting, high on the cliffs, run by a woman called Hope Maguire. Inside it was unpretentious and yet very stylish, with simple, square, bleached oak tables and chairs and walls painted a metallic greeny-gold. And although the food was notoriously slow to arrive, when it did it was so good that people had been heard to talk about it afterwards in their sleep. Waiters threaded their way between the tables, carrying

huge white china platters just too high to be able to see
what was on them, so it was possible to catch only tantaliz-
ing glimpses of crab claws or lobsters' legs trailing over the
sides, encouraging waiting diners to frantically return to
their menus to work out which dishes were which. Between
May and October the Pelican was full every night and it
was necessary to book weeks in advance.

If Arthur had been able to choose he would have
booked them a table near the huge floor-to-ceiling windows that looked out to the sea, but, understandably, they
were the first to go, and only having booked that morning,
he had been lucky to get a table at all. He led Emily across
the room, Emily drawing everyone's eyes as she walked.
Instead of the shirt she had packed for the evening, she
was wearing a cream lace vest. High necked and sleeve-
less, it was more than a little transparent, but as she
wouldn't be getting it wet, she thought she'd get away
with it.

As they were led to their table, Emily saw there was a
girl in a tailored black jacket with long black hair sitting
alone with her back to them.

'There she is,' Arthur muttered nervously. 'Do you see
how she's plaited her hair. Isn't that great?'

It was amazing hair, a heavy, shiny curtain that had
undoubtedly been washed and conditioned and brushed
a hundred times before being plaited on either side in a
series of tiny intricate plaits that met at the back while the
rest of her hair hung loose beneath. Emily's heart sank,
because all too often the effort of producing such hair

seemed to destroy the sense of humour entirely. She imagined a face plain and unsmiling, bare of even the merest scrap of make-up.

As Emily and Arthur slowly made their way towards her Jennifer slowly turned and rose from her chair to greet them and Emily could see her for real and see that she had been completely wrong in her predictions. For a start Jennifer did believe in make-up. Lots of it. Black eyeliner ringed her huge eyes, emphasizing the translucent whiteness of her skin and the ruby red of her lips.

Emily greeted her with a smile and an outstretched hand, taking in battered stiletto boots and flared low cut jeans. In contrast the black jacket was made of a dull brocade and was very tight, nipped in around a tiny waist. Why hadn't Arthur warned her! Not that Emily knew what he might have said. All she knew was that she felt silly and overdressed, even though all she was wearing was a vest and velvet trousers.

Jennifer meanwhile dropped her eyelashes and gave Arthur a provocative lingering smile. *And Arthur thought this girl collected sea shells on the beach?*

'Hello,' Emily said smiling at her.

'This is Emily,' Arthur encouraged Jennifer.

Jennifer managed a faint smile back.

'Sam's late,' said Arthur.

'He'll be here,' Emily reassured him. She looked at her watch. 'We're five minutes early.'

There was another awkward pause.

'Shall we sit down?' Emily suggested then, seeing how

behind her a log-jam of waiters had quickly built up, all balancing heavy trays and impatient to serve the nearby tables. 'Jennifer? Can we sit down?'

Standing in front of Emily and blocking the way, Jennifer either didn't hear or ignored her deliberately.

Emily gave the waiters behind her an apologetic smile and Jennifer a gentle nudge in the small of her back. 'I think we should get out of the way of the waiters,' she repeated to Arthur over Jennifer's shoulder.

Arthur nodded. Then Emily saw a look of alarm widen his eyes. She turned and saw that the waiter nearest to her, carrying a heavy glass jug of water in one hand and four glasses in the other, was in trouble and, anticipating what was about to happen, she shoved Jennifer forward, trying to find some space. At Emily's push, Jennifer tipped forward into Arthur who stepped backwards, Jennifer in his arms and out of reach but there was still no room for Emily to escape to. Even so, if Emily had been able to resist looking back once again, she wouldn't have got quite so wet. As it was, she turned just in time to catch a jug of icy water full in her face. With ice cubes in her hair and down her neck and water pouring down her face and down her skimpy cream vest, she stood in the middle of the restaurant, gasping with shock.

The first thing that Sam thought, when he walked through the door and saw her standing there, with her eyes closed and her shoulders thrown back, was how she might as well have been wearing nothing at all.

Sam, who had seen it all before, became her saviour

again. Emily opened her eyes and watched, frozen to the spot, as he steadily made his way towards her, pulling off a jumper as he came, so that he could reach her and slip it around her shoulders all in one movement.

'Hello, again,' he said, coming even closer. 'Another happy coincidence, I think.'

He took a napkin off the table and gently wiped her face. She stared at him, so close, and when he had finished couldn't resist falling forward to rest her wet cheek against his shirt.

When she moved away again she saw that she'd left a large round wet patch behind. She slipped her arms into his jumper and pulled it over her head. It was warm and soft and smelled of him. 'Can I keep this?'

'For good?'

'No! For tonight.'

'Of course you can.'

She looked down at herself. Her trousers were only damp and her vest, wet through, would dry out beneath Sam's jumper. She took the napkin off him and wiped her face again and then her hair and the back of her neck, then shook the water out of her ears and reassured the horrified waiter that she was fine.

Sam pulled back her chair but she was in no rush to sit down.

It seemed that neither was Sam. 'Did you get the job?' he asked her.

Emily shook her head. 'Didn't bother going to the interview.'

'You realize that wasp made my day?'

She laughed. 'I'm so pleased. Did you find another skirt for your sister?'

'No, I bought that one I showed you and she loved it.'

'That's impossible,' Emily said, catching Arthur's eye, and finally making a move towards her chair.

Sam paused. 'I'm lying. I spent half an hour in Jigsaw choosing something else.'

He moved around to his own chair and sat down too. 'Emily helped me choose a present for my sister,' he explained to Arthur and Jennifer.

'Did she?' Arthur nodded impatiently. 'Are you all right, Emily? I'm so sorry about that. Do we need to find you some dry clothes?'

She shook her head, feeling very happy inside Sam's jumper. She leaned in to Jennifer. 'But if you'd moved sooner I'd have got out of the way.'

Around them a couple of waiters were hurriedly mopping, while others had brought dry glasses and cutlery. Surprisingly the glass jug had bounced on the wooden floor and survived.

'I didn't hear you,' Jennifer muttered. 'I didn't realize what was going on.'

A complimentary bottle of champagne was brought to their table, even though to Emily's mind the blame rested not with the waiter but entirely with Jennifer, who had twice ignored her plea to move and who should have been listening better and who wasn't apologizing.

'Perhaps I could fold you a dry outfit out of table napkins,' Jennifer offered then, with an utterly straight face.

Was it meant to be a joke? Emily had no idea. 'That's a very kind thought. But I'm fine in Sam's jumper.' Seeing Arthur's troubled face she shook her head. 'I'm fine apart from some water on the brain.'

'Your hair's certainly gone fluffy,' said Sam.

'Let's start again,' Emily said to Jennifer. 'We've hardly even said hello.'

Jennifer held out a narrow white hand and Emily took it and shook, noticing short fingernails painted dark green and a heavy silver thumb ring. 'And you know Sam?' she checked, still sounding painfully polite.

Jennifer nodded and glanced across at him and he gave her a little surreptitious wink back. Maybe it was only a wink of reassurance, but Emily was surprised to see it, and wondered if he was laughing at her. Certainly if there were sides to be on, it made her think Sam was on Jennifer's and she'd thought that he'd be on hers.

He caught her eye and she realized she'd been staring at him. 'Traitor,' she whispered, then couldn't help her face breaking into a smile realizing she hadn't taken him in before. She hadn't noticed whether he was tall or short, fat or thin, couldn't have said what colour his eyes were or his hair. Now she was looking at him properly and liking what she saw, held for a moment by his lovely wide smile and rather sad brown eyes. And he was attractive, in a rugged, messy kind of a way, with thick brown hair, spiky surely with wind and sea spray, not gel. And, in contrast to Jennifer, he was wearing reassuringly familiar clothes, faded blue jeans, and the navy shirt she had dried her face on. Fleetingly she remembered how it had felt to press up close to him, remembered his warmth and the lean hard body against her cheek.

Yet, even as she saw his charms, he left her unmoved. It was as if they'd met on an escalator, him travelling down, her travelling up. There was time to watch him as he came into view and to think idly that he looked nice, strong and attractive, lucky the girl who got him. But that was it. A few seconds later and he would be forgotten because she was on her way somewhere else, somewhere that was taking all her attention because it was her destination that was important, not whom she passed on the way.

'So how well do you two know each other?' Emily enquired politely, looking from Sam to Jennifer.

'Only a little. We've met once before, haven't we, Jennifer? Through a friend of a friend.'

Jennifer nodded her agreement.

'And you both knew the other was coming tonight?' Emily asked, taking a piece of bread and spreading it with butter.

'Yes, we did,' Jennifer said. 'Arthur certainly told me about Sam – ' she took Arthur's hand – 'and I think he warned you that you'd see me here, yes?' She turned and included Sam in her little smile.

For a long moment nobody said anything. Then Sam followed Emily's example and took some bread for himself and Jennifer picked up her napkin. She sounded relaxed, her voice low but clear, and yet Emily watched the napkin tremble in her hand, then shake all the way from the table to her lap. She had to stop herself from staring at Jennifer's face, wanting to see if the tension was reflected there too. The next moment the napkin slid right off Jennifer's lap and as she bent to retrieve it Sam leaned forward and whispered so not even Arthur could hear, 'Be nice. She's worth it.'

Then a waiter came up and began loudly to run through the menu, and Jennifer leapt up in alarm, flicking her head around at the sound of his voice, so that Emily, sitting beside her, was whipped in the face with a fast-moving mouthful of hair.

Out of sisterly support for Arthur, she didn't react at all, even as she could see Sam struggling not to smile. She discreetly removed the strands stuck to her eyelids, and her top lip, and concentrated instead on her menu and on listening to the waiter. But she couldn't resist letting her eyes drift slowly over the top of the menu and back to Sam. *See?* she beamed to him, without saying anything aloud, *See what she did to me*? He returned such a deadpan stare that she quickly had to duck back behind her menu and stop herself laughing.

Emily attracted a good deal more of Jennifer's hair during that evening. Perhaps being damp made her very static. And each time she lifted a hair away, Sam would notice and would be looking at her with bright, laughing eyes.

Arthur, on the other hand, noticed nothing. Jennifer Aniston could have come to sit beside him and he wouldn't even have been aware of it. For Arthur there was nothing else but his Jennifer. It was obvious that he couldn't believe his luck.

'Do you ever come to London?' Emily asked her,

determined that Arthur wasn't going to monopolize her all evening and that they would leave at the end having had at least one proper conversation.

'London.' Jennifer stabbed at a bread roll with her knife. 'The first time I went to London I was ten years old and I got accused of shoplifting.'

'You didn't! What happened?'

'We'd come for the trooping the colour, but I got arrested in Hamleys.'

OK, it wasn't particularly funny, had probably been a horrible experience, but the complete lack of animation in Jennifer's voice and her utter refusal to smile had Emily clutching the sides of her chair in her effort to keep a straight face.

'If you look anything like you do now, I can understand why,' said Sam. 'I don't somehow imagine you were ever a pigtails-and-pinafore type of girl.'

Jennifer grinned back at him.

'You're right,' she agreed. 'Think Carrie and you're getting close.' She turned back to Emily and dropped her voice. 'Actually, I did steal something.'

As Jennifer spoke, her knife went straight through the bread roll, hit the plate on the other side with a terrible glass-shattering screech, then clattered to the floor.

There was silence around the table and way beyond. Then Arthur said, 'Boom-ching!' and Jennifer collapsed into giggles.

'It was a cuddly puffin,' said Jennifer. She reached down for her knife. 'I knew my mother would never buy him for me.'

'So what else were you to do?' Emily said, laughing too, still not knowing what to make of her but at least deciding she liked her now.

'The police eventually believed it was a mistake. I said I thought my mother had bought him.'

'So they let you keep him?'

'They would have done but my mother said she didn't want him in the house, that he was *polluted*.'

For no good reason, that made Emily laugh even more. She was just so relieved that Jennifer had a sense of humour after all, buried deep, but there in the end.

'I'll buy you another one,' Arthur interrupted, grinning delightedly at Emily and Jennifer. 'We'll go shopping tomorrow and I'll buy you one.'

Jennifer had picked up her knife again, and had her buttered roll halfway to her mouth. 'You don't think I took any notice of her? Not after all I'd been through! He's in a shoe box under my bed.'

'But you must come back to London,' Emily said eagerly. 'You should come with Arthur. He could take you to the trooping of the colour,' she joked.

'Please, no. Anything but that.'

'Jennifer is an interior designer,' Arthur interrupted with pride. 'Of course she's been back to London hundreds of times.'

Emily nodded. Of course she had. Stupid to think she wouldn't have done. She tried but couldn't quite imagine the kind of interior design Jennifer would produce.

'Jennifer's booked up for the whole of the year.'

'You should have told me!' Feeling wrong-footed once again, Emily criticized Arthur.

'It's how we met,' Sam interrupted. 'Jennifer did a friend of a friend's beach house.'

Waiters arrived with a steaming, fragrant fish soup, again compliments of the house. Emily, Sam, Jennifer and Arthur leant back from the table and waited as the bowls were passed to each of them.

The soup tasted sublime. As they ate, Sam turned back to Emily, allowing Jennifer gratefully to slide back to Arthur.

'I remember the summer I met you.'

Emily couldn't look at him. 'I do too.'

'You told me how you came to St Brides every summer with your parents.' She nodded. 'But then you never came back.'

'You're right. That was our last year.'

'Was it something I said?'

She finally met his eyes, smiled and shook her head.

'Why didn't you come back?'

'I suppose I grew out of holidays with my parents.'

He looked at her, knowing that she was thinking of Oliver.

'You know, I was so angry with him!' he admitted. 'I'd seen you first – the day before, walking through the sand dunes from the car park – and I'd told him about you. And that evening when we saw you on the beach, that was meant to be my big chance.' And he laughed in a way that told her it was all in the past, that they could joke about it now, because whatever had happened had happened so long ago, it didn't matter any more.

Even so, Emily realized how it had once been for him and she was touched. In truth, she'd been so instantly bowled over by the golden figure leaning down towards her that evening on the beach that she hadn't even seen his friend, waiting there behind him. All she ever remembered about that moment was how it had felt when Oliver pulled her to her feet, and later the feel of his arm around her shoulders, a long brown arm, with soft sun-bleached hairs, and how, later still, she had touched the hairs with her fingertips and gently rubbed away the fine grains of white sand caught between them.

'Are you going to see him again, now that he's back?' Sam asked.

There wasn't an easy question. There was now a tension in Sam's voice that hadn't been there before and yet the opportunity to talk about Oliver, when he was all that was on her mind, was irresistible.

'I think so. I hope so. I missed his party, the one you came down for. I know you saw Holly there, but I was away for it.' She was aware that she was saying too much but she couldn't stop speaking.

'You know Nessa and he . . .'

She nodded, not looking at him, waiting for him to say something more but knowing she wouldn't like what she heard.

'Watch out for him, Emily.'

She was right.

'He wouldn't make you happy.'

She looked at him in surprise, still said nothing.

'Am I overstepping the mark?'

'I think you are.'

Sam was undeterred. 'I could tell in that shop – Ruffles – that it was all the same as ever. I can see it now, in your face.'

She stared back at him. It was outrageous that he could say such a thing, when he had so little, nothing, to go on at all.

'He has just left his girlfriend of nearly five years.' Sam was speaking quietly still with a smile and yet Arthur's head shot up from the sweet nothings he was murmuring to Jennifer to check what was going on. Emily rolled her eyes at him in mock desperation and he smiled back at her, convinced all was well and turned back to Jennifer.

'I know you think he's a great guy,' Sam went on. 'Thoughtful, kind, not just to you but to everyone. And he's good-looking and charming and funny and sweet, but right now he wants to be a selfish bastard, too, and you should remember that or you might get hurt. He wants to look out for himself, he wants to have some fun. After Nessa, don't think he's going to want another relationship for a while.' He paused. 'It might be hard to believe, but he's quite good at being a selfish bastard, when he concentrates on it.'

'I want to have some fun too!' she retaliated. 'With or without Oliver . . .'

'Don't be angry.'

Emily could see that Arthur's antennae were still

twitching. He kept looking over to them, giving her little worried glances.

'It's you who's sounding angry. With me,' Emily hissed.

'The last thing I am is angry with you.'

'Whatever, you've got it wrong. I haven't even seen him.' But she was going to, on Saturday night.

He nodded. 'I'm sorry. I didn't mean to say anything to offend you.'

Abruptly, he pushed back his chair, tipped the last of the champagne into her glass and picked up the wine list. 'What shall we have now, white or red?'

And the conversation was over as quickly as it had begun, almost as if Sam had never said anything. Certainly as if it had had no effect on him, saying what he'd said. As if reading the wine list was all that was on his mind.

But Emily was wrong to think that. The reality was that the conversation had been difficult for Sam. And what had been even harder was not shouting out what he really wanted to say. *Emily! Look at me! Couldn't you have fun with me?*

Awkward as it was, Emily found she couldn't drop the subject of Oliver. 'Do you see him much?'

He shook his head. 'Cornwall and London. We live too far apart to see each other very often,' he shrugged. 'And we've grown apart, too.'

'But you still came down to his party last weekend.'

'I thought I might see you there.'

She didn't know how to take it. Was it a throwaway remark that meant nothing at all, or was Sam telling her he'd travelled three hundred miles in the vague hope of seeing her? She hoped not. She hoped it wasn't that. And why would it be true? She hardly knew him, she'd met him perhaps only three times before the time in Ruffles. He couldn't have meant that.

'Come outside with me,' Sam said, startling her. 'Come and see the sea.'

'Are you joking?'

'We can't see the sea from the table.'

'No, we can't,' she laughed.

'It's a full moon tonight, did you see it?'

She shook her head.

He looked across to Arthur and Jennifer, deep in conversation. 'Who will notice? Not those two, and the next course won't be here for at least another half an hour – if we're lucky – so come outside with me. It's too warm in here. I need some air.'

And so she found herself standing up, laying down her napkin on her chair, and when Arthur and Jennifer looked over to her, she explained where they were going and that they'd soon be back.

Outside, there was a bite in the air and Emily was very glad of Sam's jumper.

'Aren't you cold?' She rubbed her arms as he led her around the side of the restaurant and through a little gate onto the terrace.

'Not at all,' he lied, teeth clenched to stop them chattering.

She had had lunch on the terrace many times but never been out there at night, and she hadn't realized how beautiful it would be with the thousands of lights twinkling and glittering against the sea – lights from the fishing boats setting out to sea, lights from cars travelling along the coast road, lights from the town and from the houses high in the hills, and at least a thousand others that she couldn't identify.

As she looked, Sam dragged a couple of wooden chairs over to the furthest edge of the terrace. There was a low stone wall, about a foot high, that marked its end and after that nothing but the rocks that dropped away to a tiny pebbly beach a couple of hundred feet below. Sam placed their two chairs side by side and Emily sat down and then Sam sat down beside her, shifting his chair close enough for his shoulder to be touching hers, and they sat in the darkness in conspiratorial silence, listening to the waves unfurling down on the beach below.

'Listen! You hear the grating roar of pebbles which the waves draw back, and fling . . .' Emily said in a low voice. She took her time, slowly remembering the words. '. . . Begin, and cease, and then again begin, with tremulous cadence slow, and bring the eternal note of sadness in . . .' She stopped.

'You don't know any more, do you?' Sam teased.

'I do, I do,' she protested, laughing, and then she was seized by a sudden shiver of cold. 'I'm sorry.'

'Do you want to go in?'

'No.'

'Come here, then.' Sam shifted closer and put his arm around her and she let herself fall in against his warm body. 'That was lovely. What comes next?'

'I can't remember any more.'

They sat in silence, Sam fighting hard not to bend his head and kiss her.

'What do you do here?' she asked him suddenly.

'I'm working with my father,' he said. 'We grow roses together.'

It was all he said but there was something in the way that he spoke that caught her attention and made it important that she know more.

7

Emily knew already that Sam had been born and brought up in Cornwall. What she hadn't known was that Sam's family home was called Trevissey and that six months earlier Sam had come back to live in Cornwall to start working with his father.

'Trevissey has a lovely garden,' he told her simply, 'famous for its roses.'

If Emily had known the first thing about roses, the names Finch and Trevissey might have meant something to her, but she hadn't and they didn't. Warmed by her enthusiasm, Sam tried to explain in two minutes what it had taken him all his life to learn about roses. Then, at Emily's insistence, he stopped and, with a few better chosen words, started again.

'If you thought of a rose, what would it look like?' he asked.

Still sitting with his arm around her, Emily closed her eyes and thought about it. 'It would be long-stemmed, very straight and elegant, with one single flower,' she decided. 'A beautiful, crimson rose.'

'Would it smell?'

'Yes. Wonderful.'

'Unlikely.'

She opened her eyes and looked at him in surprise. 'Why?'

'You've described a modern rose and they don't usually have much of a scent.'

'OK,' she said cautiously, 'presumably *some* roses do. Which ones might they be?'

'Which was the right question,' he said.

'Tell me.'

'The ones that do smell are the old roses. The rose you've just described is a modern rose, probably a modern hybrid tea.'

'Who would want a modern rose that doesn't smell of anything?'

'Lots of people. They're the ones for sale in all the garden centres. People buy them because they're more likely to flower all summer rather than for just a few weeks. Most people don't realize there's any other choice.'

'But do they look the same, old and modern roses?'

'No, they don't. Modern rose bushes stick up out of the ground very tense and stiff, as if they've been bound up for so long they can't quite get the hang of being free. They can't mix and entwine with the rest of the garden like the old shrub roses do. And their colours are usually very, very bright. Lots of fluorescent oranges and lipstick pinks. You know the type – huge petals, enormous heads. They're nothing like old roses. The old roses are usually a shade of pink, but not always, some of them have the most gorgeous colours, and their flowers are the most wonderful shapes.' He cupped his hands into a bowl.

'Like this. Sometimes their heads are so heavy with petals they can barely support themselves.'

'Let me guess which sort grow at Trevissey!'

'No, it's not as straightforward as that.'

'Why not? Which ones do you grow?'

'Neither.'

She frowned at him. 'Tell me.'

'I'm explaining as fast as I can,' he insisted. 'The old roses divide into different classes, there are the Gallicas, the Damasks, the Albas, and lots of others too, they're mostly French and they've been with us for centuries. Then, about a hundred years ago, came the modern hybrid tea rose, bred to be strong and bright and to flower over and over again. It had to be there at the start of the summer, and it had to last all the way through. The fact that it wasn't as nice to look at, or smell, seemed almost irrelevant. Once it had arrived it took over so quickly that the old roses went completely out of fashion. For a while it looked as if some of the most wonderful varieties were going to die out altogether.'

'Didn't anyone want to protect them? Is *that* what you do?'

'In the twenties and thirties, some of the great English gardeners like Gertrude Jekyll and Constance Spry did start to champion them again. Vita Sackville-West grew them at Sissinghurst, and they saved the old roses for us. Wonderful roses like "Rosa Mundi", said to be named after Henry II's mistress in the twelfth century, "Belle de Crécy", "Cardinal de Richelieu", "Comtesse de Murinais".'

When Sam spoke their names, he made them sound so beautiful and precious that Emily, who'd never given a moment's thought to roses, ancient or modern, sat beside him entranced.

'Then other gardeners followed their lead and now there are wonderful collections of old roses all over the country.'

'Including Trevissey?'

'We do have some but no, that's not what we do.' He paused. 'Some of the old roses are very similar to their wild relatives, and although that means they can be utterly beautiful, they only flower for a very short time and they're not very hardy, often less able to withstand disease than the modern roses. The short flowering period doesn't matter if you have a huge garden with hundreds of different varieties but most people don't have gardens like that – it's one of the reasons the modern hybrid tea became so popular. Then, in the nineteen sixties, a solution was pioneered in Shropshire by a rose grower called David Austin and in Cornwall by my father.'

Emily was back in the crook of his arm, enjoying the rise and fall of his voice in the darkness.

'They began cross-breeding some of the best of the old roses with several modern hybrid teas, trying to persuade the resilience and repeat flowering of a modern hybrid tea rose to combine with the scent and beauty of an old rose. And, eventually, they managed it. They managed to create an entirely new but traditional rose. David Austin called his collection "English Roses", my father called his "Heritage Roses".

'So, today, forty years on, in the gardens at Trevissey, we are growing them together, ancient varieties alongside our Heritage Roses. They blend in together and into the landscape of the garden. Our roses look and smell as beautiful as their old French relations but they do flower repeatedly and most of them are disease resistant – they don't get black spot and powdery mildew.'

'Thousands? Hundreds? How many do you have?'

'Most years we introduce three or four. Last year it was only two. "Gabriel's Daughter" and "Song for Summer". We launched them at the Chelsea Flower Show last May.'

'So is it still very difficult to cross-breed? It must be if you're only producing one or two a year.'

'It takes years to develop a new rose. And we don't want to produce any more than one or two at a time. We're deliberately keeping our collection fairly small.'

Emily thought back to her childhood. 'Modern hybrid teas,' she said, surprised at what she could remember. She was nine years old, in a rain-drenched garden full of rose bushes and the flowers were just as Sam described them, long stemmed, huge heads, orange and lilac and cerise. She remembered trailing along behind her mother through long grass that soaked her legs, hearing her mother speaking more to herself than to Emily. 'Why are modern hybrid teas always such ghastly colours?' Emily had been convinced they were about to turn a corner and find a table piled high with orange and red and green fairy cakes and biscuits wrapped in purple foil – a modern, hybrid *tea*.

'When did you start working at Trevissey?' she asked.

'When I was six or seven. Then summer jobs when I

was a teenager. I've always been involved but I only started full-time six months ago.'

She wondered what it was like for him, working with his father.

'And we get on fine together,' he said and she could hear from his voice that he was smiling. 'He tells me what to do and I shut up and do it.'

'Really?'

'No. He's amazing. He knows intuitively what will work and what won't – helped by forty years of trial and error.'

'Presumably it's all written down somewhere? It's not all inside his head?'

'We write down every cross we make.'

'There must be so many thorns,' she said, then shook her head apologetically. 'How dumb did that sound?'

Sam laughed. 'You get the hang of where to hold them. It becomes a sixth sense. Look. No scratches.' He spread his hands.

She took hold of one and looked at it closely. 'It's so green,' she teased. 'You really do have green fingers.'

He laughed, happy to leave his hand in hers. 'Dirty brown, I think. If you'd like to see Trevissey, I could show you around tomorrow.'

'I'm spending tomorrow with Arthur. And then I go back to London the next morning.' She gently disentangled her hand from his.

'Busy all of tomorrow?'

'Arthur will have to go to work . . .'

'So give me an hour?'

She nodded. 'I'd love to.'

'Nothing will be flowering,' he warned her. 'It's completely the wrong time of year. March is much too early. June and July are the best months. You'll have to promise to come back then. At the moment the only roses you'll see will be in the greenhouses.'

'I could come after we've been to St Brides. I could get Arthur to drop me off.'

'Do that.'

By unspoken agreement they stood up together.

'Do you think we've been a very long time?' Emily asked.

'They won't have noticed. They'll have been pleased to have some time together alone.'

When they re-entered the restaurant Emily was relieved to see Arthur and Jennifer still waiting for their main courses. She caught Arthur's eye across the table and he gave her a quick encouraging smile and she guessed she was in for an inquisition the moment they got in the car. She knew, absolutely *knew*, that Arthur would think Sam one hundred times more suitable for her than Oliver.

'What about your brother and sister?' Emily asked Sam, when they'd sat back down. 'Do they work with you?'

Sam shook his head. 'My brother is a teacher in Exeter, my sister is a fund manager in the City.'

Emily pictured her arriving for work in Sam's pleated brown and yellow skirt.

Out of the corner of her eye Emily could see Arthur turning to Jennifer, taking one of her hands in his, turning it over and slowly stroking her palm with his finger. He's going to remember nothing about us leaving the room, he'll remember nothing else about this evening at all, she realized.

And afterwards, after they'd waited a further ten minutes, and had then been served with great platters of *fruits de mer*, after she and Arthur had driven home and she had said good night and got into bed, it was Trevissey that she thought about, the details of Trevissey that she could recall almost word for word. And she found she was looking forward very much to the next afternoon, when she would be able to see it for real.

8

But before Trevissey, St Brides had to be explored.

In the morning the sky was clear again but the temperature had dropped and the wind was blustery and very cold. It licked the tips of the waves far out to sea and sent Arthur and Emily huddling deep into their coats for warmth.

They left Arthur's car in a car park next to the beach and walked into the heart of St Brides and it seemed to Emily that they were almost alone there, certainly the only people with nothing to do but wander the streets.

It was a good thing to see St Brides at its quietest but it was also somewhat disheartening. Though Emily had been there so many times before, in pouring rain and snow as well as in the heat of high summer, somehow she always pictured St Brides bathed in hot sunlight and buzzing with people. It took her aback to find it like this, the one time she was hoping it would show itself off to her. She told herself that it was only early spring, not high summer, and that she shouldn't have expected to find it any other way, but somehow she hadn't ever realized how truly quiet it could be, emphasized by the bowed heads and silent treads of the few people who passed them by. Neither had she realized that at least half the shops closed down for the winter, several having signs in their windows announcing that they wouldn't be opening again until 31 May, still over two months away. In only a few minutes, the reality of opening her shop became not just difficult, risky and challenging but rather grim. Looking up and down the narrow streets she knew for sure that whatever she put inside the shop, passing trade would be non-existent, that St Brides wasn't a town already stuffed full of art galleries and craft shops that attracted browsers, apart from in the few months in high summer when holiday-makers poured in everywhere and were found happily browsing in the ironmongers and locksmiths, as well as the more obvious places. For the rest of the time, it was the full-time residents who shopped in St Brides and they came because it was a simple, working town with shops full of things they needed, rather than things they hankered after. And so she would have to be good enough to draw people, to bring them out on a special trip to see her, and her stock would have to be irresistible.

Emily wasn't put off completely. She was convinced that St Brides was moving upmarket, that more and more people were coming there for their holidays, and would be looking for opportunities to spend their money. The success of the Pelican proved it could be done. And if she had to shut up shop for a few months in the winter, that would be when she could concentrate on her suppliers, visit the trade shows and discover the wonderful artists and milliners, handbag makers and ceramicists who worked in the Cockpit or Great Western studios in London. She would be able to talk to the local artists, some of whom she'd met already through Arthur: one made wooden boats that bobbed across a painted sea at the turn of a handle and another designed gorgeous spiralling mobiles from coloured stones and shells and sticks washed up on the beach. She also had a friend from university who made beautiful birds out of driftwood, and who had already hinted that Saltwater could be her exclusive stockist.

'Let's go,' Arthur said after less than five minutes of wandering. He walked away from her, then turned so that his back was against the wind. 'If you want to come and live here,' he shouted to her, 'I'm sure I could find you a job. You don't *have* to open a shop.'

'Are you serious?' Emily moved over to him. 'Are you saying that because you really don't think I should do it? Or are you saying it because you're in a bad mood with me this morning?'

He shook his head. 'You could do it, but it would be bloody hard work.'

'Wait a second.' There was an estate agents on the other side of the road and she pulled Arthur with her towards it. Together they looked in through tiny leaded windows.

'If I found the right place,' she said to Arthur, after they'd scanned all the pictures in one window, 'you know I could do it. I have the right contacts, I know where to look for stock, I've got all the ideas, all the enthusiasm. I'm artistic-ish. Even though there's nothing for me here today, something will come up. And I'll make it work.'

'So, you are serious?'

She shrugged. 'I think I am. Don't you think I should be?'

'I thought you were serious about staying in the theatre? I thought that was why you held out with it for so long . . .'

Emily sighed. 'That's true. But I think it was more to do with being stubborn. Not wanting to be pushed out by her, leaving when I wanted to, when I was ready and had something to go for instead . . . Not that I managed that.'

'And how much money have you got?'

'Not enough. I'd have to do a business plan and get a loan from the bank.'

'I think you should open somewhere bigger than St Brides.'

'Or do you mean somewhere further away from you?'

'No!'

'Even after last night?'

'What about last night?'

'I thought perhaps I didn't behave very well . . . with Jennifer. And the way Sam and I left you . . .'

'Did you?' He smiled. 'I don't remember.'

Emily remembered Arthur kissing Jennifer's fingers, leaning in close, the two of them giggling together most of the evening, and knew it was true.

They moved away from the estate agents' window and down the high street. 'If I opened in a bigger town, then the rates and rent would be even higher.'

'I suppose so.'

They cut down an alleyway, then along another and up and down the flights of steps that linked the narrow streets, onto a street called Flass Street, which took them back to the sea.

And then, just as she sensed Arthur was about to say something more about Jennifer, a shop called simply 'Number Seventeen' caught Emily's eye, and of all the places that they had passed, she saw that this one came closest to what she wanted. She touched Arthur's sleeve, stopped him walking off in the wrong direction and they wandered down towards it.

From the outside it looked sweet. It was painted fondant pink, part of a little terrace of shops all painted in different colours, with a large bow window in the front and two small steps leading up to the half-open door. Curious, Emily looked in through the window at the items displayed for sale.

The effect was pretty, but not sufficiently enticing. Cautious rather than original. As she leaned in to get a better look, Emily caught the eye of a smart, dark-haired woman sitting alone behind a white-painted desk, hands folded in front of her, and she felt an overwhelming urge to climb the steps, go in and spend a huge amount of money, if only to wipe away the defeated look in the woman's eye.

'Go on. She could be you,' Arthur said encouragingly.

'No, she could not be me.'

Emily went up the steps, Arthur behind her, pushed open the door and they went inside.

She stood for a moment, breathing in the warm scent of lavender. A piano concerto rippled gently in the background. Emily cast an appraising eye around the room, giving the woman a bright smile.

The central feature of the room was an ornamental wooden stepladder with a card balanced on the top step,

stating in neat black ink that it was 'Not For Sale'. The
other steps were laden with terracotta pots of blue artificial
hyacinths that presumably *were* for sale. Behind the stepladder was a pretty wooden chest of drawers, painted
antique white and distressed, on which were displayed
various delicately patterned glass bottles. Emily walked
over to them, lifting each one and turning it upside down
to see the price. They were astoundingly expensive. She
moved away again, aware that every movement she made
was being watched intently.

The piano concerto finished and in the silence Emily
turned slowly around, and then around again, letting tea
towels, white china soap dishes, wooden bowls filled with
wooden pears, brooms made out of twigs, wicker baskets,
silver photo frames and floral biscuit tins blur before her
eyes. Behind her, Arthur muttered that he would wait for
her outside and she heard the clunk of the door shutting,
leaving her alone.

She wanted to leave but couldn't empty-handed. What
to buy? What to buy? Beside the till was a rack of flowery
wrapping paper and a stand of boring flowery cards. To
her right an open drawer was filled with napkins and
napkin rings and above the drawer was a lavender collection – bottles of lavender water, egg-shaped lavender soap
and bundles of dried lavender tied with raffia bows neatly
laid out in a trug. What could Emily buy? She grabbed an
egg soap and turned to the woman, only to remember that
she'd no cash and she couldn't face writing out a cheque
to this woman for just two pounds ninety-eight pence.

She looked out of the window, hoping to catch Arthur's

attention, but he'd wandered off down the road. There was nothing else to do. She turned back and guiltily replaced the soap in the drawer, feeling her face flush with embarrassment.

All she was aware of now was the door and the prospect of walking through it.

Then in the corner of her eye she saw something red and she stopped and turned towards it. It was in a half-open drawer in the little white painted chest. What it was she couldn't tell, but it did look interesting.

Curiosity beat back the need to escape. She peered at it more closely, and even as she was telling herself to *go, go, go*, she couldn't resist pulling it free of the drawer. Behind her, she heard the scrape of the woman's chair and Emily waited for her to come near.

'I bought it months ago,' she said with a sigh. 'There's not much of a market for it in St Brides but I couldn't resist.'

Emily held it out to look at, letting the material drop in front of her, still unsure what it was. It was definitely beautiful, made from gossamer-thin silk as delicate and translucent as a web, a deep pinky red top with three-quarter-length sleeves and a low scooped neck. She took it over to a Venetian-glass mirror hanging on one wall to see it against herself, but even before she looked she knew that she was going to buy it and not only to make the dreary woman happy but because it would be perfect to wear to meet Oliver the following evening.

She didn't look at the price tag or ask how much it was, just smiled and nodded and handed over her credit card, but the way the woman coloured with pleasure as she took it, and then the reverence with which she wrapped the top in tissue paper, gave Emily a good idea of the size of hole she was blasting in her bank account.

In less than a minute she was running down the steps, calling out a hasty 'Thanks, goodbye!' She caught up with Arthur and grabbed his arm.

'I hope you wouldn't end up like her,' he said straight away. 'I couldn't bear it.'

'Lonely and miserable?'

'Creepy and strange.'

'Of course I won't. Especially not if I have people like me coming in.' She swung her bag at him. 'I think I've just spent enough to keep her afloat for the next six months. Enough to send her on safari,' she added, seeing his smile.

The truth was that, apart from the brief flush of pleasure at the sale, the woman's eyes had never lost their mournful look. Emily doubted those eyes smiled even in the summer when her shop was crowded with holiday-makers itching to spend, people who would leap at the chance to buy a whole fruit bowl's worth of her expensive, wooden pears.

Her shop was so clearly pictured in her mind that every tiny detail was in focus. It would be light and white, the colour coming from the gorgeous things she had to sell, not from the room itself. And not a big room because she wanted it always to be full. Emily knew how hard it would be constantly to keep it that way.

In the middle of the room she wanted a big wrought-iron and glass table, like one she'd seen once in a gorgeous shop in Barnes. She wanted it so people were drawn to the table first, to find the items on it irresistible, impossible not to touch and pick up and buy. What those things would be she didn't yet know. Knew only that they would have to change all the time, and that her biggest challenge would be finding enough items to sell, and still to be able to run the shop. She knew that as soon as she could afford to, she would have to take on an assistant to free her up to go hunting for new stock.

Back in Arthur's car, when warm air finally came through the heater and Emily had stopped shuddering inside her coat and was ready to talk again, they returned to the subject of the evening at the Pelican.

'I liked Jennifer,' she told him as they drove along the sea front.

'Thank you. You told me so last night.'

'I know I did, and I'm telling you again. At first I wasn't sure I was going to, but I really did.' She could see sailing boats out at sea, bright sails stretched as tight as drums by the wind, and a lone windsurfer streaking along the shoreline, kicking up an impressive wake behind him. 'She wasn't at all like I expected.'

'What did you expect? What makes you have me down for a particular sort of girl?'

'Nothing. Of course I don't.' Something put her in mind of Caitlin and their conversation in Holly's drawing room. She remembered how she'd pulled up Caitlin with almost exactly the same words.

'I think I imagined someone more straightforward,' she

said carefully. 'Someone more *normal*, someone who wore jeans and watched too much television and liked fish and chips, who I knew would look after you and Dodger Point, who'd want to play with Clara and have a little garden outside the house.' She turned back to Arthur and grinned. 'I suppose I wanted you to meet someone safe ... someone I could push around a bit. Not some amazingly talented designer with a lovely face and so much hair.' Arthur laughed. 'So at first, I thought, *get her away from me* – and *get away from him*. I'm sorry, but I did. I was so taken aback. Then I looked at her again, took her in, stopped being so overprotective – of myself, not of you – and I realized I was wrong. Then I thought she was great.'

'She's better than great. Last night, while you were outside with Sam, I looked across at her and realized I was so incredibly lucky. I've known her for less than two weeks and now I can't imagine my life without her.'

Listening to him, Emily thought how lucky she was to have him as her brother. He was so expressive and so honest. She loved how his dazzling confidence in Jennifer allowed him to cast aside all his defences and speak the truth. He would be happy to tell the world how he felt, not just Emily, and she felt her heart pierced with tenderness and admiration for him. How she would love to be as comfortable with her own feelings as Arthur was with his, and how she would love to find someone the way Arthur had found Jennifer. Her own muddled, troubled feelings for Oliver felt somehow furtive and inferior in comparison.

Back at Dodger Point, Arthur pulled on the handbrake and turned off the engine and Emily looked through the windscreen towards the house and didn't move. 'She might have great taste, but I'm scared at the thought of what she'd do to this place.'

'Tear it down and start again, she says.'

'That's what I meant.'

'Of course she wouldn't!' Arthur got out. 'She loves it. She especially likes what you did to the tower.'

He slammed his door shut and left Emily still inside the car, feeling disproportionately pleased that Jennifer liked her tower. She opened her door and called after him, 'Oh, I *really* like her now.'

She got out of the car and caught him up.

'And by the way,' Arthur told her, 'she does wear jeans, and eats fish and chips and watches television. And she was only saying yesterday how she'd like to do the garden. So you can relax.'

He blocked her way into the house.

'And Emily, if those are the things that are important to you –' he counted them off on his fingers – 'if you'd like someone who ... wears jeans, enjoys gardening ... Not sure about the television but I could find out ...'

She smiled as she realized where he was heading.

'There's someone I know just like that. Someone we both know ... who you happen to be seeing this afternoon.'

'Not interested,' she insisted, pushing past him and going into the kitchen. 'Not interested at all. Don't you understand anything, Arthur? There is someone else. I have been waiting for him for nearly ten years and I will be seeing him again in approximately thirty-one hours. And the anticipation is killing me. His name is Oliver. It is not Sam. Sam is a lovely guy but all I can think about now is Oliver.'

After lunch Arthur drove her to Trevissey. It was twenty minutes inland from Dodger Point, through thick woods and steep-sided valleys, until they passed through the little village of Leswidden and then turned in through a pair of intricate and beautiful wrought-iron gates made of intertwined roses and up a short, straight gravel drive through an avenue of lime trees. Standing square in front of them was a perfectly proportioned Georgian house, built in dark grey stone.

Rather than follow the drive in its sweeping arc to the front door, Arthur turned instead to the right, taking a second, smaller drive that met the first and led them away from the house and on behind a high yew hedge, where it opened out into a car park. It was, Emily noticed, completely screened from the house and garden. There was a separate area for coaches, and signs in dark green and gold for an arboretum and herb garden as well as for the visitor centre and garden centre. Emily hadn't expected Trevissey to be on such a large, business-like scale.

She sat for a moment. Then, through an unobtrusive archway cut into a grey stone wall, came Sam.

He waved to Arthur and then opened Emily's door and leaned in to her with a rush of cold air and kissed her cheek. 'There are no wasps. No jugs of water. I promise you're safe here.'

Emily laughed and took his hand and let him pull her out of the car. His hands were cold, too.

'Isn't this wonderful,' Arthur said to Sam, turning and looking all around him.

'Join us, if you like,' Sam offered. 'I can show you both around.'

'No, I can't. I've got work to do in the village.'

'Then let me drop Emily home for you,' Sam offered.

'No, I can come and pick her up on the way home.' He got back into the car. 'Call me when you're ready,' he said to Emily, then he waved to them both and was gone.

Sam took her back through the archway and they came out in a small courtyard against one great grey wall of the house. Then they turned down a narrow gravelled path between two low box hedges and came out in another small courtyard, on the left of which was a garden centre.

She'd not expected buildings and customers and shops. She'd imagined long avenues and large empty gardens, and silence, the roses invisibly getting on with the business of growing with little help from anyone beyond a bit of pruning and perhaps a forkful of manure. When Sam had said he was joining his dad, she'd imagined it would be just the two of them with a few extra pairs of hands employed at the busiest times of year.

Now she saw how very wrong she'd been. Everywhere she turned there were young, busy-looking people, wheeling wheelbarrows, moving briskly in and out of the plant

centre, helping customers, talking and laughing, all looking incredibly healthy with shiny hair and great skin, all
wearing bottle-green hooded fleeces embroidered with a
tasteful gold rose underneath which appeared, in gold
letters, 'Thomas Finch Roses'.

Instantly Emily thought that she didn't want to open
Saltwater at all, she wanted to come to work here, learn
about roses and be part of it all.

'Shall I show you around now?' Sam asked. 'Or would
you like a cup of coffee? Or tea or a beer? Whatever you
like.'

'No. I'd like to see it now.'

'Are you warm enough?'

'Too warm,' she said, squinting up at the sun, pulling
off her hat and stuffing it into her jacket pocket. Chilled
by the trip to St Brides, she'd come to Sam's in a long-
sleeved T-shirt, polo-necked jumper and a quilted jacket.
Seeing Sam in just a shirt and jeans she realized she'd
rather overdone it.

Planned and laid out to show off the roses, the gardens
opened, one after another, like rooms in a house, pergolas
and arches inviting them through to each new space
beyond. It was all so imaginatively and beautifully
designed that even now, with not a rose in bloom, it still
took Emily's breath away.

They walked side by side. There was so much to see,
even though what buds there were were all tightly closed
and dripping with recent rain, and the new green shoots
were only just beginning to take hold of the trellises and

fences. They walked around statues and hidden benches and gazebos, past an eighteenth-century dovecote, and everywhere there were the roses waiting for the sun to shine down upon them to ripen the buds until they burst. It was a dormant garden, a green garden, and Emily knew she would have to come back.

Dipping beneath a stone archway covered in lichen and moss they came out in a perfect square of grass and Sam led Emily across it to an ornate Victorian wooden summer house. 'A revolving summer house!' he told her. 'Get up those steps and I'll show you.' She did as he said, climbed the two wooden steps and went to sit down on the rather flimsy-looking garden chair left out on the veranda and Sam put his weight behind the summerhouse and suddenly she was moving in a slow dignified swing. 'Moving to follow the sun,' Sam explained, jumping up beside her. 'Don't you think that's a good idea?'

'It's a lovely idea.' They stopped again and she looked at him. 'I wish I could see the roses. I'd like to see this garden as it's meant to be.'

'You can imagine it instead. Look. Over on that wall.' She looked, waiting for him to go on. 'Think there's magenta and red and purple. The red is a Thomas Finch rose called "Helen of Troy". It has dark foliage and crimson petals and it's huge, it will be spreading all across the back of the wall, all along to the other side. And then, beneath it, we have a velvety Gallica rose called "Tuscany Superb". It's a darker red than "Helen of Troy" and it doesn't flower for so long, but if we were here in late June, we would probably be catching them both out at the same time. And then, all around the garden – ' he swept his arm around to the right – 'the colours are changing, slowly moving from the dark reds to orange and scarlet and then, right there – ' he pointed directly opposite them to a bare grey stone wall – 'imagine that wall covered in pale frothy pink. The pink of iced buns.' He made a small circle with his finger and thumb. 'Sweet, tiny, pink roses, not a Heritage Rose, it's called "Long Goodbye" because it flowers until the first frosts.'

And she could see it all, as clearly as if she was there one hot July day when the beds were full of roses and the air sweet and full with all the scents of summer.

'Thank you,' she said, not wanting to stand up again and move on, to leave the lovely garden behind.

After they had left the summer house Sam took her to the boundary of the gardens and they looked over a fence, Emily casting her eyes over the fields beyond, and loving the fact that the crop, stretching away as far as the eye could see, was roses, not corn.

She found herself telling him how she wanted to stay, how much she wanted to move to Cornwall. How Saltwater might be the way to make it happen. Standing here, with this view, it was so much easier to be sure of herself than it had been in London. Looking out at all the space, at the beautiful rolling hills, at the sapphire sea glinting in the distance, she wondered aloud what had taken her so long.

Then Sam took her to the greenhouses where he attempted to explain, simply enough for Emily to begin to understand, how unpredictable it all was, how one couldn't set out to breed a new rose and expect to know in advance how it would turn out. Emily listened and meanwhile nearly expired with the heat, pulling off her jacket and handing it to Sam when he insisted on carrying it for her.

In the first of the greenhouses thousands upon thousands of delicate seedlings, all just a few weeks old, waited for Sam and his father to work their way through them selecting the best plants. Thousands of crosses were made each year to produce just three or four new roses. And they would be ready in six or seven years' time, Sam explained. The narrowing down happened very gradually, year by year.

The best of the seedlings in front of them would be propagated and left to grow and, after a few more years, there might be ten that they wanted to keep. These ten would then be re-propagated, perhaps producing a hundred more of each of the plants, which would then be watched for a few more years. And at the end of the line, six or seven years on from the plants that Emily was looking at now, perhaps two, perhaps three or four, would be named and patented and put on sale.

Sam led her down to the end of the greenhouse to a large cupboard and pulled open a drawer. Inside was tray upon tray of fine sable paintbrushes. 'We use these to transfer pollen from one plant to another. That's how it's *physically* done. We take the pollen from the anther of one rose, at the top of the stem, and we paint it onto the stigma of another flower. The stigma is female. The pollen is male.'

'And propagating? How do you do that?'

'By budding.'

'Of course, *budding*!'

He grinned at her, a long, slow, appreciative smile and she remembered the night before, how it had felt to be sitting beside him with his arm around her shoulders. 'Budding means we transfer the leaf bud of one rose onto the neck of a root stock.'

'I know that.' She shook her head. 'No, I don't. I know nothing about this at all.'

'We're not manipulating genes,' Sam said. 'Some other commercial gardeners do, but this is not genetic engineering. Everything we're doing here could happen in the wild. All we're doing is steering the roses in certain directions. We make the critical selections for them rather than letting the pollination happen at random. Arranged marriages, if you like.'

'What about making roses disease resistant?' Emily countered.

'It's still a natural process. Whatever scientists do to a tomato's genes to stop it bruising or softening does not happen here. We're simply taking the best of one rose and introducing it to the best of another. And we hope to make a lovely new rose at the end of it.'

In the next greenhouse, roses were already flowering, their sweet scent catching in the air. A huge area at one end was devoted to the preparation of the Thomas Finch Garden for Chelsea Flower Show. The plants would be carefully orchestrated so that all the display roses would flower at the same time and be at their peak for the five days of the event. This year, Sam told her, they would be launching three new roses.

Emily wandered over to look at them.

'Here – ' Sam took her hand – 'smell this one.' He lifted a pale pink flower towards her and Emily dipped her head and breathed it in.

'It's wonderful.'

Then he took out a pair of secateurs from a drawer under one of the tables, carefully snipped off a rose and handed it to her.

'Don't tell Dad because he would explode. But he'll have lots more to choose from.'

Emily took it. It was one of the most beautiful roses she'd ever seen, the flower was a perfect cup, its colour a soft blush pink and the petals within the cup each placed with exquisite perfection. It had a smooth stem, only one or two thorns, and the most wonderful lemony scent.

'This is "Gabriel's Daughter," Sam told her. 'We bred her from an old Portland rose called "Gabriel Delphine."'

'Do you know who Gabriel was?'

'All we know is that he lived in Paris at the beginning of the eighteenth century.'

'And now, two hundred years later, you've given him a daughter.'

'Yes,' Sam agreed. 'I hope a gold-medal-winning daughter.'

They walked back through the gardens to the house. She had loved it all so much she didn't want it to be over, didn't want to go inside. Emily twirled the rose between her fingers, looking down at it. 'I can see why you had to come back,' she said.

He looked at her speculatively, then walked away. 'Come with me.'

She followed him along a narrow, grassy path that ran between two hedges and for the first time she was acutely aware of being there alone with him, of the stillness of the air, and the silence. Then Sam stopped beside her, put his hands around her waist and, without warning, lifted her towards the branches of an old pear tree. There were places to put her feet and she pulled herself up until she found herself on a wet wooden platform a few feet above him. In the summer it would be hidden behind the leaves and would have a bird's-eye 360-degree view of the gardens.

' "Rambling Rector" climbs up there,' he told her, looking up at her.

She looked down at him. 'Disgraceful. He shouldn't be allowed.'

'Don't you think that's the perfect place to spy from?'

'You snoop on people from up here, do you?'

'I see people taking cuttings and picking roses when they think nobody is looking. Once a woman stuffed about six up her jumper.'

'Ouch!' she laughed.

He lifted her gently down again and took his time letting her go. *He likes me. He's flirting with me*, she thought. But her mind skittered away from the realization because she didn't really want to know. Yes, she was aware of Sam still standing close beside her. They were alone in his gardens, and the air seemed weighted with expectation, but how could there be any desire, any sexual tension on her part, any desire to get close to Sam, when she felt only half with him, while her other half was already on the train back to London, was putting on her make-up in her flat, then locking the front door, catching a cab to Caitlin's flat, where, after so long, she would finally, finally, see Oliver again?

She turned away from him, not meeting his eye. 'Is most of your business done here in Trevissey?' she asked, walking away.

For a long moment he neither answered her question nor followed her. She walked on, then stopped and turned back to him.

'Trevissey is our flagship,' he said, sounding all businesslike and professional, back on the script. 'It's where people come to see what we're doing, but we sell only a few roses here. The real business rests on the roses we breed and sell to nurseries and garden centres. We can copyright those.'

'And do you get a pink rose if you mix a red one and a white one?' she asked, one safe question after another.

'Sometimes. Other times you might get another red one, or a yellow one or even a purple one. Because you have little idea of what went on in the generations before, you can never be sure about what's coming next.'

'How would you get a pink one, then?'

'You'd select and select and select. And hope.'

'And would you say there's a rose for every shade of pink?'

Instead of answering, he stopped beside a door into the house.

'Come in for a while? Or will your protective brother be wondering where you are?'

He's changed, Emily noticed. He's gone cool on me.

The door opened into a scullery and boot room and Sam led them through, up stone steps into an enormous high-ceilinged kitchen. There was a long-haired black and white cat curled up asleep in the middle of a large empty fruit bowl on the table and Sam stroked it absentmindedly as he passed by. A huge honey gold oak dresser, so big it had to have been built for the house, took up the whole of one side of the room.

'You think Arthur's protective of me? He's not as bad as you!' Emily didn't know why she suddenly wanted to be so provocative. She copied Sam and stroked the cat, but obviously not with Sam's special touch, because it immediately rose up and leapt out of the fruit bowl and off the table.

She pulled out a chair and sat down as the cat stalked out of the room. Meanwhile Sam disappeared through another doorway and came back with two mugs.

'Talking about being overprotective,' he teased, 'I saw how you were with poor, defenceless Jennifer.'

'What did I do? I'm not protective of Arthur. Not in an unhealthy kind of way! And Jennifer's hardly defenceless.'

'I'm teasing you.'

He went through yet another door and reappeared with a pint of milk. Obviously, where most people had a cupboard, Sam had a whole room.

She hung her coat over the back of an old rocking chair, then balanced her rose on top of it.

But the kitchen was a very warm room and Emily wanted to take her jumper off too. She waited until Sam had his back to her and then quickly pulled her jumper up and over her head. But Sam turned back at the worst possible moment, when not only her stomach (hastily pulled in) but also her bra (old and grey) were showing. At least he couldn't see her flaming red face.

He put down the milk, leaned over to her and firmly held down her T-shirt while she pulled the jumper clear, then said from a few inches away, 'You've got to stop doing this to me.'

'I'm sorry, I will.' Surprised by the feel of his hand on her waist, she felt her heart start to bump in her chest, and colour flame again in her cheeks. She turned away and looked around the room. 'Who did these lovely pictures?' Hanging on the walls were framed watercolours, some of individual roses, others of the gardens at Trevissey.

'My mother.'

She went over to look at the one hanging furthest away from Sam. 'Does she live here too?' She asked because there'd been no mention of her and the house, lovely as it was, seemed to lack her presence.

'No. It's just me and Dad. She died.'

'I'm sorry.'

'Five years ago now. She died here.'

'How sad that she didn't see you come home to live here again.'

Sam nodded. 'But then I probably wouldn't have done if Dad hadn't been alone. It's still very strange being back here without her. But she knew I would come back to work here one day. It was always going to happen.'

'And how is it, living with your dad again?'

'We've had the last six months together and sometimes it feels much too long. Other times it's just great. I'm sure Dad would say the same. I suspect we'd get on better if we lived apart, especially with working together all day, but I guess neither of us likes the idea of living alone.'

What she couldn't deny was that she was looking at Sam clearly now and liking what she saw. Strip away the outside world and inevitably you see much more of the truth about someone. She was sitting at the table where he had breakfast every morning. There, against the wall, was a neatly folded pile of his socks and boxers and T-shirts – she presumed they were his, presumed his dad didn't own a Radiohead T-shirt. There was a book lying on a small table beside the window, *Nightwatch, a Practical Guide to Viewing the Universe*, and underneath the table a pair of muddy-soled Caterpillar boots. Hanging over the back of the chair she was sitting on was a bow tie, a proper one, untied now, and fleetingly Emily imagined Sam dressed in a dinner jacket and wondered where he'd gone. Who had he been with? Upstairs was the bed he slept in, the books that he read, in the bathroom was his toothbrush. Somewhere up there was the room where his mother had died. The cartoon hero who'd rescued the damsel in distress was gone and there was so much more in his place. He was Sam, who lived here in magical Trevissey, and she couldn't deny that she would have liked to know more.

'I should go,' she said, draining her cup and standing up.

Sam nodded. He was standing at the other end of the room, leaning back against a dark red Aga.

She didn't know where it came from but the thought was suddenly there in Emily's mind that he was waiting for her, expecting her to come to him, waiting to kiss her. While the impulsive mad side of her told her to fall into his arms, that it would be fantastic, the more powerful rational side forbade her from doing any such thing. She knew that Sam liked her and she knew that if she kissed him now, he wouldn't want to walk away afterwards. She would be entangling him in her life and she didn't want him there, not while there was so much else already waiting to be resolved. So she went to him and brushed his cheek briefly with her lips and didn't meet his eye, then turned back to the chair with her jacket hanging on its back.

'You think you've given Arthur enough time?' Sam sounded relaxed and unconcerned.

'Yes, I think so. I was wondering where my phone had got to. I'll call him.'

'Use ours,' he offered, indicating a telephone half hidden under a heap of unopened post.

She nodded her thanks. Her heart was thumping and all she was aware of was a dreadful sense of anticlimax. 'I'm going back to London tomorrow,' she told Sam while she waited for Arthur to answer the phone. Not mentioning the fact that she was going home to see Oliver.

9

Anticipation washed over her again as the train pulled out of St Brides. Speaking with Arthur the previous night had made her see everything differently, made her realize how pointless it was to try to predict how Oliver would react to her, how, in this case, worrying about the future would effectively stop anything happening in the present. And as a consequence Arthur had freed her up. Fired her up. The thought that at last she would be seeing Oliver again drove every memory of Sam clean from her mind.

Oliver is free, she thought as the train slowly gathered speed. There's no Nessa. As her carriage was pulled along the coastal track, twisting left and right, rolling from side to side as only ancient British trains do, she looked out of the window at the landscape flashing by and thought, *Here he is, here he is, all these years and here he is.* Then, when the train turned away from the sea and headed inland, running now through rich green fields full of cattle and spring lambs that skittered in fright at its sound, she thought, *It could be me, it could be me.* It felt as if, at last, the moment was upon her.

But then, halfway back to London, Emily took out Sam's rose, the lovely 'Gabriel's Daughter', which she had tried to press between the pages of her book, and held it in her lap, stroking the soft, damp, battered petals. The rose hadn't had a chance to dry out, and it lay there, not pressed so much as squashed and, inevitably, it reminded her of Sam, of standing beside him in the greenhouse as he snipped and he was there, not forgotten at all, vivid and vibrant, warning her to stay away from Oliver. She felt a flash of unease which she smothered quickly. Sam was wrong: wrong to presume he knew what Emily was looking for, wrong to think she was in danger of getting hurt, wrong to condemn Oliver. She knew Oliver, she'd spent more time with Oliver in the last few years than Sam ever had. And she knew herself too, knew how skilled she was at looking after herself, knew she could avoid being swept off her feet. She wanted to believe in Arthur's advice, not Sam's. It would be Arthur she kept in mind as she went to Caitlin's that evening, and she would arrive unhindered by any doubts or preconceptions, there to have fun, to take the moment as it came and find out which way it could take her.

Once off the train she hurried down the platform into the hurly-burly of Paddington Station, and stood for a while to regain her bearings. Ahead of her she saw the signs for the underground and she walked towards the steps, handbag and rose in her left hand, hold-all in her right.

Just as she was shifting her grip on the rose, ready to negotiate her way down, a thorn pricked the soft pad of her thumb and she cried out and dropped it. Around her, the sea of commuters separated around her and then closed again, oblivious. She picked up the rose gingerly. She could see a man in a fluorescent vest leaning on a broom beside the ticket machine, with an open wheelie bin beside him. Emily took the rose over to his bin and found, hard-hearted woman that she was, that she could drop it in with no remorse at all.

In the early evening, as Emily pulled the red top she'd bought in St Brides over her head, she heard the beat of music coming from the flat above. It was a familiar enough sound on a Saturday evening – Rachel, having partied away Friday night, would have got into bed at about nine on Saturday morning and would be rising now for a second dose. Emily was seized by the temptation to go upstairs, find her friend and spill the beans. Impulsively she grabbed her front-door keys and ran up the rickety stairs, dressed only in the new top and a pair of knickers, to find her.

It was only on the stairs that she realized she was galloping up to tell Rachel all about Oliver, about how she felt and what Arthur had said, and how she was going to see him that evening. In the past she'd never have contemplated telling Rachel anything so juicy and personal, but excitement and anticipation were making her uncharacteristically reckless. She knew that telling Rachel would lead to a fresh torrent of opinions and endless advice and interference that she really didn't need. And yet Rachel was a friend and the new Emily wanted to trust her, wanted to do as Arthur had advised and stop evaluating the consequences of every action she took and be more instinctive. If her instincts told her to tell Rachel what was on her mind, she would tell Rachel . . .

Her friendship with Rachel had crept up upon her. Emily had left school with little intention of keeping in touch and yet Rachel was now the only school friend she still saw. Hard not to when she lived only a floor above Emily, but in the years that they'd lived here Emily had been endlessly grateful that fate had worked out the way it did. She and Rachel had slowly but certainly become good friends.

But Rachel didn't answer the door. Emily stood on the stairs, thinking how she'd done this half-naked thing once too often and that she should go back downstairs. Perhaps she'd imagined the sound of Rachel's music above her. And then, just as she was turning to go, a croaky voice called out a hello.

'It's me,' Emily hissed back.

The handle slowly turned and 'Let Me Entertain You' blasted through the door. A bemused, pyjama-clad, hung-over-looking Rachel peered around it and rubbed her eyes at Emily. 'Have ... you ... brought ... me ... some ... Nurofen?'

Emily took in the tiny bloodshot eyes, the pale, shiny face and the wild hair.

'I'm ill,' Rachel groaned.

'I still haven't brought you any. I thought I heard your music.'

'I was trying to make myself feel better. Where did you lose your trousers?' Rachel squinted at Emily's bare legs.

'I haven't put them on yet. I was getting dressed and I heard you and I thought I'd come up.'

Rachel beckoned Emily into the flat, shut the door and led the way to her bedroom.

'Sit on the bed and talk to me. I'm just trying to get up.'

Emily did as she was told and sat on the end of the bed. 'It's seven in the evening ... As good a time as any, I suppose.'

Rachel got back into bed and pulled up her duvet. She looked at Emily and was about to speak, started to cough, then bent down and held her head in her hands for a moment. 'Where have you been again?' she croaked.

'Cornwall.'

The room was dark and Emily reached over and switched on Rachel's bedside light. Lemsip and Lucozade sat convincingly on her bedside table.

Rachel winced at the light. 'You haven't asked so I'll tell you anyway. I've been in bed since the morning after Holly's, ill enough for more sympathy from you. Ill enough for flowers even, if I had anyone kind enough to bring me some. This is not a hangover.'

'I'll buy you some. I thought it was a hangover, but now I can see. You look terrible. Can I get you anything?'

Rachel shook her head. 'I'm feeling better having you here to talk to. Tell me about Cornwall. No, tell me about tonight,' Rachel said, changing her mind. 'Is that what you're wearing?'

Emily nodded.

'It's wonderful – ' Rachel nodded approvingly – 'absolutely beautiful.' Then she said provocatively, 'So what will it be like seeing Oliver again?'

What was going on? Emily stiffened. What had changed since Holly's party when Oliver's return had barely made a ripple of interest? What did Rachel *think* she knew?

'I haven't really thought about it.'

'Come on. You must have done.' Suddenly Rachel was sounding bright and alert.

'There's no big deal about Oliver.'

'But you must be excited about seeing him again?'

'Not particularly,' Emily said defiantly and the disbelief on Rachel's face made her add recklessly, 'I met someone in Cornwall.'

It produced such a wonderful look of surprise that Emily started to laugh.

'No way? You can't have done!' Rachel sat bolt upright, held her head and groaned.

'Yes . . . It's Sam Finch.' Emily gave Rachel a look with just the right mix of coyness and suggestiveness to be completely convincing. 'I couldn't believe it.' Emily hadn't realized she was going to say that either, but she was tired of Rachel, tired of the lot of them always acting like they knew her so well, with just that hint of superiority, as if their experiences had given them a wisdom Emily didn't possess. 'I can't have done what?'

'Nothing important happened between you two, did it?' Rachel asked right on cue.

Emily let out a deep sigh. 'Why is it so bloody impossible?'

Now it was Rachel's turn to laugh, making her clutch at her head again. 'You're the one who kept telling us it was. But of course it isn't impossible – you're gorgeous and it's up to you – and if it happened in Cornwall just a day after meeting someone, and if you're OK about it . . . I suppose that's fine. Join the club!' Emily nodded, encouraging her to go on, encouraging her to believe it. 'But I'm so stunned,' Rachel said. 'Remember, I saw you only a few days ago and there was no talk of going to Cornwall then, certainly not of Sam Finch and . . . I didn't think you would go and do this on the spur of the moment. So understand, seeing as it is the last thing in the world I expected you to say, I'm a little taken aback.'

'I understand.'

'I'm pleased for you, I suppose. You look very happy . . . But – ' she wrinkled up her nose – 'OK, I'll admit it, I thought you were waiting for better things. I'm gutted. I liked the way you were. I thought it was great, everything you said . . .'

Touched as she was, Emily wasn't quite ready to let her off the hook. 'But you have to admit, Sam Finch is a lovely name.'

'A lovely name,' Rachel agreed.

'And he is the one who rescued me from the wasp.'

'Oh, so *that* was the elusive combination. *That's* why it's taken you twenty-five years to find the right man. He had to rescue you from mortal danger *and* have a nice name.'

'Whereas all you had to do was find was a guy who went to the same school as you and was called John,' Emily teased, 'so it took you only sixteen years.'

'And don't I regret it.' The shock on Rachel's face made Emily falter. How had it got to this? Where had it started?

'I'm sorry. So sorry. John was lovely. I'm teasing. Don't worry,' she went on, unable to keep up the lie any longer, 'I'm still pure, I'm still innocent. I'm still there, on the side of the angels.'

Rachel failed to come up with a good reply, sank back on her pillows and closed her eyes. 'So that was just a joke? It's not true?'

'No,' Emily confirmed, 'it's not true. Nothing happened. I'm as pure and innocent and all alone as I was before I left.'

'Thank God for that.'

Because how inconvenient it would have been if Emily – Emily who had managed to go twenty-five years without a man in her life – should find one almost on the very day that all her friends were moving into action with the perfect man and a simple strategy for getting him. Holly had called the morning after her party and had filled Rachel in, cautiously at first because she knew that, of all Emily's friends, Rachel was her most ardent fan and more convinced than anyone else of the value of what Emily was holding out for. But as Rachel had listened and agreed, Holly had happily told her everything, stressing how important it was that Rachel was involved too, that she was too much a part of Emily's life not to be told what was going on (whatever Caitlin might have said to the contrary). And ever keen to please, and to say and do the right thing, Rachel had been easily persuaded. And then Holly had asked Rachel whether she'd like to come skiing too – defying Caitlin again and sighing with relief when

Rachel said that she was tied up with a huge family party and so wouldn't be able to.

Rachel kept her eyes shut, trying to force her thick head to gauge whether or not Sam was a danger to their plans for Emily and Oliver. In the midst of the joking, had she detected something genuine? Did Emily feel more for Sam than she was letting on? If there was any danger at all that Sam might divert attention away from Oliver, she would have to quickly get back to Holly before she called Sam and invited him skiing.

'I don't understand why,' Emily said in a small voice.

Rachel opened an eye and looked at her.

'You don't understand why what?'

'Why it's "thank God" that I haven't met anyone.'

'Because otherwise I'd be the only one without a boy-friend. No, Emily, I'm joking. I'm joking. Really. There's nothing I'd like better than for you to fall in love. We all want you to find someone.'

'Now it sounds as if you've been having a class discussion.'

'No. Of course we haven't.' Rachel slid out a pile of old magazines from under her duvet and dropped them on the floor. 'And you know how I feel about you. I want you to find someone, of course I do.' She paused. 'So, tell me. Did you really fancy Sam Finch?'

'Is that all that's important to you? You're not really interested in who he is, what he does, or how I met him again. You only want to know whether I fancy him or not? Whether I might have slept with him?'

'Absolutely.'

'No,' Emily said, irritated, 'I did not fancy him.'

She got off the bed and wandered over to the window. She knew she shouldn't have even thought about talking to Rachel. Rachel might support her stand, but she didn't know her as Holly did. Holly would have been different. Emily could imagine telling Holly all about Oliver and Sam and Arthur and everyone else. But not Rachel.

'So who do you want?' Rachel asked, almost as if she'd read Emily's mind. There was a stillness to her face, again as if she knew exactly who Emily would say.

'Nobody! You're obsessed! Leave me alone.'

And, seeing how wary she was, it was clear to Rachel that Emily mustn't ever be told that her friends were on to her. That if she did find out, it would only make her run a mile in the wrong direction.

'But you do want to meet someone?'

'Of course I do, in theory. I don't want to hang around for ever.' Emily's smile softened. 'How was I to know it would take me this long!'

'And is it still marriage that you're waiting for?' Rachel asked cautiously, in case Emily became even more defensive.

Emily came back at her immediately. 'You know exactly what I want. Not necessarily a ring and a cake, but lifelong commitment. You know the score.'

'I know that was how it always was for you,' Rachel said. 'I wasn't sure whether you'd changed, that's all.'

'Nothing has changed. I still don't see the point in

sleeping with the wrong guy,' Emily said, 'not if it's clear he is wrong from the start.'

'And what would make him wrong?'

'Wrong as in you know he's not the guy for you, that you won't last.'

'So if it's not going to last it must be wrong?'

'Yes – ' Emily nodded – 'surely you don't want to be with someone who you know you're going to break up with?'

'Sometimes I do,' Rachel admitted. 'Sometimes I don't think that far ahead.'

'I know that living like that would make me unhappy,' Emily said. 'I'm sure sex is fun and exhilarating and good for your skin and great exercise and I can see how it brings you closer to your partner . . . but that's not enough for me. It never has been. If that's all you want, play tennis.'

'You may not believe this, but people say sex is even better.'

'I don't believe you!'

'And much better exercise, too.'

'But sex isn't like tennis, is it?' Emily said, becoming more serious. 'You don't get something stuck inside you during tennis.'

'For God's sake, Emily,' Rachel exploded. 'Why do you have to put it like that?'

'Because it's true!'

'There speaks a true virgin.'

Now Emily was getting seriously defensive. 'I know

that if I am contemplating becoming physically joined to someone, then I want to be emotionally joined to them first.'

'And I agree with you.' Rachel rubbed her face and stared at Emily. 'You know I am not some girl who runs around screwing everything in sight. Neither are your friends. You don't have to convince us about that. But an emotional commitment at the time and everlasting love are not the same thing.'

What was bothering Rachel most wasn't the implicit criticism of herself and the others, but that Emily seemed to think it was the easiest thing in the world to *know* who would provide her with everlasting love. As if she was the only one to have thought about such things. And, for the first time, Rachel – loyal supporter that she had always been – felt rather irritated with Emily for seeing it all in such black and white terms. 'Don't you think we're all looking to be happy, too?' she asked.

'Sometimes I think you are.' Emily bit her lip and looked at Rachel as if unsure whether to go on. 'And sometimes ... I'll admit it, sometimes I look at a guy you're with and I think you must be blind not to see where it's heading. And I look at Caitlin and I think how sordid she is to take home men she hardly knows.'

Rachel had never heard Emily be so judgemental. And she was filled with misgiving. It was as if rational, worldly Emily was there one moment and gone the next, diving below the surface of some sugary, pink, romantic world that Rachel didn't know and no longer wanted to follow her to. She wondered if this was truly how Emily saw them all, the walking wounded, battle-scarred, soiled and half-defeated, while she marched past, untouched and invincible?

'Those are the extremes,' she retaliated, aware how strange it was to be provoked into defending a corner she hadn't even realized she wanted to protect. 'Most of the time it doesn't happen like that. Look at me! I'm not wrecked by the love affairs that haven't worked out, I'm having fun! And so are Jo-Jo and Holly and Caitlin. OK, maybe Caitlin enjoys herself more often than I do and, OK, sometimes I expect she does wish she could turn back the clock. And, yes, sometimes her men are gross. But I don't think it's destroying her. And neither am I being destroyed. My relationships haven't worked out so far, but I've not been left less of a person because of them.'

'I think Caitlin is miserable,' Emily replied. 'I think she feels worthless. I think her self-esteem is shot to shreds and she doesn't like me because I remind her of it. You're suggesting it's possible to sleep with someone and walk away and it doesn't matter who they are,' Emily went on, 'and I don't think that's true. I don't think you can.' She repeated it deliberately. 'I don't think *you* can. And I think you're fooling yourself when you say otherwise. You, you especially, Rachel. You get hurt! Admit it. You try on their surname after the first date and you collapse into bed when they don't call. And it's because you've *slept* with them that it gets you so hard. You wouldn't feel so vulnerable, so bad, if you hadn't slept with them. So don't pretend it's all just one long laugh. I know it's not.'

'Until you fall madly, passionately, overwhelmingly in

lust with someone, not in love, you won't know that you're wrong.'

'I will meet the right guy. I have faith that he will like me just the way I am and he will wait with me. I'm not arguing for abstinence. I'm arguing for patience. I'm saying, what's wrong with waiting? I'm saying I'm sick of instant everything. Fast food, fast tans, fast sex. I hate the way nobody is prepared to wait, *for anything*. It's as if things are only worth having if they're had now. But I say waiting is good, patience is good.'

At that moment, Emily saw it in Rachel's face, the surprise and confusion, scorn even. It made her flinch. 'I don't judge you,' she said, 'so don't judge me. I judge myself. I don't mean to suggest your attitudes are wrong.'

'But I'm suggesting yours are.'

Emily looked at her.

'It is wrong to be so afraid of getting hurt. Don't think it's an advantage to be so cautious and afraid of everything. You survive getting hurt and you learn and move on again. And you can't ward it off, you can't stop it from happening, however much you try. You might get bullied at work, or your dog might get run over, or your mother and father might abandon you and bugger off to New Zealand ... You still survive, don't you? And those events make you grow up, teach you what you want and what you don't want. What you care about, what makes you hurt terribly and what makes you happy too. And whether or not you have sex is *everything* to do with it.'

Rachel got off the bed, turned her back on Emily and started to dress.

'I'd shut the curtains,' Emily told her, with a weak smile. 'Or is that just me being a prude?'

Rachel whipped them closed and turned back to her. 'On this subject, you've always gone it alone and I still think that you're amazing for doing so, brave and so right in so many things that you say. But – ' Emily looked down at the bed and waited – 'at the same time you are too afraid of making mistakes. You fear that you wouldn't be able to cope with one, you fear that if you give yourself up to someone that they will inevitably hurt you. Yet it would be no better or worse for you than it is for any of us. And coping with it when it goes wrong is what makes us strong.'

'I am not frightened of making a mistake. So far it has not been a dilemma for me. So far no guy has come close. I haven't been near anyone who's made me want him that badly.'

'And when you do?'

'When I do, I believe that everything I've said now will still hold true. Because they're good, valid reasons, Rachel, they're not easily ditched. Not when I've held on to them for so long. I will prove that my way can work. I will prove that it is possible to find someone and be sure of them, that being patient, saving the moment, making sex the last thing you do with someone rather than the first will make you happy, *happier*. Because, for me, sex will never be just another way of having fun. I know that I will never want to share the innermost part of me with someone who doesn't love me. I do not want men walking the streets who have known me in the most intimate way possible and who no longer think about me at all.'

Rachel nodded. 'I hope you find him.'

Emily took a deep breath 'I know I will.'

'Such a great top,' Rachel said.

Back to normality.

'Why is Caitlin having this little party, do you think? Is it because she fancies Oliver?' Emily asked the same question she'd asked Holly, and Rachel replied just as Holly had.

'No, I don't think so. I think she wants to make things up with you. I think that's why.'

Slipping down the stairs again, letting herself back into her flat, Emily realized that Rachel's forceful words had unsettled her, and she knew too that there'd been some truth in what she'd said. Rachel was right when she said that she was cautious, afraid of mistakes – Emily knew it was true. And she wondered how much she'd be prepared to change in order to get closer to Oliver.

10

'There's something different about you.'

'No!'

'You've met someone. I can tell by the way you're looking at me.'

'Stop it!' Emily laughed, turning away from him.

Oliver put his head to one side and considered her. 'Oh, I think so. Come and tell me who he is.' He patted the sofa beside him.

'No!' she said again.

'Emily. You have to . . .'

In the kitchen, crouching down to look through the window of her oven to check up on her four towering cheese soufflés, Caitlin felt momentarily disheartened. She could hear Oliver and Emily laughing again, imagined them sitting side by side on the little sofa and wondered, sourly, what could have possessed her to come up with such a totally great idea that involved giving Emily, of all people, a clean shot at the most attractive man she knew.

When Caitlin had opened her front door and taken her first look at Oliver in over a year, her first thought had been, *She is not going to be able to resist you*. One year on and Oliver was even more attractive. Not very tall, which Caitlin liked – when he stood beside Leon he'd seem even shorter – but bigger and broader and less clean-cut than

163

she'd remembered, his tawny hair grown longer and streaked with gold, and there was a definitely naughty gleam in his gorgeous brown eyes.

Oliver had come forward, kissed her and handed her a huge bunch of frilly orange parrot tulips (and she was hardly ever given classy flowers) and her second thought, the thought that had repeated through her head ever since, was, *Do I really have to do this? Can't I have him instead?*

But when Emily had arrived and slipped off her coat to reveal a surprisingly see-through little red top and very low-cut jeans, Caitlin had felt quite proud of her, and resolved again to make the evening work. She had retreated to the kitchen as quickly as she decently could, dragging Leon with her and leaving Emily and Oliver alone in the sitting room.

But Leon was proving surprisingly difficult to control. From the moment that Caitlin got him into the kitchen he was fidgeting to get out again, all the time looking through the doorway to the sitting room opposite, as if he was trying to see what Emily and Oliver were up to, and she could do nothing to distract him. In the end, frustrated by all the chores Caitlin kept piling on him, he announced he was off to the bathroom, whereupon Caitlin knew that, for the time being, she'd lost him, that he had no intention of rejoining her in the kitchen afterwards.

Left alone, Caitlin reached for mustard, salt and pepper, brown sugar, olive oil and balsamic vinegar and a little brown jug, telling herself she would not look through the door and spy on Oliver and Emily herself until after she'd made a dressing. Which took all of thirty seconds. Still managing not to look, she reached into the corner of the kitchen for the two sticks of French bread propped up against the wall and slid them out of their cellophane.

Surely twenty minutes had passed since Caitlin last looked? Surely it was fair enough if she now allowed herself a little glimpse, another quick check on progress? She glanced. Emily and Oliver had moved from the sofa and were standing together at the far end of the little sitting room, Emily with her back to the wall (so Caitlin was able to see her clearly from the kitchen), Oliver with his back to Caitlin.

'Something has changed,' she heard Oliver say.

Glad that you've noticed, Caitlin thought. She watched Oliver pretend to peer carefully all over Emily's face and make Emily blush. He knows he's right, and he's not sure he likes it, and it's making him want to flirt with her. But what he can't see is that the change is because of him, that he's the one who's lit her up, that he's the one she can't take her eyes off now. And even though Caitlin would have said yes to him herself at any other time, even though it was still more bitter than sweet to see Oliver and Emily coming together, at that moment it seemed that the planning might all be about to pay off, and that felt good. Emily was glowing in his company, standing so close to him she was practically in his arms, and still she hadn't taken her eyes off his face. Caitlin felt like a fairy godmother to a god-daughter she'd never much liked but who was now turning out to be rather rewarding.

For so long Caitlin had felt like the flaky, irresponsible one of the three of them – at least she imagined that was how Holly and Jo-Jo saw her: the one without the proper job, the one who was broke all the time, the one who lived off her boyfriends, and her friends too if she had the chance, and who appeared to spend what little money she had on shoes and facials rather than on getting her life together. They might enjoy her company, but Caitlin knew that they didn't take her seriously. So it was great to have something positive to share with Holly and Jo-Jo, especially when it was something she, Caitlin, had initiated. Yet another reason to prolong the experience for as long as she could. Now she had Emily to work on, perceptions of Caitlin might be about to change.

'Hey, Emily!'

Leon was standing in the doorway of the bathroom. Caitlin watched in despair as he set off towards her, still zipping up his flies. He glanced in at Caitlin, gave her a smile that said it all, and stopped. But only for long enough to take a comb from his breast pocket and run it quickly through his hair and to grab a bottle of wine from her fridge.

Caitlin watched him walk into the sitting room, come up behind Oliver and purposefully move him out of the way. She watched him refill Emily's glass, turn and refill Oliver's, then stretch his arm behind Emily and put the bottle on the fireplace behind her, leaving his arm there. Fat, hairy fingers supported his weight. He had effectively annexed Emily for himself.

When Caitlin had first met Leon she'd been reminded

of a seal. Now as irritation burst inside her, she looked at his small flat nose, his ears pressed close to his little head, his slicked-down hair, his body bulging softly in his black suit, and she thought that he looked like a slug. A slug in a toupee. He moved even closer to Emily. What the hell was Leon doing? Damn him!

'Go and help Caitlin in the kitchen,' she heard him tell Oliver and, in disbelief, Caitlin watched Oliver do exactly as he was told. When he came into the kitchen she had to stop herself from shooing him back out again.

'Because I think it's my turn to talk to you,' she heard Leon say to a silenced Emily, 'or were you planning on ignoring me all evening?'

And then, belatedly, Caitlin understood. Leon desperately fancied Emily. And her heart sank because she knew Leon too well, knew how it would make him behave.

Caitlin turned her back on Oliver and stomped across her kitchen in disgust. Why hadn't she seen this coming, hadn't once thought about how Leon would react to Emily? Why, when Leon had asked who Emily was, what she did, where she came from, had Caitlin told him so much more than he needed to know? But Caitlin knew exactly why. She had told Leon about Emily because she knew how much it would fascinate him and she hadn't been able to resist. She had wanted to stun him, and at the same time tempt him with someone she knew he'd never have. *She's stunningly pretty, Leon. And, amazingly, she's still a virgin.*

She'd told him just half an hour ago, when it was only the two of them, still waiting for Emily and Oliver to arrive. And then, having told him, instead of regretting it, covering up, backtracking swiftly and making nothing of it, she'd made things even worse, had thrown him the challenge: *Don't look like that. She's hardly going to be interested in you.*

But he was interested in her, which meant that Emily was going to have him fawning and falling over her all evening. If it wasn't that he'd be getting in the way of Oliver, it would have been funny to watch.

'Anything I can do?' Oliver asked Caitlin.

You can go and be a man.

She passed him a large plate of toasted brown pitta cut into strips and a bowl of roughly chopped guacamole and he held it still while she gave it a squeeze of lemon juice. 'Give it some salt and pepper and then you can take it through to them,' she said instead. 'Split them up and save her from a fate worse than death.'

Oliver laughed and instead of doing as he was told he placed the plate and the bowl back on the tiny work surface and then jumped up beside it, took a piece of pitta and dipped. 'I think it's fair enough that Leon gets some quality time with Emily. And I think I'd rather stay with you.'

She shook her head because they were veering off the script – and yet, she thought, surely it couldn't harm. The night was young and there was plenty of time for Emily and Oliver to get close later on. Surely she didn't have to be rude to Oliver? Turn him out of her kitchen when he'd asked to stay? She hadn't seen him for a year, and he was her friend too. And perhaps if Leon was left alone with

Emily for ten minutes, he might see the other, rather more irritating aspects to her personality. Leaving Leon alone with Emily might be the best way of getting her out of his system.

'I love to watch a woman cook,' he told Caitlin, watching as she halved an avocado, peeled it, threw away the stone and proceeded to chop it at the speed of light. 'And you are cooking in the most minute kitchen I've ever seen.'

She glanced up at him. 'Chauvinist.'

What Oliver had said about her kitchen was true. Compared with Holly's gleaming industrial-sized space, her kitchen was barely bigger than a biscuit tin, and because there were only one or two small cupboards everything – all her pots and pans, the potato mashers and metal spoons with holes in, and garlic presses and egg whisks – hung from the ceiling, getting tangled in her hair and collecting dust every day that they weren't being used. In order to sit where he was now, Oliver had had to make a parting in the line of utensils swinging level with his head, and he was positioned between a sharp pair of scissors and a pizza cutter.

Pushed up against the wall tiles were her bottles of oils and vinegars and pots of flour and herbs, all specially selected for size as well as for flavour. She had a very small fridge and her little oven drove her crazy, needing telepathic intuition to judge its temperature, its door falling off its hinges almost every time she opened it. Having someone else in there when she cooked usually sent her into a frenzy of irritation. But it wasn't the same when the someone else was Oliver.

'Did I get it right about Emily?' Oliver asked Caitlin. 'Has she met someone?'

Say yes and she might whet his appetite . . . but she might put him off. Say no and she was diluting the challenge . . . but she might be encouraging him.

'Possibly.' Caitlin ran the chopping board under the tap, then wiped clean the knife, opened her fridge and brought out a cucumber. 'Rachel said she'd met someone in Cornwall,' she told him, 'but I don't think it's anything serious.'

'That'll be Sam Finch,' he said, tossing back his hair and dropping guacamole into his mouth. 'Not serious.' He agreed and licked his fingers clean.

'You know that?'

'Sam said he'd seen her. Sam's known Emily for years, as long as I have. Nothing's going on there.' He lowered his voice. 'So, she's still not slept with anyone?'

Caitlin looked at him. 'I'm not the one to ask.'

'No?'

'You should ask Emily, not me.'

'I'm going to,' Oliver said defensively. 'I'm checking with you that she's OK, that's all.'

'She's got a perfectly good brother already,' Caitlin said, sharper than she intended.

'Spiky Caitlin! I know she's got a brother.'

'So she doesn't need another one.' She started to roll the plastic wrapper off the cucumber.

'No. She doesn't need another one,' Oliver agreed, 'but I like to think I'm a friend. Someone she knows cares about her.'

'And you hope she's been good while you've been away in New York?'

'What is this?' But Oliver was laughing as he said it, distracted by the way Caitlin was loosening the plastic around the cucumber, by rubbing it vigorously up and down.

Too late Caitlin realized what she was doing. She laid the cucumber down on the chopping board and refused to look at Oliver. Then she reached into a drawer and brought out a Sabatier knife, steadied herself and chopped.

Oliver flinched.

She slid the knife under the plastic and pulled the cucumber free. 'We all like to look out for Emily.' She picked up the knife again and started to peel.

'I never realized you were such a friend.'

'She's grown on me. I want her to be happy. I think her attitudes are all wrong, of course. I hope for her sake that she starts to adapt them.'

'She's a lovely girl. She'll adapt when she finds someone who deserves her.'

Seeing Oliver sitting there, so good-looking in a heartbreaking kind of a way, someone who really meant it when he said he cared about Emily – in short, the perfect man for her – Caitlin had to fight the urge to tell him everything, to stop herself from suggesting that even if he hadn't thought about Emily like that since he was sixteen, it was now time he did.

'Sam Finch is a good friend of yours, is he?' she asked instead.

Oliver nodded. 'Great friend. Known him all my life.'

'And do you like skiing?'

Oliver laughed. 'There's a link there somewhere but I'm damned if I can find it. Sam and snow? Sam and me . . . and snow?' He laughed, giving up. 'Yes, I like skiing.'

'It's Holly's holiday. Expect a call.'

'To say what?'

Caitlin was wandering off the script, but she carried on recklessly. 'She's going to say that she requests the pleasure of your company at her chalet in Magine, in the French Alps, over Easter,' she grinned. 'For *liaisons dangereuses*.'

Oliver raised an eyebrow. 'Interesting.'

Caitlin nodded, thinking she should have kept her mouth shut. And that Holly should have asked him, not her.

Still sitting on the kitchen unit, he suddenly hooked a leg around her and pulled her close. 'And who am I meant to be liaising with? I can resist liaising with Leon. But if you'll be there . . .'

'You know I'll be there.'

'With Leon?'

'Of course.'

'Why?'

'Because he's sweet.'

She wriggled out of Oliver's reach and decided to ignore what he had just done. *Because he's my boyfriend*, she should have added, *and I adore him. Leave me alone.*

'And Emily will be there. She'll be so pleased to know you're coming too. We should go back next door and tell her—'

'Caitlin, what are you doing with him?'

'There's a lot to Leon that you don't see the first time you meet him.' She went on without pausing, giving him no chance to interrupt. 'And if you're staying here, you can help me. Chop up some parsley, then we can go through.' She pointed to where a large pot was balanced precariously on a narrow window ledge.

Without getting down, he turned and tore off a handful of the parsley. She gave him the chopping board and the sharp knife and he started to chop while Caitlin ripped open a packet of lamb's lettuce and dropped it into a china salad bowl. Then she bent to the oven and lifted out, one by one, her four soufflés. Behind her, Oliver jumped off the cupboard and went through to the sitting room. Alone again, Caitlin scooped up the parsley, sprinkled some onto the top of each soufflé, placed them on a tray and carried them through.

Caitlin walked into the sitting room just in time to hear Leon tell Emily with a lascivious smile the old cliché that he'd never met anyone quite like her before.

He was sitting beside her on the sofa, and in response Emily flicked at him with her hand, batting him away like a bluebottle. But Caitlin was surprised to see that she had a grin on her face and she didn't take advantage of their arrival to escape him. If anything, Caitlin thought, Leon was so plain bad at flirting that Emily probably found him endearing. It made Caitlin feel both irritation and affection for the pair of them. Irritation at Emily for being so hopeless, for not using opportunities to talk to

Oliver, and irritation at Leon for finding a virgin irresistibly attractive. Yet through her irritation, Caitlin knew that it was Emily's vulnerability and lack of confidence that was preventing her making any move on Oliver. And she wondered if it wasn't Leon's lack of confidence speaking too. Perhaps the thought of being with someone who couldn't compare him to anyone else was very attractive? Especially in contrast to the voracious, been-there-done-everything nymphomaniacs he usually went for, herself excluded.

The problem was that Leon's infatuation meant he was in no hurry to leave Emily alone. And he'd stick even closer to her if he ever realized what Caitlin had planned for Emily and Oliver. If Caitlin didn't do something about Leon, she could see her evening becoming a farce. She imagined Jo-Jo's lecture and felt a surge of renewed determination. She would have to get Emily and Oliver alone together, somewhere Emily couldn't run away from sometime that evening. But she wasn't sure how.

In the opposite corner of the sitting room to the sofa was a small wooden table. Caitlin went over to it and put down the tray and Oliver followed her. She handed him two plates, each with a blue ramekin holding a soufflé, and he passed one to Leon and one to Emily.

As soon as Emily got hers, she slid off the sofa and sat on the floor.

'Stay where you were,' Caitlin protested. 'I'm sorry that there's not more room to sit down.'

'No, honestly, you sit on the sofa,' said Emily. 'I'm fine on the floor.'

Possibly it had been a strategic move, designed to put her out of reach of Leon, or an invitation to Oliver to join her, but if it was it misfired, because Oliver didn't move fast enough and Leon practically threw himself to the floor next to her. He ended up half lying, half sitting by her side, supporting himself eagerly on his little white hands and looking up at Oliver in triumph. Then, as Caitlin watched in horror, he took his spoon, dipped it into his soufflé, leant forwards and tried to drop it into Emily's mouth.

Catching Oliver's eye, Emily shut her mouth tight, whereupon Leon shrugged self-consciously and ate the soufflé himself. There were a few awkward seconds, until Emily put her plate on the floor and climbed back to her feet.

'Where's the bathroom?' she asked Caitlin, pink with embarrassment.

'Oliver,' Caitlin said, seeing him standing close to the door. 'Show Emily the bathroom.'

She ignored his *how should I know where your bathroom is?* shrug, and as he and Emily left the room Caitlin moved over to the sofa, gave Leon a look and patted the space beside her. He did as he was told, sat down and looked at her warily.

There were only two doors for Oliver to choose between. Caitlin heard him make the right choice and open the door to her bathroom. She wanted to run up behind them, give them both a good shove in the back and lock the bathroom door.

'Here we are,' she heard Oliver say. Caitlin imagined him standing aside to let her pass and enter the room.

It was perfect timing. There would be no shoving necessary. Oliver stepped forward to turn on the light for Emily and momentarily disappeared into the room. And Caitlin got up, moved quickly to the bathroom door and pulled it gently shut behind him. It didn't even make a sound, and she was beside Leon almost before he had realized she'd left the room.

Quick as a flash, Caitlin returned to the sitting room and poured herself and Leon another glass of wine.

As the seconds became a minute, Caitlin felt a tug of jealousy. She imagined Oliver kissing Emily's forehead, taking her in his arms. *Ssshh!* he'd whisper, covering her mouth with his. *Let's not be rescued yet.*

Caitlin looked over to Leon, blissfully eating his supper. She was dying to say something about how long Oliver and Emily were taking, but Leon still hadn't noticed their absence and she knew she shouldn't involve him. If he realized what was happening, he'd be the first to break down the door. One more minute and she'd go back to the kitchen and on her way listen at the bathroom door.

Then, from the bathroom, came the rather disconcerting sound of a flushing loo and finally, a rattling of the door and then, at last, Oliver's voice appealing for help.

'Coming, I'm coming,' Caitlin called back, leaping up and almost tripping over herself in her haste to get out of the sitting room. Forget about leaving them there for hours, forget about keeping the door shut to allow the temperature to rise, she wanted to open the door and see their faces immediately, to work out exactly what and how much had gone on between them.

'Are you stuck in there?' she shouted.

'Don't worry. Take your time,' Oliver called back.

Leon joined Caitlin at the door. 'What's going on?'

'They're stuck,' she told him.

'In there together? I'll break down the door. *I'll break down the door,*' Leon repeated loudly, mouth to the keyhole.

'No, don't you dare,' Caitlin said, pushing him out of the way.

'I'm serious, I mean it. Take your time,' Oliver insisted from the other side.

'I've got a spanner in the kitchen,' Caitlin called to him. 'What I usually do is pass it through the space at the bottom of the door, then you can use it as a door handle.'

'You're telling me you knew about this door?' Oliver shouted back incredulously. 'Other people have met the same fate?'

'Yes. I'm sorry, I'm not very good at DIY.'

She went to the kitchen and ransacked the tiny kitchen drawers, pulling out an array of napkin rings, video repair manuals, home-delivery restaurant menus, assorted keys, tea towels, the instruction manual for her fridge, paper napkins, some nasty table mats and finally the spanner. She went back to the bathroom and fed the spanner slowly under the door and waited while Oliver got to work on the other side. Eventually the door opened.

And Oliver was standing there alone.

'Where's Emily?' Caitlin cried in frustration.

'I'm here!' And there she was. Standing red-faced in the doorway of Caitlin's bedroom, watching them.

'What the hell are you doing there?' Caitlin exploded.

'I didn't think you'd mind. I've been in your room. Not snooping, just sitting on your bed.'

'She kindly offered to let me go first,' Oliver explained.

'Isn't that just so romantic?' said Caitlin, finding it hard to stop herself banging her head against the wall.

'I was sitting on your bed, waiting for him. And I found your photographs,' Emily came over to her. 'They're gorgeous. When were you in India?'

Shut up about India! Caitlin nearly spat at her.

'I truly wasn't nosing. The album was on your bed. I didn't think you'd mind. Oliver!' she said, turning to him. 'You were ages! Are you ill? What were you doing in there?'

'I don't think we need to know the answer to that, do we, Emily? Do we, Oliver?' Caitlin butted in.

'I'm sorry,' Oliver said to Emily. 'I wish you had got locked in with me. It would have been far more fun.' He turned to Caitlin. 'How about an *I'm sorry you got locked in, Oliver*. Or *I'll make sure I fix that door before you come around again, Oliver*.'

'Sorry.' Caitlin gave him a grudging smile.

'I'll just go myself,' Emily said, sidling past them, 'if you don't mind. And I'll only push the door to, so nobody's to come in.'

Ten minutes later Caitlin came back to the sitting room to find that Leon, Oliver and Emily had all decided to move to the floor to eat their supper. Emily looked relaxed for the first time that evening, and, at last, it was Oliver she was smiling at and talking to, not Leon.

Because Caitlin's flat was so tiny, this was the way she always ended up entertaining. The room was so small that there was room only for the little table at one end of the room and the two-seater sofa at the other, so if four people wanted to eat together, the only way was for all four to sit on the floor. As it was, some of the best evenings were at Caitlin's, where the intimacy of the room, the unfailingly delicious food, the candlelight and cushions, rather than chairs, easily beat the formality of a sit-down supper.

She would let them eat and then she would try again to think of some way to give Emily and Oliver quality time together. The missed opportunity in the bathroom had to be put aside. She was somehow going to remove Leon from the room and leave Oliver alone there. It wasn't going to be easy. Leon was not going to give up his place lightly – even as he saw her struggling with a heavy dish he didn't move a muscle. It was, of course, Oliver who jumped up to give her a hand.

But in the end it was simple enough. She gave them all helpings of salad, handed around the buttery hot baguettes, the salt and pepper, the napkins, knives and forks, waited until they'd eaten almost every scrap of food, then she picked up and took out the china salad bowl. Once in her kitchen, she let the bowl slip through her fingers and hit the ceramic tiled floor where it smashed satisfyingly. She'd always disliked it and getting rid of it in aid of such a good cause was doubly justified.

'Leon, please!' she ordered before Oliver could get up. 'Come and give me a hand.'

There was something in her voice that compelled Leon to do as he was told. He came in, saw what had happened and heaved a sigh. 'Clumsy girl,' he said, daring Caitlin's wrath, as he reached for some kitchen roll, bent to her feet and carefully began to clear it up. Caitlin didn't reply. She wasn't going to say anything to hasten his return to the other room. Instead, she reached over to the kitchen door and shut it.

Crawling around at her feet, Leon gingerly picked up the larger pieces of china and dropped them into the bin while she busied herself with wiping olive oil off the wall. When that was done she turned to the washing up, which made Leon look up at her in surprise. 'Why now?'

'It'll only take a second,' she explained.

Leon, having picked up the last pieces of lamb's lettuce and rocket and avocado and cucumber, swept the floor. Then, at Caitlin's instruction, he washed it while she rinsed and rubbed clean her pots and pans.

'You'll make someone a good husband some day,' Caitlin told him, as he squeezed out the mop.

'But not you.'

'I don't think you want that, do you?'

'I don't think you'd have me.'

Their words belied the fact that this was the closest they'd been to each other all evening. Caitlin slowly walked towards him, stretched up and kissed him and he pulled her to him. 'Would you?'

'No chance.'

'I'd be good for you.'

'Would you?'

He reached down and kissed her lips and she slid her arms around his reassuringly solid waist.

Then Oliver called to them from the sitting room. 'Come on, you two. What are you doing in there?'

'We're coming. In a second,' Leon called, holding her tight.

'We should go back,' Caitlin told him, kissing him again just below his right ear. Then she pushed him away and opened the door.

'About time too,' Oliver said as soon as she opened it. 'What were you two doing in there?'

And he was irritated, Caitlin realized. She could see it clearly on his face.

She looked back at Leon, who was waiting obediently for her to tell him whether he was allowed back into the sitting room or whether there were further chores expected of him, and all at once she was tired of plotting, unsure about what she was doing and unsettled by the reality of Oliver.

She turned off the overhead light as she came in, so there were now only the dimmest of lamps lit in the room and the two candles, still burning on the mantelpiece. The room was shadowy and dark. The walls, petrol blue in the daylight, were black now.

She was encouraged to see that, left alone together, Oliver and Emily had moved closer to each other. They were both sitting on the floor, their legs stretched out in front of them, side by side, their empty plates pushed to one side, and it was clear that at that moment they were close. As she watched, Oliver wiped a tiny speck of food from Emily's cheek.

He likes her, Caitlin decided. It wouldn't be too hard to move him up a gear. Perhaps he was already more than interested? Perhaps an evening alone together would be all that was necessary to set the course for the two of them?

But then, infuriatingly, as soon as Emily saw Caitlin, she picked up the two empty plates in one hand and got up off the floor.

'Sit down,' Caitlin insisted.

'No, you sit down. I want to help. I'll take these through.' And before Caitlin could say or do anything Emily had picked up the other two plates as well and had left the room.

Leon, who had only just sat down, spied an empty serving dish and hurried out of the room after her.

Caitlin heaved a sigh of frustration then sat down on the floor beside Oliver. Why was it proving so completely impossible to get the four of them in the same room at the same time?

'It's all right, leave them to it. Don't get up again,' Oliver told her.

She reluctantly stayed put, stiff, uncommunicative, waiting for Emily and Leon to come back, planning how, as soon as they did, she'd move back to the sofa and she'd damned well take Leon with her.

But Emily and Leon didn't reappear and for every minute that they stayed away, Oliver seemed to creep ever closer towards her. This was not what was meant to happen at all. She ignored Oliver's encroachment at first and then started to edge away, all the time managing to keep the conversation going with inanities while snatching glances towards the kitchen, not sure whether it would be better or worse for Emily to come back in right now.

Through the doorway into the kitchen she saw that Leon had Emily practically pinned to the wall and Emily was flicking him away with a tea towel. Caitlin felt like laughing with despair that everything could be so back to front. Holly and Jo-Jo would never understand how hard it had been, how hard she'd tried. Or how determined Oliver was.

Oliver is resistible, she reminded herself. Lust after him as she might, it was still more important to Caitlin that when it came to recounting the evening to Jo-Jo and Holly she would be able to tell the whole truth. More important that she would be seen to have behaved impeccably.

But then, she thought, what more could Holly and Jo-Jo expect from the very first date? She'd got Oliver and Emily together again – wasn't it mad of all of them to expect some wild romance to blossom so fast? And if Emily insisted on wiping clean every surface in Caitlin's kitchen – which was what she seemed to be doing now – rather than taking advantage of the chance to get close to Oliver, was there anything Caitlin could do about it? No. She had done her bit and now it was up to Holly and then Rachel to take the couple-to-be on to the next stages. But more importantly, it had to be up to Emily too. She had to help things along herself. And surely she was only imagining that Oliver had been coming on to her?

'Come here,' said Oliver.

Caitlin laughed. 'I can't exactly come any closer. Tell me about America,' she went straight on. 'Was *The Second Guess* a nightmare?'

That was what Caitlin was so good at, remembering everything anyone ever told her, in this case playing on Oliver's ego to distract him.

'*The Second Guess* was a nightmare. But then I worked on the most wonderful thriller called *Into the Noose*.'

He told her about it, now fully stretched out beside her, and Caitlin felt him there, so close, and tried to concentrate on what he was saying, but at the same time she couldn't help sneaking glances at his face, taking in the line of his throat, the long streaks of gold in his hair, the way he kept his beautiful tawny eyes focused on her face while he talked.

Standing in the kitchen, waiting to dry the ramekins as Emily washed them, Leon was at first stuck for something to say. All he could think was to tell her how sweet the Fairy Liquid bubbles looked on her smooth slender forearms, or to point out that she had been washing the same ramekin for nearly a minute.

And while she washed up, Emily was thinking about Oliver, thinking how useless and pathetic she was – that she would prefer to stand in Caitlin's kitchen, washing up with Leon, than be sitting beside Oliver. 'Prefer' was the wrong word. Of course she would prefer to be sitting beside Oliver, but something had stopped her – a paralysis that she'd never experienced before and that she certainly hadn't expected. She despised herself for it, couldn't believe that it was happening to her, that even after the pep talks from Arthur, and the genuine conviction she'd felt that she could go for it, she'd been utterly useless.

She thought back to the year before, how relaxed she'd been in Oliver's company simply because Nessa had been there in the background, her presence keeping everything nice and safe. Of course, Emily could see now that it was Nessa who had made it possible for her to laugh with Oliver, made it possible for her to rest her head on his shoulder, to turn to him for a dance at a party, to call him up to go out for lunch. Now that Nessa was out of the picture and Oliver was available again, Emily had frozen in fear. What is *wrong* with me? she asked herself.

Still, she hadn't exactly had any encouragement from Oliver this evening. She had been aware from the moment she'd walked into Caitlin's flat that he wasn't looking at her the way she wanted him to, not as a potential girl-friend, nor as someone to have a bit of fun with. Oliver had hugged her tightly to him, had kissed her hello and had been very pleased to see her again, but he was greeting the Emily he used to know. He was seeing her as he'd always done – as someone he liked very much, someone to take care of, but not someone to fancy. And that knowledge made it cripplingly hard to behave the way she wanted to. When she'd caught Oliver's eye while Leon was trying to feed her the soufflé, she'd seen that he was laughing at her. Whereas before she might have been able to laugh back, in the present circumstances she had been so embarrassed she'd had to leave the room.

Was it simply that Oliver didn't fancy her and never would? Or was it her virginity that was putting him off? If Sam was right and all he was looking for now was a bit of fun, perhaps it was reasonable of Oliver to decided she was out of bounds.

Catching Caitlin alone in the kitchen earlier on, Emily had nearly told her how she felt about Oliver. Now, standing over the sink, she felt a hot flush of embarrassment. How could she have even thought of doing that? But Caitlin had been a revelation this evening. Even-tempered, considerate, encouraging. She'd admired Emily's little red top, she'd laughed at her jokes, she'd brought her into every conversation. She'd even seemed to know what was on Emily's mind. There'd been a moment when she'd interrupted something Emily was telling her and had said, *If you know what you want, go for it*. Emily had automatically argued that that was what she always did and Caitlin had shrugged and moved the conversation on again and they hadn't said anything more. Now she wished she had.

She ended up letting Leon make coffee for her rather than face the moment when she had to return to the sitting room. She sat on one of the kitchen units next to the sink while he found mugs and milk, and every minute she was away from Oliver made it harder to get back in there.

Leon, needless to say, seemed happy to stay with her. But finally, when the coffee had been drunk, and the conversation exhausted, there was nothing left to do but go through to Oliver and Caitlin. Emily jumped down and Leon led the way with another pot of coffee and a jug of milk and two mugs on a tray. And then he suddenly stopped and turned back, nearly crashing into her, making some feeble excuse, standing in the doorway so that she couldn't even see past him, let alone squeeze past him.

Emily laughed and tried to push him aside, once more determined to spend some time with Oliver, but then Oliver himself came through the door, with bright eyes and pink flushed cheeks.

Later, when Caitlin had finished tidying, undressed, washed and climbed into bed, she was filled with remorse. Along with the awful pang of conscience with regard to Leon there was an afterglow of affection for Emily. Emily might still talk and think like a choirgirl, but she was a choirgirl Caitlin liked more and more the better she knew her, a choirgirl who provoked little of the irritation of old, who with a couple of glasses of wine inside her had almost blurted out in the kitchen that she fancied Oliver. And the memory of that tentative, hopeful look on Emily's face made Caitlin want to curl up and die.

'Are you listening?' Oliver had asked her, his smiling face six inches from hers. How had he got so close? So close that she could see the tiny pores on his nose and the rogue hair that was sticking out at a right angle from his eyebrow. She could smell his musky warm body, hear his soft, shallow breathing, so close she could have touched him with her tongue.

'You don't have to ask me about America.'

'What do you want to talk about?'

'Who says I want to talk about anything?'

And before she realized what he was about to do, he'd leaned forward and taken her chin in his hand and gently tipped it up towards him, had slowly moved closer until he was near enough to kiss her on the mouth.

For just a second or two Caitlin didn't move, but then she jerked backwards as if she'd touched her lips to an electric fence.

This couldn't happen. This mustn't happen.

With enormous will power she dropped her head so that he couldn't reach her lips again, and she stayed like that, held herself steady, gathering herself together, and then she looked up at him again.

'You shouldn't do that,' she said very quietly, their heads still very close.

'Yes, I should. You're the sexiest woman I know.'

'You shouldn't say that.'

'Why not?'

Caitlin groaned.

'Lose Leon. He's pathetic. You can't fancy him.'

'I do. I don't want to lose him.'

'Then have me too.'

Oliver was leaning forward again, reaching with his lips for hers, and she felt her stomach flip over with lust for him. 'Are you offering me a threesome?'

'Not exactly. Even with you there, I don't think I could bear that.' He came closer still. 'And I can't bear the thought of you with him either.'

'Tough,' she said smartly, pulling away from him and sitting up. 'Because, actually, Leon and I are very happy.'

'I don't believe you.'

'I don't care whether you believe me or not.' She was amused that it seemed to bother him so much.

She said nothing more and slowly he started to believe she was serious, and then when she saw that it had worked, she kissed him gently on the tip of the nose, saying goodbye. 'I'm sorry. Leon and I might seem an odd couple, but we're good together.'

He pursed his lips, thought about it, then shrugged, recovering his bravado. 'That's cool. Forget I said anything.'

'But you will still come skiing, won't you? You weren't only coming to try to pull me?'

'You've got a nerve. Of course I wasn't.'

'Emily will be there, and Holly. And Holly is going to invite Sam too, to keep you company,' she added for good measure.

'I'll think about it.' He leaned forward again and kissed her on the cheek. He pushed himself quickly to his feet and went to the door.

11

The next morning, the phone lines were hot.

When Caitlin heard her telephone start to ring she pulled her duvet up to her chin and let the answerphone click in.

'Broadsword to Danny Boy. ' It was Holly. 'Caitlin! For Christ's sake, pick up the damn phone. It's nine thirty and you should have called by now to tell me what happened last night.'

Caitlin opened her eyes.

'I know you're there . . . and I want to know –' but the tone was changing now, caution creeping in – 'unless . . . you're not there? Oh, Caitlin, you didn't! Tell me you didn't?' Caitlin's heart leapt in fear and she looked across at the answerphone in panic.

'Did you go home with Leon?'

Better than that, I kissed Oliver.

She got out of bed and stalked out of her bedroom to the kitchen, where she leaned against the door and waited for Holly to give up.

'Or are you trying to stay asleep?' Holly changed tack again. 'That won't work either. If you're lying in bed listening to me and not answering, *la la la,*' she sang down the phone. 'I am not going to let you go back to sleep. Pick up the phone now! Please! I'm going to keep ringing until you answer. It's nine thirty, it's time to get up. You will *not* go back to sleep.'

Sometimes Holly was so irritating. Caitlin wanted to pick up the phone and tell her just that and nothing more. In a few more seconds the tape would run out, and she definitely needed a little time to think before she talked to Holly. Holly, meanwhile, tried sounding more serious.

'I understand something's happened that we didn't expect. That we might have a problem ... That there's someone who might be about to cause problems.'

Was this it? How had Holly heard? Caitlin told herself it was impossible, that nobody had seen her and Oliver, and that anyway she'd done nothing wrong.

Then the answerphone exploded. 'Sam bloody Finch?' Holly's voice picked up more speed and outrage with every word. 'How come he keeps popping up everywhere? Rachel called me last night. Emily told her she'd met *this new man*! And Rachel's worried, even though Emily then said she was joking. Emily swears that there's nothing going on, but Rachel thinks there is ... There was definitely something special about the way she was talking about Sam. And if that's true, I am worried. Did you hear he gave her a rose? Only he hadn't bought it he'd *grown* it, no, even better, he'd *bred* it. Can you believe it?' There was a pause, then, 'Oh, bloody hell, Caitlin, just call me. Call me back.' And finally Holly hung up.

Caitlin opened a drawer and took out a dessertspoon, then opened the fridge door. Inside was a bowl of chocolate mousse she'd made for the night before but, after what had happened between her and Oliver, she hadn't had the stomach for chocolate mousse.

She made herself a mug of coffee and took it and the mousse back to her bedroom. She had done nothing bad – it was just a kiss – but if she told the others about it they were sure to think she had behaved true to form and that there was much more that she wasn't telling them. And then they would feel responsible for Emily, like they always did, and they would pull Emily from the scene of danger, make it clear to her that Oliver wasn't the man for her.

But whether or not Oliver was the one for Emily or not – and after last night she had to admit she'd begun to think not – Caitlin knew that what was still important was that Emily believed he *was* the one for her, and that that was the problem that needed to be resolved one way or the other. Somehow Emily was going to have to get closer to him before she could move away. And Caitlin did not want to give up on Emily just yet. Somehow she knew Oliver's eyes would soon be opened to Emily's charms. It wasn't that he *couldn't* fancy her, he'd proved he could do that eight years earlier, it was simply that he was blinded by what she represented rather than who she really was.

But if she didn't tell the others about what happened last night, she'd be keeping a secret from them and she didn't want that either.

And then she considered what in fact there was to tell. Yes, Oliver had kissed her, but so briefly that it barely counted and certainly it hadn't been a kiss she'd invited or even very much enjoyed. In which case, surely she was free to put it out of her mind, put *him* out of her mind. She was Emily's fairy godmother, after all. She was orchestrating a fine romance. The fact that she herself had briefly fancied Prince Charming wasn't the point. And briefly fancied was all that it was, because although she was a sucker for Oliver's kind of sleepy, lazy sexiness, when she'd realized she might have been seen by Leon it provoked a far greater reaction inside her. It had taken her aback, the awful fear that she might lose him, and the urge to put things right between them was still there, very strong.

She reached across for the telephone but instead of calling Holly back, she called Leon.

'Are you alone?' Leon asked pointedly.

'Of course I am. Whatever you think you saw last night didn't happen, you know. It matters to me that you believe me.'

'I do believe you. But, for what it's worth, I didn't like Oliver. Why did you invite him?'

'Complicated reasons.'

'Keep him away from Emily.'

'You're only saying that because you want her for yourself.'

'No, I don't actually,' he said mildly. 'I'd rather have you. I was looking after her.'

'It didn't look like that.'

'It didn't look like you were pushing Oliver away either.'

'I did. He kissed me. I didn't kiss him. I stopped him.'

'Actually I believe you.'

'So why didn't you tell me that last night?'

'Because I was pissed off. I wanted to go home.'

'Leon.'

'But I could come and see you now, if you want to talk about it.'

She knew how Leon hated weekends, forced to confront the fact that he had no plans. She imagined him at his breakfast table in his white and chrome kitchen, drinking coffee and reading the *FT*, sitting in pressed jeans with a belt and a stripy Thomas Pink shirt.

'Yes please.' It was what she'd wanted him to say. It was why she'd rung in the first place. 'I'll be waiting.'

Emily rang Holly as soon as she thought it was OK. Saturday morning, about ten seemed like a civilized enough hour.

'About the skiing . . .' she said nervously.

'Don't talk to me about skiing. Tell me about Caitlin's party! How was it? Did you survive?'

'She was lovely,' Emily said. Then hurried on, 'She was just as you'd said she'd be. I have to talk to you about the skiing, it's important. I can't come.' She wanted to say her bit before Holly started arguing with her. 'I've been thinking.'

'Oh yes?'

'How I've got to grab what I want and go for it. Everyone keeps telling me I should. And I want my shop, Saltwater. Now. I need to get started. I hate not working like this, not doing anything. I've got to take a risk, and Saltwater is something I've always wanted to do. So I'm going to say no to your kind and generous offer and I'm going to start setting it up right away. I'm going back to Cornwall tomorrow.'

'You *are* coming skiing.'

'I'm sorry?'

'You are coming skiing. With Oliver and me and Caitlin and Leon. I've booked the tickets, you're not getting out of it.'

'But, Holly, I can't.' Emily knew that she had to explain some more but she couldn't face telling Holly the truth, that it had all gone so badly with Oliver the night before that she couldn't face the thought of going skiing with him.

'You've got to come to keep me company. You know Rachel and Jo-Jo can't come. How will I survive Leon and Caitlin without you?'

'But I have to stop everything sliding past me,' Emily explained. 'I've got to take charge of my life. Which means I shouldn't be going on holiday. I should be in Cornwall, checking out sites, finding stock, working out how much money I need from the bank, drawing up business plans, maybe finding an investor.'

'Emily, tell me what happened last night,' Holly urged gently, knowing that Emily's change of heart was nothing to do with Saltwater at all. 'What's changed your mind?'

Emily hesitated. 'It was something Rachel said. It was before I got to Caitlin's. She told me how I had to go after what I wanted, even if it all went wrong. That it was better to have thrown myself in than stayed on the side.'

'Are you sure she was talking about Saltwater?'

'It doesn't matter. The same advice applies for everything, doesn't it?'

'I don't know about that.' Holly paused. 'But what I do know,' she went on with renewed determination, 'is that you are still coming skiing.' Emily could deal with Saltwater afterwards. She had to come skiing.

Emily had been so sure she was going to win this one, but Holly, mild and gentle as she usually was, went into four-wheel drive when she was after something she really wanted.

'It's such a short time. Only the Thursday to the Tuesday after Easter. Tell Arthur you'll see him after that.'

'Yes, Holly,' Emily said, meekly giving in because she owed it to Holly, especially if Holly had bought the tickets.

'Good. Thank you. And was it fun last night? Did you talk to Oliver? Has he changed at all?'

'No, still the same. I hardly talked to him. I spent most of the evening washing up with Leon.'

'Why? Not because Caitlin asked you to?'

'Not at all. It just ended up that way.'

Emily didn't elaborate. At that moment the evening was not one she wanted to think about.

When you've had people around for supper the night before and you've woken once and had plenty of time to remember how much you drank and smoked and how you ended the evening kissing the one guy in the world you shouldn't under any circumstances kiss like that, and then you've fallen back into bed and into guiltless sleep, the last thing you want is to be woken up again half an hour later.

Caitlin let the phone ring six times, then reached across to her bedside table and picked it up.

'Hello, Holly,' she said.

'You guessed!'

'You're like an alarm clock.'

'So you did hear me ringing earlier?'

'No, I was asleep.'

'So tell me. How did it go?'

'We all got on extremely well.'

'And?'

'And what else do you expect? We were in my flat, not in some sauna together.'

'Did he talk to her? I spoke to Emily and she sounded rather down.'

'The point was to reintroduce them to each other and that's what I did. But they didn't exactly stick together like glue.'

'She's definitely keen on him. I'm sure that's why she's miserable.'

'So you don't think we need to worry about Sam?'

'Not at all. There's nothing going on there.'

Holly could detect something vulnerable in Caitlin's voice. 'Are you OK?'

'I'm fine.'

'It was great you organized that for Emily.'

'Yes.'

'Want to come around this evening?'

'Yes, please.'

Caitlin was overcome with a mad impulse to confess, to explain how hard it had been to reject Oliver. But she didn't say it.

'I'll get Jo-Jo and Rachel around too. They're dying to hear how it went and we can plan phase two.'

'Oliver might not want to come skiing,' Caitlin blurted out.

'I didn't know you were going to ask him.'

'I didn't either. But it was the right time and it came out of my mouth and he said yes. And then later on . . . I think he might have changed his mind.'

Holly heaved a sigh. 'I can't believe I've just been on the phone making sure Emily comes. She tried to get out of it too.'

'Don't worry. We'll get him.'

'You don't sound so enthusiastic about the idea now.'

'He wasn't quite like I remembered. He's different without Nessa.'

'Are you saying we shouldn't like him any more?'

'Yes. No, no, no. And if it's yes it's more important than ever that Emily sees him for what he is and gets him out of her system. I'm just saying, I don't know him as well as I thought. And it's going to be hard. Because Oliver's oblivious to her and Emily's too shy to make herself noticed. She's so different when she's with him. She spent half the evening hiding in my bedroom and the other half hiding in the kitchen, talking to Leon, for God's sake. It made me wonder if we shouldn't be more hands-on. Maybe not spell it out for Oliver, but hint a little, make him think about her. We certainly need to set them up together with no distractions and without her suspecting what's going on. This has all got to feel natural. That's why the skiing is so perfect. You know, high up and alone on long and winding chairlifts. We need to find places where it's impossible for them to get away from each other. That was the problem last night: there's no room here where Leon and I could have left them.'

'I think you should invite Oliver again,' Holly decided. 'You're more persuasive than me and you know him better. Be as persuasive as you can. Don't take no for an answer. And if we're sure that Sam's no threat, ask him too. He's an old friend of Oliver's, it might make Oliver come.'

'How long have we got?'

'We've got ten days.'

12

There was something so dazzling about Emily that Sam was damned if he was going to let Oliver have a clear run at her for a second time. Fate had conspired to bring Emily back into his life, and he didn't want to let her go without giving himself one more decent chance . . .

And so he started to put out word that he was looking for a shop, on behalf of a friend. A small place in a town centre, ideally in St Brides. Shops came up on the estate agents' books regularly enough, but he figured that if he could find one for Emily privately and then call her about it, she would have to come back to Cornwall to see it and, if she had any feelings for him at all, she would surely take the opportunity to see him again? Particularly if it had been he who introduced her to the shop in the first place?

And if she did come back to St Brides and she did see him again, and if the shop was right for her, she would then move in somewhere nearby. And then he'd have her on his doorstep, and far enough away from Oliver to be able to take his time with her.

Within a week Bethany Nightingale, one of the employees at Trevissey, caught up with him in the staff canteen to tell him that her sister was retiring after thirty years and that she had a shop in St Brides that she was looking to lease out rather than sell because she was going to live in the flat above, and it seemed that fate was moving into action on Sam's behalf once more.

He quizzed Bethany and found out that the shop had been unofficially on the market for a month. They were both surprised nobody had snapped it up. He wondered how much rent it would be, but Bethany didn't know. Still, he presumed that Emily had an idea of what she was letting herself in for. The fact that it hadn't been snapped up meant she might be able to get it for a good price. The fact that it was in Humble Street, the prettiest shopping street in St Brides, in the oldest part of the town and close to the seafront, was bound to appeal to her.

But it was also one of the busiest weeks of the year at Trevissey. Although the gardens themselves were still quiet, March and April were the months when the trade – not just the garden centres and other nurseries that stocked Thomas Finch roses, but the town planners, the landscape gardeners, anyone developing a garden on a large scale – wanted their stock delivered. It was still early enough in the year for the plants to have time to settle into their new soil before the summer. Some would even manage to flower. Therefore hundreds of plants were leaving the Trevissey nurseries every day. Much as Sam was itching to drive into St Brides and see the shop, he had to wait until the next day before he got the chance.

He parked in St Brides and, passing an estate agents on the way to Humble Street, he stopped and glanced quickly at what else was available. There was a photograph of another shop for rent, a new instruction, only posted that day. It was only a couple of streets from where he stood, a pretty-looking shop in Flass Street. Sam went inside and grabbed the details. Surely one of the two would tempt her.

When he set eyes on 13 Humble Street, the faded black awning still carrying the shop's name, Jack and Jill, his heart sank. It was about as shabby and grim and unappealing as it was possible to be. Like the shop on Flass Street, this one also had a pink-painted front, but that was where the similarities ended. The front of number 13 was streaked with something dirty and yellow and whereas the Flass Street property had a wide, inviting front window, the windows of number 13 were divided into small rectangular panes, several of which had round impenetrable whorls in the middle of them that couldn't exactly have been good for business.

When he cupped his hand to his eyes and peered in, it didn't get any better. He could make out a gloomy, empty, brown-painted interior. Along one wall were fitted shelves from floor to ceiling, one or two of which had been pulled away from the wall, and at the back a red velvet curtain hung crookedly from a circular curtain rail. It was much wider at the front than at the back, a poky and awkward shape. As far as Sam could see, there were a few coat-hangers lying on the floor and nothing else, nothing inside of any use or salvage value, certainly nothing that was tempting in any way at all.

For a moment he thought about getting the key and giving it a good clean and a lick of paint before Emily came to see it, even considered asking Jennifer to get to work on it for him, but he knew he couldn't, that Emily would have to see it as it was.

When it came to it, he simply called her to tell her about both properties, knowing that he had to leave her to make her own decision. It was five days since he'd last seen her. She wasn't in so he left her a message.

Ten minutes after Sam called, the Williams Office also left a message on Emily's answer phone, ringing to put off her interview until the following week. Emily, however, had left the house early to be in good time for her first temping job in nearly five years so didn't hear either message until she got home.

Setting off across London for her first morning at Bunyan Graphic Design brought back all sorts of horrible temping memories. First time around, Emily had been fresh out of university and had arrived at the offices of each unlucky employer with her heart in her mouth, knowing she was horrendously ill-equipped with snail-slow typing and no office experience whatever. Of course her agency knew this too but had sent her out anyway, into the world of temperamental office machinery and nervy, aggressive employers who had less than no time to show her the ropes.

This time she turned into a tiny dead-end road off Fulham High Street and found she was almost looking forward to the day ahead. Five years on, she was experienced, efficient, cool in a crisis, could type like a concert pianist and felt that this employer was lucky to get her.

Nice Work, her recruitment agency, had thought so too and had promised her this was a *fabulous* job, with a boss who was *a great laugh*, who headed up a *superb* graphic-design team.

Even so, Emily walked into the office at ten past nine, and walked out, never to return, in time for lunch.

From the moment she sat down at her desk in the corner of the seventh floor, the tension and aggression between the three account executives who were supposed to be sharing her was loud and clear. The fact that they were too busy fighting to pay her any attention wasn't a problem – if anything, it had been quite funny at first, sitting at her empty desk with nothing to do while they ripped each other's throats out. But then it became clear that when they weren't fighting between themselves they were turning on one junior employee who cowered at her desk and reminded Emily so much of herself that she couldn't bear to stay. To sit there, in an environment that she'd made such an effort to leave, seemed too awful for words. So she called Nice Work to tell them what she was about to do. Then she left, but not before she'd spent half an hour unsuccessfully trying to persuade the poor girl to do the same.

Setting off down the High Street again, she experienced not the slightest concern for the mail-order bunk-bed brochure, *Going on Top*, that was not now going to be *put to bed* that evening as the superb design team had been demanding. Instead she defiantly swung her bag over her shoulder and ran down the steps to the underground.

*

So Sam caught her at just the right time with his message about the two shops.

She leant against the breakfast bar in her kitchen, still in her coat, and pressed play. *Hello, Emily. It's Sam.* Hearing his voice made her smile. First he told her about the shop on Flass Street, and from his description Emily recognized it straight away as the one she had been into with Arthur. The morose woman behind the till had obviously had enough. Emily felt very sorry for her and knew straight away that there was no conceivable way that she would take on *that* shop.

Then Sam mentioned the shop in Humble Street. *It used to be a children's clothes shop called Jack and Jill. It's a dump. But I think you could transform it.* But Emily wasn't listening any more. She'd switched off at the mention of the name Jack and Jill and she felt her heart squeeze as the intensity of her memories overwhelmed her.

Two stone steps, then cautiously open the door. The bell rings, warning Mrs Maddox that she has a customer and acting like a starting pistol for Emily, propelling her across the room to the depths of the shop, to the back rail, so tightly stuffed with beautiful clothes that she has to fight them free in order to look at them.

When Emily was thirteen, Jack and Jill was the best thing about coming to Cornwall. Hitting the spot at a time when she was old enough to care desperately about what she wore, yet still young enough to want to sleep the night in a new pair of Jack and Jill maroon corduroy trousers because she couldn't bear to take them off.

But now, remembering those visits to the shop, it wasn't

the clothes that Emily recalled. It was being with her mother.

She remembered the warmth in her stomach as she walked out from behind the red velvet curtain of the changing room and caught rare approval in her mother's eyes. There was an intimacy between them when they shopped together that they hadn't found at any other time. Why it was so, Emily wasn't sure, but she remembered being aware, even then, that her mother was proud of her when they shopped together, liked the way she looked in the clothes. It was through shopping and almost only through shopping that she found pleasure in the company of her tall, pretty daughter.

As Emily played Sam's message again, she could still hear her mother's voice from outside the changing room, urging her to be quick. She could feel the pressure on her fingertips as she fiddled to push buttons through stiff new buttonholes, the breathless rush to do up zips and retie her shoes. And she remembered the wonderful high as she left the shop, striding away at her mother's side, both of them happy, the weight of a shiny red Jack and Jill bag swinging from her hand.

She rang Sam back but missed him and left a gushing message of thanks on his answerphone. And then, immediately, she called Arthur in great excitement to tell him about the shop and that, as she had no reason not to come straight back to St Brides that day, she would aim to catch the seven-thirty train. And could he be there to pick her up?

Arthur sounded tentatively optimistic about the shop,

but Emily was in such a state of exhilaration and focused energy that he decided to save his concerns for when they were talking face to face. He felt he had roles to play – as cautious solicitor and steady older brother he was duty-bound not to be too enthusiastic – but the reality was that he knew she could do it, and the prospect of Emily moving to St Brides was a fantastic one.

Once on the train, Emily finally had time to think. And what she thought about was less the running of the shop than how it could be possible that she, who was so cautious, so controlled, so safe, could be so wholeheartedly embracing such a risky proposition.

Look at me! she wanted to demand of Caitlin and Holly and Jo-Jo, who laughed at her inability to take the plunge or to stick her neck out. She knew that that was how they thought of her, and how they explained why she hadn't slept with anyone. *Watch me now! When it's the right thing to do, look how I can go for it. Look how I can follow my instincts with no hesitation at all.* But she hadn't gone for it, she reminded herself, she was just thinking about going for it. So far her money was still safe and she'd made no commitment of any kind.

Her savings would not be enough to buy her opening stock. She would have to go to the bank with a business plan. And she wondered whether Mrs Maddox, who was planning on retiring to the flat upstairs, and keeping the shop on as an investment, might take the rent in arrears. She wondered too whether she might have to lease the shop from Mrs Maddox for years or whether she could play it more gradually, take it for just six months at a time.

How quickly would she have to decide? For as long as she could remember, Saltwater had been a game, like playing fantasy shopkeeping, her stock picked on a whim and discarded just as easily. Not so now.

The next morning, Emily was alone as she walked up to 13 Humble Street, ten minutes before Mrs Maddox had agreed to join her with the key. Alone, because Emily's sudden arrival hadn't left Arthur with enough time to organize a morning out of his office.

Standing there on the step, after only the briefest of looks through the window, Emily was already sure that if she possibly could afford it, and if she was going to set up the shop anywhere, she wanted it to be here.

Where Sam saw cramped, she saw cosy. Where he saw a crooked interior and too low a ceiling, she saw character. Where he saw grubby walls, she saw paintbrushes and fresh white paint. It was so sweet and so woebegone and appealed to her far more than the well-maintained shop on Flass Street which she'd looked around with Arthur the last time she was in St Brides.

So when, ten minutes late, a sweaty and flustered Mrs Maddox turned the corner into Humble Street and saw Emily standing there on the top step, she smiled. From the way that Emily was waiting for her, hands in her pockets, Mrs Maddox knew exactly what she had decided.

It had been nearly ten years since she had last seen Emily. If Emily hadn't reintroduced herself, she would never have recognized her. But Emily remembered Mrs Maddox as well as if she'd seen her ten days ago.

While waiting for Mrs Maddox to unlock the door, Emily felt the same flutter of expectation that she'd always felt upon entering this shop. Mrs Maddox looked the same as ever, and had been one of those fierce shopkeepers permanently on the lookout for sticky faces and dirty fingers. She had several times made clear her disapproval of the amount Emily's mother spent on her. Now Emily saw a tired, lined woman in her early sixties, wearing the same brave red lipstick and still with an air of steely purpose about her, but no longer someone to be afraid of.

After Mrs Maddox had shown her around, they stood outside on the step in the cold bright sun and talked. There seemed little point in Emily disguising her enthusiasm. Mrs Maddox seemed to know from the start that she was keen, but, even so, she agreed that Emily could take a little more time to decide how she wanted to proceed, to go over her finances again with real figures rather than guesses, and to be sure she knew what she was doing. *But it's a very fair price so don't think I'll wait for ever.*

The rent was £8,000 per year, which was a little less than Emily had expected, and Mrs Maddox was prepared to take it in arrears, at least for the first six months, in order to help Emily get herself up and running. Any repairs or maintenance work would be the responsibility of Mrs Maddox, who would indeed be continuing to live above the shop. Any cosmetic refurbishment would be Emily's responsibility. Not, Mrs Maddox insisted, that Emily would be wanting to do any of that. The lighting worked perfectly well – Mrs Maddox had flicked a switch to prove it. Most of the shelves were good and solid – she had leaned her bulk upon one of them to demonstrate – and she would take care of the few that needed securing. Emily decided this wasn't the best moment to say that new lighting and shelving would be her first priorities.

She walked away from Humble Street overwhelmed with the need to talk to someone about it all. But it wasn't Sam she called but Arthur.

She didn't call Sam until she was back in London that night. She thanked him for tipping her off about the shops and told him how much she had liked Jack and Jill, how excited she was, how determined she was to make it work, how pleased she was that she would have him living nearby.

But while Emily enthused, Sam was thinking, *She came here and didn't she come to see me*, and as he took it in something shifted inside him, letting go. Emily hadn't come to see him. She hadn't noticed him at sixteen and she wasn't interested in him now and he realized then that she never would be.

And Sam was surprised at how easy he found it to put her aside in his mind. He was too confident and too happy to doggedly hold a torch for someone who was so completely blind to him. He still thought Emily was extraordinary. He still adored her quirkiness and vulnerability and was uplifted by her and transported by her loveliness. If he saw her again, no doubt he'd still fancy her rotten. But without any encouragement, without any sign from her that she had even noticed him, even when they were alone together, he told himself there was no point in thinking about her. He imagined that it would take only a couple of days before he would able to put Emily out of his mind completely.

But then, before that couple of days came and went he had a call from Holly. Embarrassed at first, uncertain whether he'd think her invitation was a bit presumptuous, seeing as she didn't know him very well, she explained they had a space on their skiing holiday and asked whether he'd like to join them over Easter. And when she told him exactly who else would be there, he saw that he was being given one more chance to get it right. That it would be crunch time. Him or Oliver.

13

They were leaving for Magine on the Thursday before Easter and returning the Tuesday after.

Snow reports warned that it was warm enough to sunbathe and that mountain flowers were appearing on the lower slopes, but Magine was linked by a high-speed cable car to the massive Trois Vallées, with its glacier and year-round skiing so Holly could tell the others that the skiing was on, whatever the weather.

Caitlin wouldn't have minded if there was no snow at all. She could ski well enough but it had never been high on her list of favourite activities. She went to Magine because she loved Holly's chalet and because the men were gorgeous, and the warmer the weather the better. On really hot days she sunbathed at the mountain cafés in her bikini.

Like Emily, she'd been invited by Holly twice before, but either by accident or design, Caitlin wasn't sure which it was, she'd never crossed over with Emily before.

At six thirty on the Thursday evening, Emily, Holly and Caitlin were standing in Departures at Heathrow Airport, waiting for Leon and Sam to join them, and for Oliver to return to them. Oliver had arrived five minutes earlier, parked his bags and instantly disappeared again.

'Passport-tickets-money, passport-tickets-money,' Emily muttered to herself over and over again, until, with a sigh, Holly snatched her ticket from her with a red-leather-gloved hand.

'You, me . . .' She showed Emily the fan of tickets in her hand and Emily nodded. 'Sam, Leon, Caitlin and Oliver.' Emily nodded again. 'Watch,' Holly told her, 'they're all going in here –' she tucked them into a matching red leather handbag – 'where they will be safe.' She dropped her voice. 'Now, do you want me to take your passport?'

Emily shook her head. 'And don't let Caitlin hear you say that or I'll be crucified. She thinks you watch over me too closely, you know.'

Then Leon appeared through the revolving doors wearing a large green tweed coat and fur hat with floppy earmuffs. He caught sight of Holly, Emily and Caitlin and beamed his way towards them.

Caitlin stared at him pitilessly. Happy toad, off on his holidays, with his puffed-out chest and his dapper clothes. All that was missing was a silver-topped cane and a cravat – but perhaps he would get lucky in the airside branch of Aquascutum. She thanked God that Oliver had disappeared, wasn't watching Leon's arrival and laughing at her.

'Isn't this fun, fun, fun?' Leon said, clutching her to him and kissing her exuberantly. Seeing the look in Caitlin's eye he then held her away. 'And you, my dearest, are you happy to see me too?'

Caitlin laughed, despite herself, took his fat cheeks in her slim hands, and kissed him hard on the lips, leaving him with a look of stunned delight. 'Yes, I am. Very happy to see you.'

Keeping one arm around Caitlin, Leon kissed Emily and Holly.

'Are the others here?' he asked.

'All but Sam,' said Emily. 'And we've managed to lose Oliver.'

'Look after my bags for me and I'll go and find him,' said Caitlin. 'Come on, Holly, come with me,' she added throwing Holly a look that said don't argue about it. 'And look out for Sam, too. He'll be here any minute,' she called back to Emily over her shoulder.

The two of them walked off together through the terminal, Caitlin in a soft black leather jacket and jeans, Holly in a flowing green fur-lined cape. 'What is it?' Holly asked, turning to her.

Caitlin took her arm. 'I wanted to say that I've got a good feeling about this holiday. I think it's going to be fun.' She paused. 'And I wanted to say make sure that you put Oliver and Emily next door to each other . . . And I also wanted to say – ' she stopped, bit her lip, then looked at Holly and gave her a rather uncertain smile – 'am I mad or is Leon quite cute? In his own cuddly Kermit-y kind of way.'

'If you're going to stick with him you're going to have to stop being so horrible about him.'

'Really? Do I have to?'

Holly nodded. 'Yes, because he's sweet. I really think he is. And *very* good for you, so much better than the guys you usually end up with.'

And then, just as Caitlin was about to reply, they both caught sight of Oliver at the same time. He was some distance away but clearly on his way back to them, with one hand pushing a heavily laden trolley and a girl swinging from the other. When he caught sight of Holly and Caitlin he waved, looking very pleased with himself.

The girl was wearing a dark green denim jacket and in Caitlin's opinion was way too thin and way too pretty, with bouncy, shoulder-length hair and very long legs in her long straight jeans. At first it seemed that she was coming towards them reluctantly, but Caitlin quickly realized, watching the way she was laughing and only half-heartedly protesting, that she was putting it on and was really loving every second of being pulled along by him. 'Look at him,' Caitlin murmured to Holly. 'Look at how he's talking to her. No wonder everyone falls in love with him.'

As they drew nearer, Oliver leant close to the girl to point out Caitlin and Holly and Caitlin watched her look vacantly around and then catch her eye.

In the circumstances Caitlin was not about to pussyfoot around with a polite smile back. She gave the girl a put-him-down-or-you-die look and watched her pull up in surprise, then whisper something to Oliver.

'No, darling. That was Medusa,' Oliver replied, pulling the trolley to an unsteady halt beside Caitlin. 'This is Caitlin with her friend Holly.'

Then he introduced her to them both. 'This is Meribel. She's on our flight to Geneva.'

'Aren't you in the wrong place?' said Caitlin with a polite smile. 'Aren't you much closer to Lyon?'

Meribel gave a weary laugh. 'And I haven't heard that one before,' she said.

Behind Holly and Caitlin, Oliver caught sight of Leon and Emily coming over to join them and then his smile of relief broadened still further when he saw Sam appearing behind Emily, a hold-all over one shoulder. 'Sam! Great to see you,' he called out. 'Everyone, this is Meribel.'

Holly moved to welcome Sam. Caitlin kept her eyes fixed on Meribel.

'Oliver and I know each other through my sister,' Meribel explained to her, seemingly immune to the daggers in her eyes. Then she nudged Oliver playfully in the ribs. 'My sister who knows him rather better than I do.'

Oliver turned to the others. 'Meribel's on her own and I was saying that she should check in with us, so we can all sit together on the plane.'

Meribel fumbled in a fringed green suede shoulder bag and pulled out her ticket.

'And I was saying I wasn't even sure I was on the same flight.'

What, Caitlin raged, the *hell* did Oliver think he was *doing*?

'Good idea,' said Sam, standing very close beside Emily. 'Let's hope you are.'

'Shall I look at that ticket,' Caitlin suggested to Meribel, practically snatching it out of her hand. 'What's your flight number?' she demanded. 'What's your departure time?' She scanned the ticket quickly. 'Oh, what a shame, that's not going to work at all, you're leaving much later than we are.'

'Absolutely no problem,' Meribel said with an acid look at Caitlin. 'I've got some shopping to do. You guys go and check in without me.'

'Thanks,' Caitlin snapped. She knew she was being obnoxious, but Meribel was just poisonous and the sort of disastrous diversion they did not need. She turned to Oliver and forced a smile. 'If you hadn't disappeared, we'd have gone through already. You'll have no time to buy me that scent you promised me.'

'She's lying,' Oliver told Meribel. 'And Caitlin,' he added, 'Sam only arrived two minutes ago. I was watching out for him.'

'I'm a nervous passenger,' Caitlin joked, happy now that the threat had been disarmed.

'Then go, before you get your knickers into even more of a twist,' Meribel told her with a little laugh. 'Good to see you, Oliver.'

He kissed her goodbye. 'And you must say hi to Val for me.'

Holly glanced across at Caitlin, and Emily who'd heard him too, bit her lip and grinned at the two of them.

'Which "Val" would her sister be, then?' Caitlin asked Oliver, matching strides through passport control and on into the departure lounge. 'Val d'Isère? Val Thorens? They don't have quite the same ring as Meribel, do they?'

Listening to her, as she strode along in front of them,

Sam at her side, Emily smiled at Caitlin's words. Ahead of her Leon and Holly were already sliding their bags through the security checks and she slipped her handbag off her shoulder ready to do the same.

'And exactly when did you get to know Val so well?' she heard Caitlin ask then. 'I thought Nessa had been the only woman in your life for the past five years.'

'I can't help what you thought,' said Oliver.

'What?' Caitlin exclaimed. 'That is *news*. Are you saying you weren't faithful to Nessa?'

'More or less. One or two tiny lapses of concentration. Meribel's sister was one of them.'

'I don't believe it.' Caitlin laughed. 'So much for Mr Squeaky Clean!'

He sounded defensive. 'Speak for yourself. Don't tell me you've never done that.'

'I haven't! I've never two-timed anybody.'

If it was hard for Caitlin to take in, for Emily it was incomprehensible. Her first reaction was to feel as stunned and dismayed as if he'd been unfaithful to her, not to Nessa. Oliver did not do such things. Not Oliver. He was her champion, honourable and loyal. She wanted to turn around to him and force him to stop walking, make him stand still, look her in the eye and tell her it was all a big joke, that he was saying it to wind up Caitlin. Of course he wouldn't have been unfaithful to Nessa.

'Did Nessa find out?' Caitlin asked.

'She did about the second one. Not about Meribel's sister.'

'Oliver, I'm so surprised.'

'It happens. Nessa and I had been on the rocks a while.'

He shrugged. 'I wouldn't have done it otherwise. Change the subject, you're making me feel guilty.'

'So who was she? Who was the second girl?'

'Just a girl. No one you know. Stop talking about it, it was no big deal. I want to know why you were being so horrible to Meribel. Why did I feel I was being called to heel?'

'Because that's exactly what I was doing,' Caitlin told him. 'I wanted to remind who you'd come on holiday with because you looked as if you might have been about to forget. If you meet up with other people, make arrangements to see them instead of us – people like Meribel – Holly will think you're using her place like a hotel.' Caitlin knew she was taking Holly's name in vain, that Holly wouldn't ever think such a thing.

'Don't be ridiculous,' Oliver replied, then added so quietly that Sam and Emily had no chance of hearing him, 'I think it's because you know as well as I do that you and Leon are not going to last the holiday.'

Caitlin glared back at him. 'We're getting on better than ever.'

'Of course you are. But you were jealous of Meribel.'

'No I was not,' Caitlin whispered furiously. She looked away, watching Emily striding along ahead of them. *I wasn't jealous for myself!* Caitlin nearly said it aloud. *I was jealous on behalf of Emily. Not that you deserve her any more.*

They all made their way through the various security checks to their departure gate, whereupon Caitlin immediately dragged Leon away from the others and off towards

219

the shops, hoping she might persuade him to spend some money on her.

Following her lead, Holly then cornered Sam, sat him down and started to tell him all about the chalet, how her uncle Richard Foy had bought it in 1960, before there were even any chairlifts in Magine. She drew out the story, explaining how he'd had to walk up the mountain with his skis on his back and had managed just one run down in a day.

And Emily and Oliver looked around and found themselves left alone.

'How about a drink?' Oliver suggested. 'Caitlin's rushed us through here so damn fast we've at least an hour to kill. Let's celebrate the start of the holiday.'

'The bar?' Emily suggested.

'Or shall we buy a bottle of champagne in duty-free and go and find some corner to drink it in?'

'Let's go to the bar.'

'You're right. We could end up missing the plane, couldn't we?'

Could they? Emily wasn't sure what he meant, but knew she wouldn't mind at all if it meant being left behind with Oliver.

In what she still thought of as duty-free, Caitlin peered around the shelves of cut-price cigarettes. They're alone, he's smiling at her, she's smiling at him, they're walking off together, he's taken her hand and she's moving closer, Caitlin noted with satisfaction.

Oliver held onto Emily's hand. For a few moments she was acutely conscious of it, hot and clammy in his, and then she made herself relax. After the non-event that was supper at Caitlin's, she was determined not to let this holiday become an endless agony over Oliver. She didn't know quite what she did expect of the holiday – there had, of course, been dreamy images of falling into his arms – but what she most wanted was to be relaxed around him again, certainly not to let him see the adoring, dumbstruck schoolgirl she felt she'd become. It seemed so unfair that all the confidence which had stood her in good stead for so long should vanish whenever she laid eyes on Oliver. It hadn't been this way when Nessa was on the scene. In the past Emily had had no problem talking to Oliver. Back then, she'd have been the one to throw an arm around his shoulders and suggest they went to the bar. But the moment she'd caught sight of him pushing his way through the doors into the terminal, a battered brown leather jacket slung over a shoulder, looking around for them – for her – then seeing her and giving her the most devastating smile in the world, she had collapsed inside in a heap of hopeless lust and confused love, and hadn't been able to pull herself together again afterwards. She hadn't liked what Oliver had admitted to Caitlin, had heard the warning that perhaps he wasn't all she thought he was, but it wasn't nearly enough to spoil the fact that she was alone with him now and that stretching ahead were four more days full of him.

During supper at Caitlin's, Emily had managed to talk to Oliver alone just once, an innocuous catching-up sort of conversation where he had told her about the split with Nessa and she had told him about leaving the Carrie

Piper Agency. She'd admitted that she'd done it only a week before, and he'd laughed and said exactly what she'd imagined he'd say. So you lied to Sam! And you promised, you *promised* me you were going to leave a year ago.

Now propped up in the bar against a little round table, with a vodka and tonic doing a good job of fortifying her, she was determined to move the conversation on. To be braver and bolder. But at first the conversation again stuck stubbornly to the mundane. She told him about Saltwater and her plans for moving to Cornwall. Even as she heard herself singing the praises of St Brides, she did wonder why she was telling him all this. What exactly she was hoping to achieve by emphasizing her desire to move a good three hundred miles away from London, from him. When she told him it was Sam who had found her a shop, his eyebrows shot up in surprise.

'Sam has found you a shop?' he repeated, for the first time sounding genuinely interested in what she was saying. 'Why did he do that?'

'But I might not go. I might stay in London,' she backtracked again. 'I'm not sure where I'm going or what I'm going to do.'

Oliver leaned in a little closer and stared into her eyes. Instantly Emily felt as if it was just the two of them alone together, as if the whole noisy airport had disappeared.

'How many times have you been back to Cornwall in the last two months?'

'I went to see a couple of properties up for rent. But I

only stayed one night.' Now he was making her feel defensive and she didn't know why.

'See Sam while you were there?'

'No. Why do you ask me that?'

'Anything you want to tell me?'

'What do you mean?'

'I wondered if my old friend might have been moving in on you.'

She shook her head emphatically. 'Of course not.' How could he have got it so wrong?

'Trevissey is wonderful, isn't it?' Oliver moved seamlessly on and Emily was left wondering if she'd imagined it, the flare of interest in his face. 'When I was there a couple of years ago I had a long conversation with Sam's father. He was picking my brains about the best way to get Sam home. He said that Sam was a genius and that it was a complete waste him being anywhere other than Trevissey, where he belonged. Don't you think that's sweet? That his dad said that about him?'

Emily nodded.

'As well as understanding all the technical stuff, apparently Sam has this incredible sense of colour. The gardens he's designed at Trevissey – ages ago, years before he went back permanently – are famous. People come from all over the country to see them. I read a piece about him in the paper saying how he clashes and mixes up his colours in this absolutely brilliant and original way.'

'I wish I'd seen Trevissey in the summer,' Emily said. 'But the way Sam described it, I almost did. It was as if it was real.'

'Make sure you do go back. You'll be blown away by what he's done ... OK, act normal,' he said, smiling broadly and looking over Emily's shoulder. 'Here he comes.'

Emily leapt back from Oliver, though she'd hardly been standing very close to him. What was worse, she could feel a giant blush burn her cheeks as soon as she caught Sam's eye.

'We were just talking about you,' Oliver told him as Sam threaded his way through the tables and joined them.

'Oh yes?'

'I was telling Emily about my last time at Trevissey.' Oliver turned back to Emily. 'What I hadn't got to was the bit about nearly breaking my back digging his rose beds for eight hours.' As he was speaking he was moving away from the table. 'Let me get you a drink, Sam,' he offered. 'What do you want?'

'A beer?' Sam suggested. 'Whatever you're having, thank you.' He took Oliver's place at the little round table. 'He did ask for it,' he told Emily.

'For what?'

'He did offer to dig up the rose beds. And of course he had to show us he could dig them up faster, harder, deeper than anybody else had ever done before.'

Emily laughed. 'That can't be so! Not Oliver.'

She had been a little concerned about how things would be between herself and Sam, whether there'd be awkward teenage embarrassment hanging over them despite the fact that nothing had happened that time in the kitchen at Trevissey, but she obviously wasn't a problem for Sam at all and she was relieved, even as a little part of her was the tiniest bit regretful too.

Emily thought how typical of Holly it was to invite someone whom she hardly knew skiing. As long as she had liked meeting them – and Holly had met Sam twice: once years ago and once at Oliver's welcome-home party – then she trusted that she would enjoy seeing them again. And for as long as Emily had known her, Holly had never been wrong. Her suppers, parties and holidays were always sprinkled with interesting new people as well as old friends. And so she hadn't been surprised to hear that Sam was coming skiing too.

'OK?' he asked.

'Sorry,' she laughed, shaking her head. 'I was in another world.'

'I'm sorry I interrupted you?' He raised his eyebrows at her. 'Was I in it too?'

'Bugger off, Sam!' But she was smiling back at him as she said it.

Another pause.

'Will you come shopping with me?' he asked. 'When I've drunk that beer Oliver's kindly fetching for me? I need to buy a present for my . . .'

She looked over to Oliver. He was paying the barman, and almost under the intensity of her gaze he turned and then waved at her. She waved back, unable to tear her eyes away.

'Emily . . .'

She forced herself to look back to Sam. 'Yes?'

Ever since the evening in the Pelican his words about

Oliver had been quietly repeating themselves in her head. And now she could see from his face he wanted to say them here again.

'Sam,' she cried. 'Don't tell me!'

He flinched. 'Present for my sister,' he said.

'There's nothing between Oliver and me. I wish there was, but he's not interested.'

He looked even more shocked. 'Oh, he will be. Give him a day or two. He's just slow to react. Once he realizes what's going on he'll be all over you.'

'And what's that supposed to mean?' she asked. 'What are you saying?'

'I'm saying I know Oliver. And I know that Oliver likes a challenge.'

'I thought you were his great friend. You shouldn't talk about him like that.'

'Oliver and I were great friends a long time ago. Not so much now.'

'Stop,' Emily hissed. 'He's coming back.'

And to her dismay Sam chose that moment to take her hand. 'Don't be cross. I promise, Emily, that I will shut up from now on. I will back off. What you choose to do is up to you.'

She slid her hand out of Sam's just as Oliver arrived back at the table, a vodka and tonic for Emily in one hand, a couple of bottles of beer in the other, and Emily caught his eye and knew that she hadn't done it quite fast enough.

'Beer for you.' Oliver dropped one down on the table in front of Sam, then chinked his bottle against Sam's. 'Cheers,' he said.

From then on Oliver seemed to freeze Emily out of the conversation, bombarding Sam with questions and anecdotes and jokes about their past together that deliberately excluded her, and even though Sam tried to steer Emily back in, she never lasted more than a couple of sentences. It was as if she was being punished. Eventually she gave up, knocked back her vodka and picked up her bag off the floor.

'I'm off. If you want me to help you choose that present for your sister, come and find me over there,' she told Sam, nodding towards the shops.

'No, stay with me, Sam,' she heard Oliver say as she moved away. 'We'll catch her up later.'

Emily headed first to WH Smith and bought Chris Manby's new novel, *Seven Sunny Days*, and then on into what used to be duty-free, where she wandered the aisles. In one of the mirrors, she caught sight of her pale washed-out face and she sloped over to the make-up section to sort herself out, brushing her cheeks with a bronzing powder before surreptitiously picking up a mascara and applying a coat, still thinking about what had happened in the bar. Why had Oliver suddenly become so unfriendly? He'd been like a big sulky kid. But what was it that was bothering him? Could he really have been jealous of her and Sam? What was he thinking?

'I don't know how you do that without a mirror,' Sam said behind her, making her jump.

'Ow!' she cried, wiping her eye, and what had been a tiny splodge streaked across her cheek.

'Isn't it great, what make-up can do?'

She rubbed at her face. 'Has it gone?'

'Not quite.' He came up close and gently rubbed her cheek with his thumb. 'Now it has. I'm sorry about that. And don't let Oliver upset you. He can be a moody bastard sometimes.'

'He doesn't fancy you, does he?' Emily asked. 'Perhaps that's what it was about?'

'No!' Sam shook his head. 'Definitely not. This has happened before. It's you he's bothered about, not me.'

'How do you know?'

Sam shook his head. 'Let's not talk about Oliver any more. Not now.'

'I agree,' Emily said, stepping back from him. 'We'll talk about Magine. You're going to love it, you know.'

'Hello, you two.' As Emily spoke, Caitlin's head popped up from the other side of the display cabinet.

'Oh, hi!' said Emily.

'What happened to Oliver?'

Sam couldn't miss the irritated disapproval in her voice. 'He's having a drink with Holly at the bar,' he said.

'But weren't you two having a drink together?' she asked Emily, ignoring Sam's explanation. 'Holly said she was going to buy some sunglasses. I thought she'd be here.'

'No,' said Sam. 'She's definitely at the bar.'

'Dammit,' said Caitlin, looking across to where Holly and Oliver were standing drinking together.

And then, belatedly, Sam understood everything. He saw what Caitlin was trying to orchestrate, the lengths she was going to in order to help things along between Emily and Oliver. He presumed Holly was in on it too, and even Leon perhaps. And what an irony it was that he, of all Oliver's friends, should have been invited along as a spectator.

On the plane, Emily slipped into her seat and watched Holly manoeuvre herself and a large hold-all down the aisle towards her, but when Holly reached Emily she smiled and then moved purposefully on, and Emily turned to see her take the seat two rows back, next to Sam.

So if Holly was sitting there, Emily thought, and Caitlin was going to sit beside Leon – she craned her neck to get a better look and saw Caitlin and Leon behind her, already sitting down across from Holly and Sam – then it had to be the man making his way down the aisle who was going to sit beside her.

Oliver swung his bag and his jacket up into the over-head locker, then slid around and into the space next to hers. When he turned to face her he was so close that she could breathe him in, feel the warmth of his body now pressed against hers.

'I was hoping you were going to be Caitlin or Holly,' she told him.

'I was hoping you were going to be Nicole Kidman.'

'Fair enough.' She grinned.

'At least you weren't wishing I was Sam.'

'Don't start on that again.' She looked away from him then, out of the window, seeing the great stiff wing of the plane there just in front of her, and a momentary burst of panic immediately overwhelmed the pleasure of sitting beside Oliver.

'I'm glad it's you and I'm very disappointed that you're not glad it's me. What do Caitlin and Holly do that I don't?' he asked the back of her head.

She looked at him. 'Sometimes they let me hold their hands while we're taking off. They let me bite them, if I get really scared.'

'Bite your own hand.'

'That's what I thought you'd say.'

He dropped his hand in her lap. 'There you are,' he said, obviously enjoying the way the conversation was going. 'How hard would you bite? Show me.'

They hadn't even taken off and instantly possibilities were fizzing between them. Emily had only a few seconds in which to make her choice: to go with it or to run away.

'Oliver!' She broke the moment, stumbling on his name, not knowing what else to say. She looked down at his hand in hers, at his stubby tanned fingers and short pink nails, and knew that the last thing she could do right then was pick up his hand and bite him.

Instead she lifted the hand off her lap and gave it back to him.

'So you've spared me?'

Then the engine noise increased and he saw her face drop in fear.

'Come here.' Instantly he put an arm around her and pulled her close. 'You *are* scared, aren't you?' She nodded. 'Poor baby. But you weren't nervous in the airport?'

'In the airport we were on safe, solid ground.' She sat back in her seat. Even Oliver's arm around her couldn't distract her now.

The plane started moving, taxiing out towards the runway.

'Go on, bite my fingers if you want to. Do whatever makes you feel better,' he offered.

She shook her head. 'I'll be OK. Talk to me about something. Distract me.'

'Sure.' He thought for a moment. 'So, which is the worst moment? Is it now? Or is it worse when we actually leave the ground?'

'Maybe you might choose a subject other than flying?'

'Oh, right, of course.'

Bing-bong went the intercom and the lights flickered off, then on, then off again. Emily watched the flaps lifting and dropping on her wing and she presumed final tests were being carried out, and that the wings were doing as they should. 'And nothing about how it's far more dangerous to cross the road, or about how I'm more likely to win the lottery than be in an air crash,' she told him.

'If I was going to distract you, I'd be much more effective than that.'

The lights came on again and she closed her eyes and folded her hands in her lap.

He paused. 'I could say, Emily King, that in eight years, I've never stopped thinking about you.'

'Oh, God!' Against the tight restraining safety belt, Emily turned as far away from him as she could.

'Nice reaction! Thank you. Exactly what I was hoping for.'

'But, Oliver . . .' she said looking back at him. She wanted to say she couldn't believe he'd said it, and said it so soon. That in eight years, she'd thought only about him, too.

'And stop smiling like that,' he told her. 'You're not allowed to smile. I'm being serious.'

'It's not a smile. My face has set like this. It's the shock.'

'Emily, don't joke.' He dropped his voice. 'I'm telling you, I adore you, every inch of you. I always have done. Ever since I met you and your rather enchanting pink bikini, three weeks before your seventeenth birthday. But I know you won't believe me. I know that you've forgotten about that time and that now you don't see me as anything other than a friend . . .' He waited but she still said nothing. 'This is probably the last thing you want to hear, but I had to tell you.' He was sounding anxious now, pleading almost. 'Since I've been back, it's been driving me crazy not telling you. And now, having you beside me here, I've got no choice. I have to tell you how I feel. I didn't mean to, not straight away. I'm sorry.'

'Oliver, I can't believe it.' It came out as a whisper.

'No, let me speak,' he insisted. 'This is the first opportunity I've had to talk to you properly since I came home, so you have to listen. When I saw you at Caitlin's – I knew that you were going to be there – I thought I'd leave with at least a date to see you again, but it didn't happen. How could it not happen? We were in a one-bedroom flat and yet we never seemed to be in the same room at the same time long enough for me to say more than two words to you.'

'Oliver!' She was elated. She couldn't believe it. She turned to tell him so again, opened her mouth to say the words and saw clouds through the window opposite. And she realized that they'd taken off without her even noticing.

'Or I could say there's this book you might read called *Fear of Flying*,' he said more loudly, the gentleness and tenderness leaving his voice, 'which isn't actually about flying. We could talk about that. Have you read it? Do you know what it's about?'

'You bastard!' She turned back from the window and looked at him desperately. 'Don't think for one second that I believed any of that.'

'But, sweetheart, it worked! It worked! You weren't scared at all. You didn't even notice when we took off.'

'Oliver! You are horrible.' But her heartbeat was steadying again after its awful free-falling in shock and the only thing she was really thinking was *Thank God I didn't tell him how I feel.*

'Why am I?'

'Because you sounded so sincere. You went into so much detail. Remind me never to believe anything you say about anything ever again.'

'But are you OK? Now that we've taken off? You're not scared any more. You seem really pissed off now, so I presume that means you can't be scared at the same time?'

'I'm pissed off because you shouldn't joke about something like that.'

'Who said I was joking?'

Not again!

'I wasn't. You make me melt inside. It's the truth but
you'll never believe me, will you?'

'Not now I won't.'

Teasing each other had been so much a part of their
friendship in the past. She should have been ready for him
– she would have been if everything else hadn't changed
and got in the way. A year ago she'd never have been
caught out so easily.

But even as the old familiarity returned, Emily was
aware that something had shifted between them. Even
joked about, Emily and Oliver *together* had been mentioned aloud and had therefore become a possibility, and
there was a new awareness between them as a result.
Twice she looked up from her book to find him watching
her, and, looking down at his forearm and broad flat wrist
– a Breitling now in place of the Swatch watch she
remembered – and at her own narrow arm beside his, she
thought how good they looked together, his arm and hers.

And she could tell that he was as aware as she was of
his bare arm touching hers as they both read, or poured
their drinks, or simply sat in silence. She leafed through
the in-flight magazine, but didn't really read it at all.
Arthur's voice was in her head, telling her that she was
not to run away from this, that she had to stop worrying
about what happened next. Let the future take whichever

direction it chose. And listening to him again, she realized that it was panic that was making her feel this way, not a sudden distrust of Oliver. Enjoy the movement, she told herself. Have fun.

As they gathered around the carousel and waited for their baggage to reappear, Holly took Caitlin's arm and led her away from the others, ostensibly on a hunt to find a couple of trolleys. As soon as they were out of earshot of the others, Holly blurted out her confession to Caitlin. She'd had a rather difficult conversation with Sam.

'You didn't tell him!' Caitlin hissed. 'Not that we want to set Emily up with Oliver.'

'Yes, I did,' Holly admitted, shamefaced. 'And I told him why, too. But it wouldn't have made any difference if I hadn't. He'd already guessed everything anyway. I'd never have said anything to him but he was the one that brought the whole thing up.'

'And, let me guess – he thought it was a really good idea,' Caitlin said bitterly.

'Sadly, no.'

They found a line of trolleys and Holly felt in her pockets, found two euros and got one for each of them.

'Does he know she's never slept with anybody?' Caitlin asked.

'He does now,' Holly admitted.

'And I suppose he was really surprised?'

Holly shrugged. 'He was, a little, because it's unusual after all, but he seemed to cheer up after that, he said she must have had to withstand other Olivers before now, and what made me think this Oliver was going to be any different?'

'And you explained what made this Oliver different?'

'I did.'

'And what did Sam think about that?'

'He wondered how close she'd have to get before she realized she was wrong.'

'Glad he understands the problem.' They started to push the trolley back towards the others.

'Don't let's go back yet,' Caitlin stopped her. 'Wait with me here. We can see when the cases come through.'

'Walk back very slowly,' Holly suggested, 'or Emily will notice us talking and wonder what's up.'

'And what's up is that Sam obviously fancies Emily himself,' Caitlin said. 'Which is quite funny, in the circumstances.' She turned to Holly. 'What a good choice *he* was to bring on holiday.'

'I know, I know. Rachel did warn us—'

'That Emily liked him, *possibly* liked him. Not that he was besotted with her.'

'Maybe he's not.'

'But would it surprise you if he was?' Caitlin asked. 'Look at her.'

Fifty feet away, Emily was standing alone in the baggage-reclaim area. She had put on a pale blue wool coat and she stood tall and beautiful with her thick, wavy honey-golden hair tumbling down her back.

'If Sam's in love with her, he can't realize how hopeless it is,' Caitlin went on as they walked slowly back to join her. 'He didn't have much chance before Oliver appeared on the scene and he certainly doesn't have a hope now. The only chance for Sam is for Emily to get Oliver out of her system. Perhaps we should ask him to help us.'

'Which is sort of what I suggested to Sam.'

'You didn't! How did that go down?'

'Not brilliantly. He knows that Emily is infatuated with Oliver. But did not like the idea of us setting her up.'

'He wouldn't want Oliver to have first shot?'

'I suppose,' said Holly, 'and although of course we want things to work out for Oliver, I have to say I think it would be sweet if she ended up with Sam.'

'What else did Sam say on the flight, Holly?' Caitlin asked suspiciously. 'What's he done to you?'

'He asked how Emily would react if she knew what we were doing.'

'Perhaps a little badly?'

'Sam said that we shouldn't do something that we know she'd hate.'

'She'd go ballistic because she hates anyone controlling her. Who doesn't? But one day she'll be grateful to us. And, come to that, what *have* we done?' Caitlin stopped the trolley, pulling it to a sudden standstill. She didn't want to reach the others before they'd finished the conversation. 'Think about it. I've invited her around to supper and we've organized a skiing trip for her. Where's the big conspiracy? We're not talking *Dangerous Liaisons*. This happens all the time. It's what friends are for. You're getting distracted by her virginity again. And so is Sam.'

'Move,' Holly hissed, pushing the trolley forward again. 'She's watching us.'

Ahead of them, they could see that the carousel had started to turn. Caitlin caught Emily's eye and waved.

'We should talk about this again,' Holly said.

'I don't think so. What's there to say? What's done is done. Whatever happens next is not going to be because of us. It'll be down to Emily and Oliver. And Sam.'

In spite of the snail's pace, Caitlin and Holly had almost reached Emily.

'Sam said it was about the worst time to be doing this,' Holly added urgently. 'That now he's without Nessa, Oliver is determined to have some mindless fun.'

'He had some *fun* when he was with Nessa too.' Caitlin turned back to Holly. 'He told me about it on the way to the plane.'

'So what are we doing?' Holly asked, dismayed. 'Have we got him all wrong?'

'No, Holly!' Caitlin whispered, pulling a conspiratorial Holly-drives-me-mad face at Emily as she spoke. 'The point is that Emily needs to get him out of her system. If they end up having a one-night stand, so what?'

'But it would be so awful.'

'Perhaps it would be fun.'

14

As Holly had explained to Sam at Heathrow, Magine was a perfect hideaway, which was why he hadn't heard of it. A large village rather than a town and certainly not big enough to attract the tour operators, it had some lovely shops, just two hotels, one pizza house, one very good restaurant and less than a dozen commercially run chalets.

From the moment the six of them got onto the train it was clear that they need not worry about the snow. It was arriving with them, falling fast during their entire journey, so that when they arrived at their station, in a little town called Valorias, an hour and a half later, it was already deep. The taxis waiting to pick them up and take them on up the mountains to Magine had their snow chains on.

It was a further half-hour's drive up to the village. By the time they arrived, the snow had finally stopped falling but lay thick and even on the roofs of the buildings, and the few cars parked beside their chalet, had become soft vague bumps under a heavy white duvet of snow.

It was past midnight and Magine had shut down and gone to sleep, leaving a silence in the little village square.

Emily, who had been there twice before, looked around, at the little floodlit church in the corner, at the familiar pathways and shops and chalets. There was Holly's chalet, snow piled up against its grey stone walls, pale pink shutters all closed for the night. It had once been a barn and stood to one side of the village square, two minutes' walk from the cable car, one minute from the boulangerie. She took a deep breath of the clean, cold air and was hit by a childish rush of exuberance that made her grab hold of Sam, who was standing beside her and dance around him in her long blue coat.

'It's fantastic! It's so beautiful here,' Oliver agreed, catching her mood and spreading his arms to the sky, his breath rising up in a plume into the night sky. And watching him, Emily felt overwhelmingly happy, not just because he was there with her, but because they were all there with her. She realized she couldn't imagine having come with better friends. There was no tension between her and Sam, and even Caitlin was continuing to thaw faster than Magine in late April.

The chalet was warm and softly lit, homely rather than showy, with one huge main room with low beams and walls painted a washed-out china blue, rugs on the old stone floor and a couple of armchairs and two deep sofas pushed around a fireplace, the fire dying down in the hearth. Off this main room was a little kitchen. The fridge was already well stocked with food. Lying on the table was a note from Delphine, Richard Foy's housekeeper, to say that she would be coming in the morning with crois-sants for breakfast.

A narrow twisting staircase in the corner of the main sitting area took them all upstairs to two double and two single bedrooms and a couple of bathrooms. Holly divided them up, putting Caitlin and Leon in one double room and herself and Emily in the other, Sam and Oliver each getting a single room to themselves. Oliver's next door to hers and Emily's.

Perfect, Caitlin thought, walking into the bedroom she would share with Leon.

She dropped her bags on the floor, went over to the window and stood in the darkness looking out at the little square imagining the days ahead. She pictured the others leaving to ski while she'd take her time to get up, then perhaps she'd have a little wander around the town, then, later in the morning, she would take the cable car to meet them for lunch.

She heard Leon come into the bedroom behind her, put down his bag on the bed and take off his coat. Then he came over to join her at the window, and she felt his arms slide around her waist and pull her back against him. She'd known he would come to find her. They'd got too close on the plane for him not to take the first opportunity to get her alone.

She closed her eyes as she felt his arms tighten around her. He bent his head and slowly kissed the back of her neck, so lightly that she could hardly tell when one kiss ended and another began. She turned in his arms, her mouth reaching for his, and felt his hands slide under her sweater and she shivered as his fingers stroked her back. She touched his stomach and heard him groan.

The problem with Leon, Caitlin thought, as he pushed her back upon the huge double bed, undid first the buckle of her belt, then the button of her jeans, then pulled them down her legs in one fast, determined movement . . . The problem with Leon was that however critical of him she was to her friends, Caitlin found him irresistibly sexy. Get close to him and all those things she told everyone she couldn't stand, like his hairy body and his luminous white skin, she suddenly couldn't get enough of.

He was kissing her stomach, his rough chin grazing her skin, turning her insides to syrup. She reached down for him, pulling him up on top of her so that she could kiss him properly, and then she pulled the huge goose-down duvet over them both.

The next morning Caitlin woke up hungry, with a dry, foul-tasting mouth and her contact lenses stuck to her eyeballs.

She rolled her eyes to get the lenses moving again, then glanced across to Leon's side of the bed and saw that she was alone. She looked at her watch and saw it was just past ten. She got out of bed and cautiously opened her shutters, just wide enough to let a dazzling arrow of sunlight pierce the gloom of the bedroom. Seeing how glorious it was outside, she pushed them open all the way and looked out at a perfect blue-sky day.

Down in the square below her window people were walking about. Holidaymakers, dressed in brightly coloured ski clothes, carrying their skis and boards on their backs and making their way in twos and threes towards the cable car. She could hear the distinctive squeak of their ski boots against the fresh snow. A girl was pulling along a child and a bag of groceries on a plastic sledge, and some shopkeepers were sweeping snow away from their shop fronts, while others were shovelling paths across the village square.

The crisply perfect scene, all the fresh snow, the blue sky, the golden sun, the fact that it was the first morning of their holiday, that she had woken feeling full of love, all this combined to tell Caitlin that her dislike of skiing had to be put aside, that today she had to join the others.

And so, in a sudden panic that she was already too late to stop them leaving without her, she pulled on a T-shirt and a pair of jeans and ran out of the bedroom.

In the kitchen, she found Emily, Sam and Oliver dressed but clearly in no hurry to leave. She stopped in the doorway and smiled at the scene.

Emily was standing between her two men, eating a piece of toast, leaning against the kitchen cupboards in black lycra ski trousers and a heavy Equadorian sweater, standing on one ski-booted leg, while the other leg dangled in a bright pink ski sock. On her right was Oliver, looking gorgeous in dark red O'Neill trousers, sunglasses already in position holding back his hair, and concentrating hard on the task of making her a cup of coffee. As Caitlin watched him, he carefully poured in the milk, peered into the mug, then poured a little more, added half a spoonful of sugar, thought no one was looking and tasted the drink with the spoon, stirred once, twice, three times, then carefully handed it over to Emily.

Meanwhile, on Emily's left, was Sam. Dressed like

Emily in a thick sweater, he had on a pair of dark grey trousers and a moth-eaten bandanna, with a pair of sunglasses hanging around his neck. He had his head down and was busily adjusting Emily's other ski boot.

As Oliver handed over the coffee, Sam declared that the boot was ready. He undid the clips, knelt down on the floor and gently pushed it onto Emily's foot.

'Good on you, Prince Charming,' said Caitlin from the doorway.

Emily looked up. 'Good morning,' she said. She put down her coffee and stamped her boots on the floor. 'Thank you, Sam. That's so much better.'

'If I'm quick, will you all wait for me?' Caitlin asked. 'Please?'

'Take your time,' Emily told her. With Holly sitting in a towel upstairs, blow-drying her hair, there was no rush. She pulled out a breakfast chair for Caitlin and put another croissant in the oven to warm.

While Caitlin waited for her breakfast, she and Emily looked at a map and talked about where they might ski. Of the six of them Emily was definitely the least experienced, and she was determined that the others shouldn't be held back because of her. But Caitlin was just as determined to make sure that Emily and Oliver spent a good proportion of the day together. If Emily had a few crashes, there'd be all the more opportunities for Oliver to prove he was the perfect mountain hero by helping her back on her skis.

With sincere promises to look after her, Caitlin succeeded in persuading Emily that they should spend the first morning together. Oliver and Leon could snowboard another day and then Caitlin would retire from skiing altogether, but this morning they would all catch the Mont Julien cable car and then several chairlifts to reach the best snow on the upper slopes. They would spend the rest of the morning skiing back down to the Mont Julien café, which was to be found just beside the cable car. Most of the skiing would be very easy and Caitlin assured Emily that when they came to the two more difficult runs, both very short, her friends would help, even if it meant carrying her down. Emily was persuaded.

While Holly dressed, Caitlin browsed through her cupboards, eventually selecting a pair of ski boots that she recognized as ones she'd borrowed previously and then a familiar pair of skis, too. She pulled on a boot, trod down on a ski to test the bindings and found that they fitted OK – well enough to last the morning.

By the time she'd chosen herself an old pair of trousers and a jacket, Holly had abandoned her to join the others waiting in the square outside.

Caitlin emerged, ten minutes later.

'I can't believe what I'm seeing,' Holly told her, handing her a ski pass.

'It's me, isn't it, baby?' Leon crunched over to her in a pair of purple snow boots and gave Caitlin a warm kiss on the lips. 'Admit it.'

Caitlin predictably grimaced, then relented and kissed him back.

*

Caitlin hardly skied any more but she could remember which parts were fun and which were to be avoided. While she was happy to carry her own poles, it was Leon who found himself with her skis to throw over his shoulder and carry to the cable car with his own.

The cable car might have looked state-of-the-art, but their journey was still more reminiscent of the London Underground at rush hour. Nose-to-armpit, the six of them were pressed tightly among seventy or so other skiers and snowboarders for an uncomfortable fifteen minutes swinging up the mountain before they were disgorged at the summit.

Caitlin was the first to jump into her skis. She pointed out the Mont Julien café where they would end up at lunchtime and then she set off in a wide, gentle curve towards the first of the chairlifts. Watching Emily struggle to make a simple turn to join her, she hoped again that Oliver would take advantage of the chance to pick up the pieces.

Caitlin led them, turning all the time to see how the others were doing, skiing with effortless style and leaving deep regular waves in her wake. She was followed by Leon, Holly, Sam and Emily and then finally, bringing up the rear doing his duty and keeping a close watchful eye on Emily, Oliver.

The snow was deep but powder-fine and the further they went the more Caitlin forgot the others and concentrated on the wonderful skiing. Then, just as she was remembering to slow down and check on everybody again, she heard someone coming up behind her and turned to see that it was Oliver, obviously unable to bear any longer the slow pace at the back. Caitlin watched as he streaked past her, head down, leaning into his turns, kicking up great clouds of snow. Finally he reached the brow of a hill, brought up his knees, took off and disappeared over the edge and out of sight. *What a prat*, she thought furiously. Absolutely typical that he'd had to show off.

Emily didn't at all mind being left at the back. On her previous two holidays here she had survived skiing rather than relished it, but this morning she was loving every minute of it, especially since Oliver had disappeared, leaving her to relax and ski as badly as she usually did. The cold air whipped at her cheeks and, as she rounded the first bend and confidently moved her skis closer together, she cried out with exhilaration. It was a perfect, perfect morning.

With Oliver gone it was Holly who became Emily's minder, occasionally looking over her shoulder to check her progress and to ask if she was OK, and each time Emily managed to waggle a ski pole at her to show her that she was fine. Two more minutes and she saw Caitlin, Leon and Sam all waiting on the brow of the next slope.

Emily skidded to a halt just in front of Sam. 'What happened to Oliver?' she asked them all.

'Oliver is such a show-off,' Caitlin told her and she took Emily by the shoulder and pointed way down the slope to a tiny waving figure, waiting far below them. 'He had to make it clear how good he was. He'll relax now and be lovely.'

Immediately, before Emily had time to recover her breath, they were off again, this time obviously judging that it was OK to speed up a little, and Emily braced herself for the fall that she knew would come as a result. Just watching the others forever zig-zagging just ahead of her was enough to make her lose control.

After the first three falls, she got up happily enough, gamely dragging together her skis, taking her time, finding her poles, knocking the snow off her boots and setting off again, but gradually it became more difficult to recover the confidence that she had started out with and she began to think longingly of the café by the cable car.

Seeing them in a line waiting for her at the bottom of the run she knew that she was holding them up and that they'd enjoy themselves more if they could ski faster. *She'd* enjoy herself more if she could be left to ski more slowly. When she eventually reached the others, who had by now joined Oliver, she suggested to Holly that they should go ahead without her, arguing that in the time it would take her to ski the final run to the café, they could have got to the bottom, caught the chairlifts up once more and skied back down again to meet her.

It was agreed. One by one, Oliver, Sam, Holly, Caitlin and Leon skied over the brow of the hill and disappeared, leaving her alone. And because she knew that she could now relax completely, her skiing went to pieces.

Within seconds of setting off she was completely out of control, coming to a halt only by colliding with an old man and knocking him flying. She knew that he could have used some help getting up but Emily struggled to get over to him and in the end he waved her away. Just a few seconds later she fell again, losing a ski and sending a bright stab of pain through her left knee.

She got up carefully, tempted to take her skis off and walk the rest of the way to the cable car. But she didn't give up, found her poles and set off again, gingerly testing her knee with her weight and finding that it was bearable, just.

Now the fun had absolutely and completely gone. She'd thought she'd be fine alone, but the truth was that she would have loved to have someone else with her. As she made her way, heart in mouth, towards the last big run before the café – the slippery slope as she'd labelled it on a previous holiday – she kept hoping that she'd turn a corner and see them all waiting for her after all.

She began it knowing she was doing it all wrong. The certainty that she was going to fall again meant that she couldn't stop herself leaning backwards instead of forwards, though she knew she was committing the cardinal sin, and, of course, she was soon out of control again. Picking up speed, she found herself leaning further and further back until she was almost horizontal to her skis and hurtling faster than she'd ever skied before, frequently taking off as she streaked down the mountainside, able to do nothing more than cry out to anyone reckless enough to be in her way.

And then, with superhuman effort, she managed to turn both skis away from the downward slope so that she began to traverse across the mountain instead, still at extremely high speed, but at least going across the slope rather than straight down it.

She knew she had flashed past flags marking the edges of the piste but had no option but to keep going. The snow was getting deeper now, and every so often one ski would suddenly slow down without the other, forcing her to do the splits, but she somehow managed not to fall. Not until she slid into a thigh-high drift and came to a complete and sudden halt, toppling forwards head first into the snow.

At least she'd stopped. She had her head deep in the snow but she'd stopped. She tried to get up but her legs were twisted beneath her, still attached to both skis, and she fell sideways instead, buried up to her waist, half laughing, half crying, thankful that there was nobody to see her.

But there was. Following her tracks, determinedly poling himself along through the deep snow, came Sam.

When she saw him she fell back into the snow again and closed her eyes, thinking, *Why does it always have to be Sam*? But, of course, it was never going to be Oliver.

'I told them you'd need some help on this run but they said you'd be fine,' Sam said. 'So I said I'd come and find you and prove myself right.' He sat down beside her, letting her get back her breath. 'I've just won myself lunch.'

'No, *I've* just won you lunch.'

'Absolutely.'

He got down on his knees and dug into the snow,

scrabbling like a determined dog, deeper and deeper, until he managed to release her legs enough for her to be able to wriggle them out. Then he stood up and held out a gloved hand, pulled her to her feet and helped her snap her boots out of her bindings.

'Do you want to ski to the café or shall we walk?'

'I don't know,' she moaned, looking back the way she'd come. The rest of the slope now looked like a precipice. 'Can you help me?' She knew that she sounded pathetic, but she was so tired now and couldn't face another fall.

She followed him on foot, tramping along behind him, back through the deep tracks that her skis had made in the snow, back to the piste, and then he held her steady while she clipped herself back onto her skis.

'I'm fine,' she said for her own benefit more than Sam's, and they set off together once more, Sam skiing very slowly just in front of her, telling her exactly what to do, reminding her to lean forward on her skis, just a little, to keep her shoulders facing downhill.

Then a snowboarder whistled past Emily's ear, spraying a great cloud of snow all over her, and thwacked straight into Sam, sending him tumbling down the slope, and Emily immediately lost her balance and fell too, and again her knee twisted beneath her and once again she lost a ski.

She looked around for Sam and saw him about thirty feet below her. Picking up her lost ski, she stumbled slowly towards him.

She reached Sam and looked down at him, waiting for her, spreadeagled on the snow. Seeing her stony face, he started to laugh and reached up for her hand. 'And I'm meant to be helping you,' he said.

She took his hand and was assailed by dizziness, overcome with the desire to fall to the ground beside him. 'You must remember to keep your upper body still,' she joked weakly, 'and to flex your thighs.' His hand was still in hers. 'You were all over the place just then.'

'Do you think we'll make it to the café?'

She looked down towards it, not so far away, and nodded.

'How about I hang on to you and if we go down again, we go down together?'

'Very reassuring,' she smiled.

He stood behind her and wrapped his arms tightly around her waist, and they set off, Sam snowploughing outside her skis, checking her speed all the way down, his strength stopping them from running out of control. In this way, folded between his thighs and cocooned within his arms, she glided safely down to the café.

Once there, Emily thankfully jumped away from him – she had been much too close, she thought. Uncomfortably close. He took her skis and his and rammed them into the snow, then hooked both sets of poles around their tips.

They queued for two hot chocolates, which came in tall glasses, topped with Chantilly and shavings of chocolate, took them out into the sunshine, found a table facing the slopes and positioned their chairs so that they could sit side by side. There they sat, in companionable silence, watching the other skiers making their way down the slopes either to the café, or on to Magine.

How could it be, Emily thought as she watched Sam, that she could wait eight years for somebody, could finally reach a point where she could have a real shot at him, and then find herself interested in somebody else? After eight long years, yes, it was still Oliver uppermost in her mind, still the same old story, that if he called out her name she'd come running, but she couldn't deny any longer that she liked being with Sam. Sam who now seemed to have nothing on his mind at all beyond sitting beside her in the sun, getting a tan and enjoying the spectacular wipe-outs as people came too fast over the brow of the hill, and failed to stop in time for the café.

What had she hoped for? That Sam's feelings for her would last indefinitely without any encouragement from her? Until that moment she hadn't even properly admitted to herself that they had ever been there. Subconsciously, of course, she'd known they had, she'd been aware of them even in Ruffles Department Store, but she'd ignored them, pushed them aside even as she'd felt flattered by them, because there was no place for them in her life. And if now those feelings had gone, if the fact that he was sitting beside her now, so still, so at ease, without any urge to look at her, making little attempt to talk, happy simply to watch the slopes and wait for his friends to arrive, if that meant that he had changed, Emily missed the old Sam very much.

Through her impenetrable sunglasses, she stared at him, sitting handsome and relaxed beside her, his long legs stretched out in front of her in his battered, grey ski trousers, his small neat nose just starting to turn pink from the sun, a tiny smear of chocolate on his chin and his thick brown hair sticking up in vertical tufts, and told herself that as long as she still wanted Oliver, she had no right to miss Sam.

15

One by one, Emily watched the others ski up to the café, and pull up short at the sight of her and Sam sitting side by side in the sun. *You're too late*, she felt like politely informing them. *Not any more. He used to like me but he's stopped thinking like that now.*

They stayed at the café for lunch and when they rose to go Emily announced – firmly – that she'd had enough and was taking the cable car back down to the village. What she hadn't expected was Oliver overruling her, telling her that she wasn't going home, that she was spending an hour with him, having a lesson.

Anyone else but Oliver – *anyone* else – and the lure of the cable car would have been too strong. But he was offering to take her far away from the others, somewhere, he said, where they could concentrate. When Emily asked where exactly, he got out a map and showed her how it was possible to do as she wanted – go back down in the cable car to Magine – then walk through the village to the other slopes on the other side, the nursery slopes.

'The nursery slopes?' Emily spluttered.

'Not *to* the nursery slopes,' Oliver told her, '*beyond* them.' High above them, where, according to the map, there was a bubble lift. 'And above that – ' he pointed – 'all these wonderful, easy runs.' He showed her, tracing them down the mountainside with his finger. 'Perfect for you to get your confidence back.'

And so, while Caitlin, Sam, Leon and Holly left for more difficult slopes, Oliver took her away.

All too soon it became clear that while Emily was thinking romantic rendezvous, Oliver was thinking energy-sapping workout. She'd had a few lessons during her first skiing trip but knew she'd fallen into bad habits – Sam had spotted them too and had done his best to correct them before her legs turned into jelly and she could do nothing but fall over.

'Get your bum in . . . Tuck your elbows in, weight forward, weight forward, look ahead, look ahead,' Oliver hollered at her as she skied past him again and again, and it was clear that he was getting more out of the afternoon than she was. After an hour, when she was finally getting the hang of parallel turns, of keeping her weight forward and her upper body still, she said she could ski no longer and Oliver was finally persuaded to take pity on her.

'You were like a man possessed,' she teased him, as she walked with wobbly legs towards a café for a quick drink before they made their way back to the bubble lift that Oliver had agreed they could travel in rather than ski all the way back to the village. 'You were terrifying. It was like you'd forgotten who I was, forgotten that you knew me at all.'

'I loved it. I loved telling you what to do. And it worked too. You improved so much.' He put his arm around her and said confidently, 'I could teach you so much more.'

Emily was sure he had said it innocently, that he had only skiing in mind, but once he'd spoken, the other connotation was the one left hanging in the air between the two of them.

Oliver responded to the long silence by laughing, enjoying himself as ever, and he squeezed her shoulders. 'I think you'd have a lot of fun.'

They sat opposite each other at a small square table, in the last of the afternoon light, glasses of brandy in front of them. It was getting colder now and Emily could feel stiffness spreading across her shoulders and a dull ache in her knee. She was weighing up the undoubted pleasure of looking at Oliver against the thought of getting back to the chalet and lying in a deep hot bath.

He took one of her hands in both of his and started to rub it gently. 'Are you cold?'

She looked down at her hand in surprise, then back at him, and he stopped rubbing and held it still.

'Why do I think you like Sam?' he asked her then.

She gawped at him. *Take your time to reply. Don't say the first thing that comes into your head.*

'I don't know.'

'Perhaps it was seeing him holding your hand, like this?'

She shook her head. 'Not like this.'

'Or perhaps it was seeing the two of you sitting side by side at the café just now, sitting so close.'

And it could have been you, she thought irritably but didn't say it. If you're jealous, if you're worried about Sam, why wasn't it you sitting beside me then?

'Do you find him attractive?' Oliver asked.

'I suppose I do.'

'I thought so.'

'Oliver. Nothing's about to happen between me and Sam. I don't want Sam.'

He was meant to ask her what she did want, and then she would have told him, but he didn't.

'Good,' Oliver said instead. 'Don't you think he's such an old woman?'

'I thought he was your friend!'

'A long time ago.'

'Sam said the same thing.'

'Yeah, he would. Oh, bollocks,' he said, dropping her hand. 'We're not such good friends any more.'

'Why not? Since when?'

'Since we fell out over a girl Sam was keen on. Years ago. He's not forgiven me.'

'Was it me?' Emily whispered.

'No! It was not you!' He shouted with laughter, making her jump. 'God, no. I'd forgotten that Sam liked you then. No wonder he's really pissed off with me now.' He sighed. 'Oh, Emily, stop looking at me like that, like you want to spit me out.'

'But you can sound so hard.'

Oliver drained the last of his brandy. 'I'm not hard. But I do have this urge to shove Sam away from you. I don't like him getting too close.' He abruptly stood up. 'And we must go or we'll miss the lift,' he finished. 'And they'll have used up all the hot water in the chalet.'

'Oliver, are you OK?'

'I'm fine,' he said impatiently. 'I just don't like to think of you and Sam. Do you mind me saying that?'

She shook her head. Mind? Did she mind? All she minded was that he was getting up and walking off just as he was starting to talk, but then what he was saying was true. If they didn't go, they *would* miss the lift and the thought that she might have to ski down to the village, in pitch darkness, overrode her wish to keep him talking.

They made it to the bubble lift with only a minute to spare. All the way down, alone in the little car, swinging gently in the darkness above the mountainside and then as they walked back through the quiet streets to the chalet, Oliver with her skis on his shoulder and his hand in hers, she waited for him to say something more. But he didn't and Emily, happy to have his hand in hers, didn't push him. Because it was clear that something was happening between them at last.

Back at the chalet, there was a brief lull in the early evening when Oliver, Sam and Leon were all asleep upstairs and Emily, Caitlin and Holly sat downstairs, already dressed for the evening, sprawled across the sofas in front of the fire eating crisps, reading yesterday's newspapers and drinking wine. Emboldened by two glasses on an empty stomach and by a new confidence that she could talk freely to Emily, that she no longer had to worry that Emily would flounce off in a huff, Caitlin found she had the courage to try a gentle interrogation.

She started off innocuously enough, asking about Emily's ski lesson with Oliver.

'It was fun,' Emily told her. She finished her glass of wine and refilled hers and Caitlin's. 'I could have done without Oliver taking it quite so seriously, but it was still fun.'

'You were so late back,' said Caitlin, 'we were getting worried about you. We were wondering what you'd got up to.'

'Nothing,' Emily said immediately, and then realized that she wanted to tell them. 'But he said if there was anything I'd like him to teach me, to let him know.'

Sitting in a deep armchair, out of Emily's direct line of sight, Holly chipped in, 'Will you take him up on it? That's the big question! Are you ready to learn?'

'No! Not like that,' Emily told her, serious now.

Caitlin quickly sat up on the sofa. 'Emily,' she said, full of purpose, 'let's not pretend any more. We know how you feel about Oliver. Is he what you've been waiting for? If he turned to you now and made it clear that he really badly wanted you, said all the right things, would you think this is it? He's the one? Would you jump into bed with him?'

'No,' Emily said. 'If that was all I was waiting for I'd have been to bed with someone else by now, wouldn't I?'

'I thought Oliver might make you feel it was worth it.'

Emily shook her head. 'Holly understands,' she said, looking over to Holly's chair. 'That's why she's not asking me these questions. It'll take more than someone saying all the right things.'

'Why? Give me a reason.'

Emily smiled. 'Whatever I say, just remember that they're my reasons. Not that I think you should have done the same.'

'Tell me,' Caitlin said more eagerly. 'Can you give me six reasons. And do make me think I should have done the same! Make me think *If only I'd thought of it like that!*'

'No chance.' Emily laughed. 'My reasons wouldn't have worked for you.'

'But I really would like to know what they are – hear it from you, for once, rather than from everyone else,' Caitlin said. 'I've wanted to ask you for ages.'

'Aren't there loads of reasons?' Holly piped up again from her armchair.

'No! Tell me what they would be,' Caitlin challenged. 'And none of that *sex is sacred* rubbish.'

'I'm serious,' Holly insisted.

'I am too.'

'I think of how Rachel was after Felix,' Emily said, interrupting them. 'That's my first reason.'

Caitlin shrugged, remembering.

'She made me realize that if the physical intimacy isn't matched by emotional intimacy, it breaks your heart. Like it broke Rachel's. And I've seen it happen too many times to want it to happen to me. That's why I know I shouldn't sleep with Oliver. Not for a long time. Not until I am sure he isn't going to leave me.'

Caitlin nodded. 'That's true. But that was how Rachel chose to deal with it. I'm not like that, I could have walked away with a smile on my face and he'd never have known.'

'Good for you. I couldn't.'

'But you can solve that simply by being discriminating, you don't *have* to stay a virgin,' Caitlin argued.

'And I am discriminating. Very discriminating. I want to do it with someone I love, who loves me. That's all. Reason one.'

'Because ninety-nine per cent of your friends exaggerate. Reason two.' Into the silence Holly piped up again from behind the sofa, 'And reason three,' she went on, 'because most of the time it's a bit disappointing. Emily shouldn't risk losing it all for a button mushroom. My advice is at least look before you leap.'

'Really?' Emily said laughing. 'Is that true? Everyone's making out it's better than it is?'

'You won't know until you try,' said Caitlin.

'It's a reason,' Holly insisted.

'Three reasons,' Caitlin said. 'Three reasons for staying a virgin. Aren't there any more?'

'Other reasons I've told you about already,' Emily went on. 'I like the anticipation. I wonder what's wrong with waiting, why we think we have to have everything so fast.'

'Fast tans, fast food, fast sex,' Holly interrupted. 'I agree with you. And endless foreplay sounds like a marvellous idea.'

'And I suppose it means you don't have to sleep in the wet patch,' Caitlin joked. 'There's another reason.'

'No, seriously,' Emily interrupted, 'think about the guys you lost your virginity to. Can you remember it? Do you still care about them now?'

'I never cared enough about him,' Caitlin answered. 'That was the problem at the beginning.'

'But he was completely in love with you, wasn't he?' Holly said. 'I remember you telling me about him, how bad you felt.'

'What about you, Holly?' Emily asked her. 'Do you still think about the man you first slept with?'

'Not if I can help it.'

'But don't you think that's sad? Don't you wish it could have been something special?'

Holly pushed herself upright so that she could look at Emily properly. 'Not really,' she admitted. 'I understand exactly why you do, but it simply wasn't like that for me. I didn't ever see my virginity as something I wanted to look after. It doesn't mean that I sleep around, doesn't mean I don't agree with you that sex can lead to emotional entanglements that can make you fall apart. But I don't believe it has to be like that. I think it can, simply, be good fun. Not something to worry about for twenty-five years.'

'I can only lose it once,' Emily said stubbornly. 'I want to get it right.'

'Five reasons. You have five reasons to stay a virgin,'

Caitlin said to Emily. 'I don't think that's enough. Not when I can tell you so many more reasons why you shouldn't.'

'Just give me one.'

'Because you'd enjoy it. Because it's such good fun.'

'I'll find out. And I'll find out with the man I'm going to stay with. And that'll make it even better. That's my sixth reason. Because if it happens with the right man, it's surely as good as it gets?'

'But that's so boring!' Caitlin retorted. 'You can't want to do it with only one man. That's such a waste.' She looked at Emily curiously. 'Have you *ever* been to bed with someone?'

'Once,' said Emily. 'I was sixteen and we did nothing at all.'

'Not Oliver, was it?' Holly asked, only half joking.

'No, not Oliver,' Emily confirmed. 'Before I met Oliver. And it was lovely. I'd do it again, if it felt like the right thing to do and whoever it was understood what wasn't going to happen. But it's not come up again, as it were. It just hasn't happened to me.'

'Emily,' Caitlin said, leaning in to her, 'all those reasons . . . the truth is, I don't need to be told what you believe in and why it hasn't happened to you yet because I know you better now. And I had just the same choices as you did, I listened to the same arguments. I don't regret the route I took, but I do respect you for choosing a different one to the rest of us. I used to think that you were too good to be true, that it was all part of an act, but I don't any more.'

'What do I say to that?'

'And now, I'm thinking "please hold on" and I never thought I would.'

'Why?'

Caitlin looked down at the floor, thought about it for a moment. 'In about twenty seconds, I think I may regret saying this.' She looked up at Emily again, and across the room Holly held her breath. 'I certainly wasn't going to say anything tonight. But now I'm going to.' She took a deep breath, sensing Emily bracing herself for some kind of an assault. 'I don't think Oliver's your man. I don't think he's ever going to be the one.'

Out of the corner of her eye, Caitlin could see Holly looking at her steadily but Caitlin was far more interested in Emily's reaction and she could see straight away that she had struck a nerve.

'Why? What do you mean?'

'I know how much you like him,' Caitlin said gently, trying hard to keep her voice very steady and calm, 'and while I have huge respect for your reasons for not sleeping with anyone, I still think Oliver is the main reason why you've not even come close. Oliver is the reason why you've not been tempted, why it is that you've not found yourself in bed with another guy since you were sixteen years old. I think you've come out on this holiday wanting to put everything you believe in to the test, hoping that you might get together with Oliver, that you might discover he's the man you've been waiting for. I think you're vulnerable. I think you might make a mistake.' She paused. 'And I'm not even sure that I like him any more.'

As Caitlin finished, Emily glanced quickly over to the staircase, the fear that Oliver might somehow overhear what they were saying there on her face.

'It's OK,' Caitlin reassured her. 'He's in his room and I'm talking too quietly for any of them upstairs to be able to hear a word I'm saying.'

'Anyone listening would know you were talking rubbish,' Emily finally retaliated half-heartedly.

'Really?' Caitlin asked. 'Are you sure?'

The anger was fleeting. Now Emily rubbed a hand across her face, more muddled than angry. 'I don't know . . .'

'I think what I'm saying is true,' Caitlin told her. 'Until this holiday I thought he was the one for you too. But I don't any more. I only hope you've got close enough to him to realize that for yourself. But I'm scared that you haven't, that you're still going to get swept off your feet by him.'

'Why don't you like him any more?' Emily asked.

Caitlin bit her lip. 'This morning, after we left you to ski on your own, Oliver started messing around, setting out to wind us all up, especially Sam. It was obvious that he had something on his mind.'

'What was it?'

'You.'

'Me?' Emily cried, and in her voice Caitlin still heard the hope.

'Yes, but it's not what you think. You were on Oliver's mind because he had finally picked up on the fact that

Sam likes you. *Really* likes you. He does, and you know it,' Caitlin went on quickly, sensing Emily was about to protest. 'You might not feel the same way but don't pretend that you haven't noticed. We all know he does. As soon as Sam walked into the airport it was obvious that you were the only person he wanted to see there.' Caitlin dropped her voice again. 'Sam adores you. And Oliver knows it.'

Caitlin caught sight of Holly frantically shaking her head and ignored her. 'And realizing that has got Oliver's juices flowing. It's made him want you for himself.'

'Is that what you think too, Holly?' Emily turned to her. 'Do you think what Caitlin is saying is true?'

It was difficult to interpret Emily's feelings at this point, hard to tell if she was terribly hurt or emerging unscathed, whether she believed a word of what Caitlin was saying or was dismissing it entirely.

'I think Oliver can be very competitive,' Holly told her carefully, 'and I agree with Caitlin that he was very bothered about Sam this morning. He kept challenging Sam about you, needling him.' Emily shrugged. 'But I'm wondering whether that's simply because he likes you and he wants to make sure you're OK.'

'I don't think so,' Caitlin said emphatically. 'Oliver wants to get one over Sam. That's what his interest in Emily is all about. That's why he suddenly decided to take Emily off for a lesson this afternoon, having paid her barely any attention at all. He hadn't realized how much Sam wants her.'

Emily remembered the look on Oliver's face when he

came up to her and Sam at the bar in the airport and how he had reacted to what he thought he was seeing then.

Caitlin went on again, 'I think Oliver gets turned on by other guys' women. He always has done. He sees it as a challenge, and he loves a challenge. He saw me kissing Leon in the kitchen and it turned him on. The next thing I knew, he was trying to get me to do the same to him.'

'At your party?' Emily looked at her. 'When? When I was washing up with Leon? I thought Leon went a bit strange.'

Caitlin nodded. 'But he's cooled off me now because he has you and Sam to think about. And you are far more important to him than I ever was. Think what you represent . . . Don't you see? And the thought of Sam getting to you first . . . That's a big problem for Oliver.'

Had Oliver done this to Sam before? Emily wondered, wishing that she could stop herself. Was that why Oliver had suddenly appeared with Sam on that empty beach in Cornwall, when she was sixteen years old?

But even as a part of her acknowledged the possibility of truth in what Caitlin was saying, she had to deny it straight away because she hoped so badly that it wasn't true. Over the years she'd known him, there had never been any sign of this. Then a sneaky little voice inside her head told her, *But over the years there'd never been a Sam on the scene, never anyone with whom Oliver had to compete*. Yet she had made such progress with Oliver that afternoon. She'd just begun to feel that something might happen, really happen, between the two of them. And she wanted it to. She badly did. Why did Caitlin have to say this now, when she had finally, finally begun to feel there was hope between them?

Emily could see the concern on Caitlin's face, and on Holly's too as she peered at them over the side of her armchair, and she knew that neither of them wanted to hurt her, that both of them were looking out for her.

'I'm not angry with you for saying what you said. I appreciate your concern. But I'll show you that you're wrong.'

Caitlin shrugged. 'I had to tell you. But if I'm wrong, I'll be very pleased. I suppose you'll do whatever you think is right. I won't be judging you.' She grinned. 'As if *I* could ever judge *you*.'

And then they heard a heavy thud, thud, thud down the stairs and a freshly pressed Leon appeared around the corner of the staircase, closely followed by Oliver.

Oliver threw one quick glance around the room and went straight over to Emily, bending down towards her on the sofa. 'OK?' he asked affectionately. 'Not too tired? Not too stiff after the battering I gave you this afternoon?'

She shook her head, looking up at him, and he dropped his head and kissed her cheek and Emily put an arm around him and held him still for a few seconds.

He's working on her, Caitlin thought indignantly. It couldn't be a coincidence that Oliver was behaving like this right now. He was staking his claim. He probably knew that Sam was about to come down the stairs behind him and was waiting for him to catch them like that.

But Sam didn't come down. Caitlin looked back at Emily, at her perfect profile, her just upturned nose and her clear, flawless skin, her slender arm holding tightly onto Oliver, and thought she understood why Emily now mattered so much to him. He had always liked beautiful girls – especially when his friends liked them too – and Emily wasn't just beautiful. She was a rare prize. And Caitlin hoped very much that the prize was not about to be claimed.

Sam had still not appeared half an hour later. When Leon and Oliver disappeared into the kitchen offering to cook supper, Holly volunteered to go upstairs and fetch him down. She came back down a minute later, stood on the bottom step of the staircase and beckoned to Emily and Caitlin to follow her up.

Only half understanding where they were going and why, Emily found herself getting up and following Caitlin quietly up the stairs. At the top Holly led them along a short corridor and stopped outside Sam's door, which she carefully and quietly opened, and all three of them stood in the doorway and looked inside.

It was dark, the only light thrown in through the open door and a panel of glass above it, and the room glowed with a soft, intimate light. Emily's first thought was what a sweet but very feminine little bedroom it was, with a low ceiling painted a deep red pink.

The walls were painted white and in the middle of the room there was a bed surrounded by floating gossamer-fine drapes, gathered together into a bunch, creating the effect of a romantic billowing tent. She wondered suspiciously whether Holly had been let loose in this room, knowing it was just to her taste, and then her attention was caught by the bed itself.

Lying on it, half hidden by a cerise satin eiderdown, lay Sam. He was asleep, blissfully unaware of them all looking in at him. A long arm stretched out across the bed, his sleeping face turned towards them.

Emily had never watched a man asleep before. Her eyes flicked warily from his face to the bunched knot of muscles in his shoulder and then to the delicate skin that curved into his armpit. With an unexpected jolt in her groin, she caught sight of his nipple, dark and flat against his smooth tawny skin, and she felt herself blush.

'Doesn't he look flushed?' Caitlin joked, breaking the spell. 'Best we take off all those nasty covers.'

'Doesn't he look divine, you mean?' whispered Holly. 'Are you sure you don't want him, Emily?'

'We should wake him up. He's got to come and have supper,' said Caitlin.

'Make a noise, then. Say hello,' Holly told her, 'Don't just stand there staring at him.'

'Or shall we jump on him?' Caitlin suggested. 'All three of us? Don't you think he'd enjoy that?'

'You can't,' Emily managed to say. 'You mustn't wake him!' And then she turned away from them, towards the stairs, calling out as she ran that she thought she would go and help Oliver and Leon in the kitchen.

16

The next day everything changed.

When they awoke, it was not to the clear skies of the day before. The temperature had dropped and the clouds were low and heavy with the promise of more snow.

When she opened her curtains and looked outside, Emily's first reaction was to get straight back into bed, deciding there and then that she would not be skiing that day. She had gone up into the mountains in low cloud once before and found it utterly terrifying. She had been able to see nothing, had had no sense at all of where she was or where she should put her feet or where her friends had gone, and she was absolutely certain that she did not want to go through that again.

When Emily finally did get up and make her way down to the kitchen, still in her pyjamas, she found that Leon and Caitlin were already kitted up and eating breakfast together. And, as far as they knew, were expecting Oliver, Holly and Sam to join them.

'You?' Emily protested to Caitlin. 'I thought you hated skiing. What are you doing going up when it's like this?'

Caitlin shrugged. 'I've surprised myself. I had such a good day yesterday, I thought I'd do it again. And,' she said, blowing Leon a kiss, 'I like being with him.'

'Sweet,' Emily said, thinking how things had changed.

Then Sam came in, barefoot and dressed in jeans and a T-shirt.

'Sleep well?' Caitlin asked him.

'I'm starving,' Sam told them. 'I've spent the whole night dreaming about steak and chips. I can't believe you didn't wake me up.'

'You were too sound asleep,' Caitlin told him. 'We decided we couldn't do it to you.'

Sam wandered over to the fridge, found nothing that he liked and started opening and shutting cupboards. 'Have you eaten all the breakfast too?'

'There wasn't much. Delphine hasn't been yet,' Holly told him from the doorway, also barefoot and obviously having just woken up. 'If you're that hungry, you'll have to go into the village and buy something.'

'Come with me, Emily?' Sam asked.

She nodded, not meeting his eye.

'Croissant? Pain au chocolat? What do you fancy? Whatever, I need to go soon. I need to go *now*.' He looked her up and down. 'And you're wearing pyjamas.'

'I'll get dressed.' Emily stood up. 'Wait for me.' She brushed past Holly. 'We could buy the supper while we're out,' she told her.

'And I need to go to the bank,' Sam called after her.

'Have some fun, why don't you?' Holly said sarcastically.

'Oh, we'll have fun,' Sam said. 'Coffee, bit of shopping, perhaps some ice skating on the rink in the village. Yes?' He called to Emily.

'Definitely,' she shouted from the stairs.

'And don't you worry about Oliver,' she heard Caitlin add. 'We'll leave him a note to tell him where we are skiing. He can come and catch us up.'

Emily and Sam crossed the market square and walked on into the heart of the village. Emily knew exactly where to take him. She led the way through the narrow cobbled streets, so dark under the heavy clouds that the street lamps had come on again, and Sam followed her unquestioningly until she stopped outside a café tucked away down a little street called Rue Mathilde.

Although a few diehards were eating their breakfast outside, it seemed much more appealing to stay inside the café, with its whitewashed walls and steamy windows and red-tiled floor, the bittersweet smell of chocolate hanging in the air. Each little table was lit by an individual lamp and had a checked red and white tablecloth.

Emily stood beside Sam at the counter and looked down at all the mouth-watering patisserie and she heard her stomach instantly grumble with hunger. Each currant seemed plumper and more shiny than any she'd ever seen before, all the pastry more deliciously puffed up. Everything was so liberally sprinkled with pistachio nuts, chocolate or almonds that she wanted to eat it all. In the end she did the same as Sam and ordered a wonderfully fluffy-looking pain au chocolat and a croissant, warm from the oven, and they sat down opposite each other, pulling off pieces and dunking them in large cups of milky coffee.

It was strange, Emily thought, how despite everything

that was left unspoken between them, in that café, cocooned together for the twenty or so minutes that they stayed inside, they were so close. Nothing was said, they didn't hold hands or hold glances, and yet there was an intimacy between them and a trust that meant Emily knew she mattered to Sam, and Sam knew that he mattered to her. It lasted until they left the café. Outside, in the cold air, it didn't feel so certain any more.

When they got to the bank Emily left Sam, saying that she would wait for him in the street. She would look in a few shop windows while he queued inside. She watched him walk into the bank, then unexpectedly turn back at the last second to look at her, and it seemed to her that he was doubting whether she would be there as she'd said she would.

She wandered a little way down the street, looking in the windows of the shops, passing a toy shop that had opened since she'd been there last and then stopping outside La Coccinelle, her favourite shop in Magine. She would have gone inside straight away but for Sam's glance, so instead she made do with window-shopping.

La Coccinelle sold jewellery, all designed by its unlikely owner, Monsieur Gérard. He was huge and hairy with big fat fingers and a thick black beard, and he made the most simple, stunning jewellery. Rings, necklaces, earrings, brooches and bracelets, always intricately pretty but bold and dramatic too. Usually made of silver, but sometimes gold or platinum, sometimes with precious stones but more often with crystals, glass beads, jade, topaz and turquoise, everything was unique, and yet all undeniably M. Gérard's. Every time she came to Magine, his was the first shop she wanted to go to.

At first she'd wondered how such a shop could thrive in such a very small, traditional, conservative place as Magine, thought that only a few had discovered him, but then she'd asked Holly and had found out how famous M. Gérard was, how people came to Magine from miles around simply to visit him, that there was no danger of him closing down for lack of business. Ever since Saltwater had first taken shape in her mind, she'd been wondering if there was any way to persuade him to let her sell his jewellery there.

While she was still looking in the window, Sam caught her up.

'Let me buy you something,' he said impulsively.

'Lovely of you, but no.' She shook her head. 'For once I'm thinking about Saltwater, not me. How cool it would be to persuade him to let me stock some of his pieces there.'

'Go inside,' he encouraged her. 'Go and see if it's a good moment to talk to him. I'll wait for you.'

'Oh, God.' She swallowed. If she did, she would be confirming the reality of Saltwater.

'You are going to need stock,' he reminded her, speaking as if Saltwater was already a definite. 'Finding things to sell is going to be the hardest part of all.'

She gave him a worried look and went inside.

When she came out ten minutes later, Sam knew immediately that it had gone well. She danced her way towards him, and then hugged him delightedly.

'That's brilliant! You're on your way now.'

'He didn't say yes,' she said, smiling up at him, still in the circle of his arms. 'But he did say maybe.'

He could have kissed her then, and he knew that she'd have responded, caught up in that lovely moment of excitement, but she pushed herself up on her toes and kissed him on his cheek instead, and then before he could move she'd let him go and set off down the street again.

They spent the rest of the morning ice skating, first edging their way around the dilapidated ice rink and then getting braver. At one moment Sam caught her hand and led her around and around the rink, faster and faster, daring her not to let go, until finally she couldn't take any more and spun away from him, making it to the rails more by luck than skill rather than crashing in a heap in the middle of the rink. And Emily was angry with herself for her inconsistency, for her inconstancy, because she knew that if it had been she and Oliver here, skating together, she'd be enjoying it too and she wouldn't be thinking about Sam.

When Emily and Sam got back to the chalet it was nearly lunchtime. They walked into the kitchen together to find Oliver sitting at the table, reading a newspaper, one hand knotted in his hair, pointedly not looking up at their entrance.

'Hi,' Sam said brightly, too brightly, and Oliver glowered at him rather than smiled. It was obvious that he had been waiting for them, and waiting resentfully.

Oliver and Sam might once have been good friends,

but they certainly weren't now. Sam tossed the paper bag of pastries onto the table in front of Oliver and took off his coat. 'Help yourself,' he said, but there was no warmth in the invitation and Oliver ignored the offer.

'Where have you been?' Oliver asked Emily. He was so cross and aggrieved that Emily wanted to laugh and yet she felt her heartstrings pull.

'Getting supper, going to the bank.' Nothing about the ice skating or the coffee. 'I'm sorry we left you all alone.'

'I've been waiting for you all morning,' he said.

'Why?' Sam asked. 'Why didn't you go and find the others. They'd left a note for you. You knew where they'd be.'

'Because I was going to take Emily out for another lesson,' Oliver told Sam.

'I don't think so,' Sam said, looking out of the window.

'There's nothing wrong with the weather. If anything, I think it's brightening up.' Oliver turned to Emily. 'You are coming with me, Emily, aren't you?'

'But –' Emily looked outside, thinking if anything the weather was worse than before – 'I'm not sure I can ski well enough to go out in this.'

'Don't ask her to,' Sam interfered again. 'It isn't right.'

'Once we get high enough, we'll be above the cloud,' Oliver said, keeping his voice light, as if it was only the weather that was at issue.

'Bullshit, Oliver, of course you won't,' said Sam.

'It's all right, it's all right,' Emily intervened, hating them arguing over her. 'If you want me to come, I'll come,' she told Oliver. 'For an hour, no longer. Not when it's like this. Wait while I get changed.'

Sam looked at her and shook his head. 'Don't go.'

'Why not?' She smiled, trying to make light of it.

'Just don't go.'

I want to go. I need to resolve this. I want to know.

'No need to worry, Sam,' Oliver said as Emily moved to the door. 'I will look after her.'

'Do you mind if I come too?' she heard Sam ask him as she walked up the stairs. She stopped to listen.

'Yes, I do, mate, sorry to say. I'm going to give Emily another lesson and you'd be in the way. How about we all go out tomorrow?'

'But I'd like to come.'

'Look, Sam,' she heard Oliver say impatiently, 'you're not invited. You had her all morning, it's my turn now.'

Which was how Emily found herself alone on a chairlift with Oliver at two o'clock in the afternoon, swinging up a mountain when every other skier seemed intent on getting down.

The silence, deepened by the deep muffling cloud, was overwhelming. At first they both tried to make conversation but it didn't last, and for most of the ride up they sat listening only to the creak and occasional rumble of the chairlift.

What was she doing swinging up a mountain with Oliver? She didn't know. Was she happy to be there? She didn't know. Yes, yes, she was, of course she was. It was what she'd been wanting for so long. Beside her, he shifted slightly on his chair and then slid a familiar arm around her and she fell in against his warm body, reassured a little.

At the top, when they raised the bar and launched themselves away, Oliver immediately skied into the cloud and disappeared.

She was left all alone, once again, to think how mad she was to be doing this. How she had now set herself up for a neck-breaking fall simply because she was programmed to take advantage of every chance to be alone with Oliver. And she had vowed not to come out again, and she'd made that vow sitting in the snow in brilliant sunshine. What was she doing here in cloud so thick she couldn't see beyond the end of her ski pole? Trying to follow a man who seemed not to have thought of waiting for her, and who had now completely disappeared.

There was no choice now but to follow in Oliver's general direction and hope to pick up his tracks.

If Emily had been able to recognize where she was in the midst of this white-out, she would have realized Oliver had only skied forty feet away to where they had begun their lesson the day before. Finally she found him, his red ski jacket a beacon in the mist. She stopped beside him and told him that he'd damn well better look after her, that if he set off alone again she would never forgive him, and he apologized and after that stayed close.

In the end, Emily realized that as long as she followed Oliver and stuck to his tracks she was not going to ski over a precipice, and that softer snow meant slushier, slower snow that gave her time to regain her balance after each turn. With barely anyone else around, and silence but for the scrape and push of their own skis, or the occasional sound of their voices, Emily even began to enjoy herself again.

But she still didn't know why she was there. Oliver made little attempt actually to teach her anything and no further attempt to touch her and eventually, after half an hour or so, impatience started to build inside her again. Why had it been so important to go out together, if they weren't even going to talk? She was tired of trying to catch up with him, of feeling that he was always just out of reach.

'OK?' he asked her as she pulled up just above him.

'Just about.'

'Thanks for coming. I'm glad you did.'

She nodded.

He came side-stepping the few feet up the slope so that he was closer to her and she could look into his golden eyes, see the dent on the bridge of his nose where his sunglasses had been. He carefully edged his skis between hers so that he was standing very close.

'OK?' he asked again.

She shook her head miserably, then looked back at him and slowly he came towards her and she knew he was finally going to kiss her. He did, so gently that she hardly knew it had begun before he had moved away. *It's got to be more than that. Please after so long, let it be better than that.*

'Because you look miserable,' he said, sliding further away from her.

'I could do with a brandy.' She forced a smile.

And so they skied off again, Oliver leading the way to the mountain café they'd been to the day before. It was usually heaving with hundreds of skiers, but now there were only three other couples inside. Oliver bought two brandies and they chose a corner of the room well away from everybody else.

'You were great,' Oliver told her. 'You've done really well.'

'Thank you.' She shrugged. 'I had a good teacher.'

He took her hand across the little round table. 'I'm really glad you came out with me today. Sam was being a prat.'

She shook her head, looking down at her hand in his. 'He wasn't. He was worried I couldn't cope with the weather, that's all.'

'Sam wasn't worried about the weather,' Oliver told her. 'He was worried about me.'

'Why do you say that?'

He leaned forward across the table and kissed her again.

At first she didn't respond, then she felt his hand tighten on hers and tipped up her face to his, and let out an involuntary little sigh.

As if it was the signal he'd been waiting for, Oliver stood up and pulled her to her feet, knocking over his brandy glass so that it smashed on the floor. He wrapped his arms around her and pulled her hard against him, kissing her mouth, her cheeks, her ears, and she kissed him back, feeling light-headed, as if she wasn't really there, as if it wasn't really happening.

'So you *do* want me. Oh, yes,' Oliver murmured, his breath hot against her cheek. 'My sexy little fox. I think you want me.' He held her face in his hands. 'And I want you, Emily. I could take you back to my bed right now. I've been waiting for you for weeks. But I can wait some more, I've always wanted you,' he corrected himself hastily. He saw the look on her face. 'I can wait until you're ready. I won't rush you. I'll wait for as long as it takes.'

He kissed her again, his tongue driving inside her mouth, his teeth knocking against hers. But she couldn't give herself up to it. After all the waiting, all the longing, it still didn't feel real. She certainly didn't feel the electricity, the excitement that she'd expected. His kissing was clumsy rather than passionate, nothing like she remembered, and when he'd said she was his sexy little fox she'd had to fight not to push him away.

'Shall we go home?' Oliver asked, kissing the top of her head. His husky voice still suggested bed.

Go home to face the raised eyebrows and the smirks . . . and Sam.

It had to be done. 'Yes,' she nodded.

Unaware that anything might be wrong, Oliver dropped some euros on the table, took her hand and they left the café together.

When they reached the lift station and climbed the wooden steps to the top, it was to discover that the bubble had stopped running and wasn't expected to begin working again for at least half an hour.

'It's OK,' Oliver reassured her. 'Thirty minutes isn't long. I'm not even going to try to persuade you to ski down the last bit. We can wait.'

She looked at him standing beside her, his hand in hers and thought, *I just need more time to get used to him, that's all*. Perhaps it was bound to be a disappointment after so long.

'There is no way I *could* ski down the last bit,' she admitted. 'I'd rather stay here all night.'

They sat down on a wooden bench running the length of the station, Oliver with his arm clamped around her, neither of them talking but Oliver tapping his foot on the wooden floor, obviously more impatient to get back to the chalet than she was. Apart from the bubble operator, there was nobody else there.

When, thirty minutes later, the bubble still hadn't restarted, Oliver changed tack.

'Are you sure you don't want to ski down? We could be waiting here for hours.'

'What's the big hurry?'

He shrugged, looking at her, starting to smile. 'I want to tell everyone about you and me.'

'No!' she cried.

'What's wrong with that?'

'You don't want to tell *everyone*, you want to tell Sam. You don't care about the others but you want him to know.'

'Yes, I do. I want to put him straight.'

'You're awful,' she told him.

'No, I'm not.' He touched her cheek. 'I want the world – and Sam – to know that you're my girl.' He watched her reaction. 'And stop looking so happy about it.'

She made herself smile.

Ten minutes later, seeing that the snow was starting to come down harder and harder, she changed her mind. 'Show me the way home,' she said. 'I'll come with you if you promise to go slowly.'

'I've looked at the map and it should be really easy,' Oliver told her. 'Every run we have to do is green and we can trek through the trees just behind the chalet and ski right down to the front door. We'll be fine.'

But Oliver's impatience to get them home meant that despite his promise he skied faster than Emily could manage safely. The cloud was thick, and the snow was falling and it was very hard to see where she was going. All at once she was scared as well as miserable. What was she doing? she found herself thinking again and again, in between bellowing at Oliver to slow down. How could she have got herself into such a mess?

'We have to keep going,' Oliver called out to her for the fifth time now, looking as irritated with her as she was with him. 'It's only going to get more difficult. It will get dark and then how will we find our way back through the woods? We're going to be here all night if we don't get a move on.'

'I thought Magine was close. I thought you said it was a few easy runs and then the woods and then we'd be home,' she retorted.

'I did,' Oliver told her. 'Keep going.'

At long last they reached the woods. Again Oliver waited for Emily to catch him up and then led the way in, pushing his way past the branches of the pine trees and holding them so they didn't snap back in her face. The woods seemed pitch dark after the white world outside, but once they were used to the change of light, visibility was better than out on the mountainside. They made their way, half sliding, half tramping, moving slowly along a silent, spooky path, both of them concentrating too hard to talk.

'Go in front for a bit,' Oliver suggested after ten minutes. 'Take it at your pace.' He stopped and side-stepped off the path so that she could pass him and take up the lead.

She did so gratefully, keeping the twinkling lights of Magine as her bearing. Being in front was much easier and she began to go faster and faster, until it was Oliver calling out for her to slow down, but still she didn't stop. Not until she slid straight into a single strand of barbed wire that hooked her exactly at eye level and held her fast, bringing her to a sudden, horrible halt. She jerked her head backwards in reflex and felt her skin tear.

'I've cut my eye.' She said it so matter-of-factly that Oliver wasn't prepared for the thick red blood, creeping between her fingers and falling in fast, fat drops onto the snow.

He unclipped his boots and was swiftly at her side. 'Let me see. Take your hand away.'

'No.' She could taste the blood in her mouth, feel it running down her right cheek.

'It's barbed wire,' Oliver said incredulously. 'There's a strand of barbed wire between these trees. Who the fuck would leave wire here? What a fucking stupid thing to do.'

'Perhaps farmers graze sheep here in the summer, perhaps it's to stop them wandering off.' Her eye was cut and she was talking about local farming practices.

He stared at her hand held to her face. 'We have to keep going. You need a doctor, Emily.'

No! she wanted to bellow then. She hated that it was Oliver witnessing what was happening to her. She didn't want it to be him. She didn't want him looking at her face, have him be the one to tell her what he could see there. She wanted her mother. She wanted her mother there to look after her.

And then she thought that it wasn't her mother she wanted either. She wanted the one person who she knew could comfort her, who would be able to look after her and make her feel better. She wanted Sam. She desperately wanted Sam. She wanted to be with Sam. All she wanted was to get back to Magine and tell him so.

With that realization she could hardly bear to speak to Oliver. With her hand still stubbornly clamped over her eye, she became hell-bent on getting back to Magine as fast as she could.

Oliver followed her quietly. Perhaps sensing that he'd lost her, that it was over before it had even begun. As they walked into the empty village he caught her up and took her arm.

'Do you think this is my fault?'

'No, I don't.'

'Then stop, just for a second, Emily. Please.'

She stopped and turned, and looked at him, one hand still held to her face.

'I want to hug you. I want to make it better.'

She gave him a wobbly smile. 'And I want to get back to the chalet.'

He let his arms fall to his sides. 'It's Sam, isn't it?' he exploded. 'You want to get back to Sam.'

'What is this obsession with Sam?' She stared back at him, aware that this was a strange time to choose for a fight. 'This is not a bloody competition, Oliver. I am not a prize.'

'Why Sam?'

'It's nothing to do with Sam. If Sam wasn't there it still wouldn't be you,' she cried, as blood again seeped from beneath her hand.

Oliver saw it. 'I'm sorry, Emily,' he sighed. 'I can't believe I'm doing this, arguing when this has happened to you. I'm behaving so badly.'

'Oliver,' she said pleadingly. 'No, you're not. It's me not you.'

He shook his head. 'We'll talk about it another time. All we should be doing now is getting you home.'

At the chalet he moved in front of her to hammer on the front door while Emily waited, her boots still done up, suddenly too weak and shaky even to take them off.

But it was Holly and Caitlin and Leon who raced to the door in response to Oliver's call, not Sam.

Caitlin took one look at Emily, standing awkwardly in the darkness, one bloodstained mittened hand over her face, and took control. She padded out into the snow in her socks and took Emily's arm, helped her keep her balance while she bent down and undid Emily's boots. She led her inside, telling Holly to fetch a bowl of warm water and TCP and some cotton wool, pulled out a chair in the kitchen and pushed Emily gently into it, touching the hand still clamped over her face.

'Where's Sam?' Emily asked.

'Let me see,' Caitlin gently insisted.

Emily slowly removed her hand and looked up at her, immediately flinching at the cold raw air that took the place of her warm dark glove. She tentatively opened her poor, swollen, bloody right eye and found that she could still see.

Without flinching, without showing any sign that it was a nasty cut, Caitlin took a ball of cotton wool, smiled reassuringly at Emily, dipped it into the water and slowly and gently started to clear away the blood and, as she wiped, she told Emily what she could see.

The wire had cut Emily's lid vertically, through both her upper and her lower eyelashes. There was a tiny flap of skin on Emily's lower lid where the barb had torn. It was clear that Emily had closed her eyes at the moment of contact and her eyelids had done their job. Her lid was very swollen and she'd probably have a black eye in the morning, but otherwise it looked as if there was no serious harm done. Emily also had a cut across her nose which she hadn't noticed but, now that Caitlin mentioned it, she felt the pain there for the first time.

'Where's Sam?' Emily asked for the second time.

'He's gone,' Caitlin said. 'Having told Oliver *he* wasn't allowed to go off with other friends, we find that now Sam has done exactly that. Can you believe it?'

'Who's he with?'

'People he knows who came over from Valorias. He brought them over to the chalet for tea and they've driven him back to their resort. We were going to drive down and join them there tonight. But – ' Caitlin smiled – 'obviously we're not going to do that now. Not with you like this.'

'You can go. Of course you can. I'm fine.'

'I don't think so.'

'But someone has to go,' Emily cried, 'because someone has to bring Sam back.'

'I'll go,' Holly told her from the corner of the kitchen where she was making tea. 'It'll have to be me as I'm the only one insured to drive the jeep.'

Later it was agreed that Leon and Oliver would accompany Holly, and Caitlin would stay to keep Emily company.

A couple of hours later the shock hit Emily good and hard. She felt battered and shattered. She lay on the sofa in front of the fire with a glass of red wine and let Caitlin cook her some pasta for supper.

'Bad day for you, wasn't it?' Caitlin said as she brought the food through.

Emily nodded, on the verge of tears. Then she grinned

sadly instead. 'A very bad day. And I don't think Oliver would say it was much fun for him, either.'

'A bad day for Oliver won't do him any harm. Bit of rejection would be good for him.'

Emily knew that Caitlin understood exactly what she was saying. But she needed to talk and explain nevertheless, to run through the moment when it had all begun and the moment when it had all gone wrong.

'We all knew,' Caitlin confessed. 'We knew that this holiday was what you needed. That you had to spend time with him.'

Emily nodded. 'I did.'

'So we set you up.' Caitlin wasn't sure Emily understood what she was trying to say. 'We brought you here. We planned it all.'

'You did?'

Caitlin nodded. 'Do you mind?'

'Do I mind? I don't mind that you did that, no. All I mind about is Sam. I mind terribly about Sam.'

'What do you mean?' Caitlin asked gently.

'That I've wasted so much time over Oliver, I've probably ended up losing Sam.'

'You've done nothing wrong.'

'But I did, I did. I chose Oliver. Sam didn't want me to go out with him this afternoon. He asked me not to, and we both knew it was a kind of test. Oliver or Sam. And I went. I had to see. I couldn't trust my instincts.'

'Big deal! So what?' Caitlin laughed. 'He's a big boy. Sam will come around. Leave it to us. We can sort out Sam, just you watch.'

'No, don't,' Emily said tiredly. 'No more sorting out, please. It's the wrong time and anyway, it's up to me now. I'll talk to him tonight.'

But Sam, Holly, Oliver and Leon didn't make it back that night. While Caitlin and Emily talked, the snow came down fast, inches falling every hour, burying cars, roads, everything, and blocking off the road from Valorias to Magine.

The next morning it was still snowing, isolating Magine completely. Lower down in Valorias, the others could do nothing to help Emily and Caitlin and it was agreed, over a mobile phone call between Emily and Holly, that Leon, Oliver, Sam and Holly should go ahead and catch the train from Valorias and their flight back to London. Caitlin and Emily would have to stay put, pack for the others and wait for the snow to be cleared.

Then, on Tuesday morning, when they should all have been back in England, Emily and Caitlin woke to blinding sunshine and a brilliant blue sky. And with the sun came the snowploughs. They had left by lunchtime, managing to get seats on the afternoon flight from Geneva, and were back in London by the end of the day.

17

Six weeks after returning from Magine, Emily had moved to Cornwall. She took the lease on the shop in Humble Street two days after she arrived, after she had checked with Arthur that he wouldn't mind her moving into Dodger Point, just for as long as it took to find herself somewhere of her own to live. She had her eye on a cottage in St Brides itself, somewhere close enough to be able to walk to the shop, and close enough to Arthur's without camping on his doorstep. With Jennifer on the scene, and the two of them so obviously happy in each other's company, Emily did not want to get in their way for longer than she had to.

And thank God for Jennifer – Jennifer with her golden touch and amazing eye and her willingness to throw herself at a challenge. Since Emily had tentatively enlisted her help she was slowly, steadily transforming the little shop in Humble Street, leaving Emily to make the big decisions, but forever coming up with quirky wonderful touches that Emily would never have thought of, and that she knew were going to make all the difference.

She watched Jennifer now, painting a second coat on the walls, the rhythmic swish of her brush making the rough-cut diamond on her left hand twinkle in the light. Saltwater would open in two days' time.

Since Emily had come back to Cornwall, she had gone into overdrive to collect enough stock to open the shop in time for the start of the summer. Throughout it all, Jennifer had been at her side several times a week and they had become good friends. Opinionated and forceful when she was talking about something she knew about – and Jennifer knew about how Emily should tackle Saltwater – the reticence that Emily had encountered at the Pelican had evaporated, leaving only a disconcerting ability to go occasionally silent and a refreshing quirkiness that meant she was always fun to have around.

Jennifer had been sweetly untroubled by Emily's sudden arrival into Arthur's life, had had no problem at all with Emily moving into Dodger Point – she had known that it was a temporary measure, that once Emily had Saltwater up and running she would be looking for somewhere to live – and Emily was only embarrassed that she had taken a while to appreciate what Arthur had seen straight away. Two weeks after Emily moved into Dodger Point, Arthur and Jennifer announced their engagement.

Jennifer proved great to have around on a practical level, too. It was she who chose the stone-coloured paint for the walls, the exact shade of off-white for the stripped wooden floorboards, the deep red of the linen blinds in the window. And although Jennifer had left it to Emily to find most of the stock, she had such a good eye, and so many wonderful contacts, both in Cornwall and around the country, that Emily wondered what on earth she'd have done without her. Certainly, within a couple of weeks of taking on the lease Emily would have been on her knees in despair, because now that Saltwater had become a reality she understood how naive she'd been to think she could possibly have set up the shop without any help. It wasn't just an eye for colour and a knack for display that was needed, she realized belatedly, it was having the right contacts: knowing, or knowing of, designers and artists, handbag makers, candlestick makers, ceramicists, glass blowers, perfumiers to call on. It was knowing where the woollen mill was in Wales that sold the softest, prettiest blankets, how to track down a new scent that nobody else had discovered, which trade fairs to attend, and more besides. Jennifer knew about these things and Emily did not, and Emily remembered their bad start and shuddered at the thought of how she might have alienated her completely. It was in the back of Emily's mind to ask Jennifer to go into partnership with her, knowing that, in the longer term, she'd never be able to both maintain the stock levels and run the shop day to day. But that was something she was keeping to herself for now, at least until the opening day was behind her.

Together Jennifer and Arthur had come up with a list of local people she had to invite to the launch, and Emily again had to acknowledge how wrong she'd been, about both of them this time, not just about Jennifer. Why was it that she'd thought Arthur had few friends? Where had that patronizing preconception come from, that hardly any interesting people lived in Cornwall, that they only arrived in summer?

Among the names on Arthur's list was Sam's. She hadn't seen him since she'd returned to England. Having

flown back into Heathrow, she'd left Caitlin at the underground and got back to her flat to find a message from
him waiting for her, expressing concern about her eye,
and she'd at once called him back and told him that she
was OK.

She had put the phone down, knowing that it was up
to her now and understanding why Sam was not about to
make another hasty move in her direction. But instead of
running out of the door to catch the first available train to
Cornwall, she knew that she needed to sit tight for a
while, wait for the right moment and not make a move
towards him until her head had cleared from the fiasco of
Oliver, until she knew it was the right time.

Once she'd moved to Cornwall, it would have been
easy to drive over to Trevissey to see him but she hadn't
and Sam hadn't come to see her either. Instead she'd spent
the weeks driving all over the country finding her stock.
She also knew that she hadn't seen Sam because they were
both biding their time. There was a calmness there when
she thought about him, because she knew that he was
waiting for her to come to him, And as the weeks passed
by, and spring came and with it the opening of Saltwater
drew closer, Emily knew that the time to see him again
was drawing closer too.

She hadn't spoken to Oliver since her return. She was
surprised at how little she thought of him, finding that the
memories of him faded as swiftly as the bruising to her
eye, aware that she hadn't known him at all, relieved that
she could let him slip from her life without a backward

glance, that neither of them had ever said or done anything to make that slipping away more difficult.

Instead she felt a readiness to begin, an enthusiasm for
the future in Cornwall that she had never felt in London.
She was finally in the frame of mind that Arthur had told
her she should strive for, full of confidence to go with
what she wanted, whenever she found it.

Saltwater would open on her birthday. Holly, Caitlin
and Leon, and Rachel were all coming down to the opening, which they hoped would turn into a spontaneous
party for her afterwards. Only Jo-Jo, still filming in Italy,
was unable to make it. Her friends hoped, of course, that
it might be the occasion on which Emily and Sam got
together, but there were no plans or schemes to help things
along, none of the desperation in the air that there'd been
throughout the discussions about Oliver.

On the day of the opening, 25 May, Emily was in
Saltwater at seven in the morning, adding the final touches
to the shop. The second coat of paint had dried overnight
and a glass cabinet that had arrived the evening before
could finally be put into place. Emily spent the first hour
washing it and then filling it. The top shelf with scent
bottles, very modern with gobstopper glass tops in pale
blues and greens, and the bottom shelves with jewellery.
Nothing yet from La Coccinelle – there had been no time
for M. Gérard to make her pieces – but instead a range
of items from other jewellers, some who had provided
just five or six, others who had been able to supply a
good deal more. The pièce de résistance was a series of

necklaces from a jeweller in Ludlow in Shropshire, tracked down, of course, by Jennifer.

Emily worked hard, filling up and arranging the shop, leaving it only to buy a bacon sandwich halfway through the morning, enjoying being alone with her radio, the sunlight streaming in through her windows. Throughout the morning she had deliveries of more stock, glasses for the champagne – she'd pushed the boat out and ordered some, deciding the extravagance was necessary. And she had hired a local catering company to serve it and also to supply plates of canapés.

At around noon a bouquet arrived from Arthur and Jennifer, and then another from Rachel, Holly, Jo-Jo and Caitlin. And then, a short while later, the doorbell rang again and she looked up and saw Sam outside.

She stood up, feeling her heart start to pound, and went to let him in. The key was stiff in the lock and she struggled with it, all the time looking at him through the glass door, standing there. And all she could think was that here he was at last, her Sam, her sweet, lovely Sam and she wondered how she could have stayed away from him for so long.

'You've picked Chelsea Flower Show week for your opening. Can you imagine what my father said when I told him I was going to a party instead?'

'Oh, no!' She started to laugh. 'I'm so sorry. You shouldn't have missed it. I'd have understood.'

'He understood too, when I told him whose party it was.'

Sam handed her three perfect roses, pale blue tissue

paper wrapped around their stems, the flowers pale pink at the edges, getting slightly darker towards the centre, each a perfect cup filled with gorgeous, gently scented petals. He came closer and stroked one with a fingertip, then bent his head to smell them.

'They remind me of you,' he said.

'Thank you, Sam. They're beautiful.' And they were – the most beautiful roses she had ever seen.

'And now I have to go,' Sam said apologetically. 'I wanted to give you these now, before I saw you again tonight, but I really can't stay.'

'I'd like to come back with you, you know how much I want to see Trevissey again, now that it's all coming alive. I've been waiting for the summer.' She laughed nerously and there was suddenly a formality in her voice.

'So that's what you've been waiting for,' he teased. 'Well, the sun is out. It's hot. The roses will be opening as we speak. Come whenever you want to.'

'Tomorrow?'

He nodded, then looked around the shop. 'And this looks fantastic. I can't believe it's the same place. You'll have customers beating down the door.'

'Sam,' she said, not knowing quite what to say, but acutely aware that it was up to her this time. 'I've missed you. I've been thinking about you, all the time I've been here.' And then she added in a flustered rush, 'I'm so pleased to see you again.'

He looked back at her, warmth, love, suddenly there in his eyes. He took two steps towards her.

'And I've missed you too. More than you could ever

imagine. But now, dearest Emily, I have to go. I really have to go. And I'll see you properly tonight,' he said, leaving her giddy with longing for him. And then, before she could stop him, he had gone, saying only that he'd be back for the party.

At Dodger Point later that afternoon she sat for a while in the kitchen in feverish excitement. Arthur, listening to her, knew exactly what it was about, knowing it wasn't her party she was anticipating, not the party that was stopping her from eating or keeping her talking and talking and talking.

Then, finally, when Jennifer arrived and Arthur packed Emily off to change, she lay on her bed in her little room at the back of the house, letting her mind still. Then she got up again, stripped off her clothes and stood naked, looking at the marble whiteness of her body in the mirror, turning to look at her bottom, at the line of her thighs, at the way the whiteness gradually changed to a golden brown around her shoulders and down her arms and she wondered what Sam might make of her, whether he would like what he saw, what it would be like to make love with him. Not just how it would feel to let go, at last, but physically, what it would feel like, whether it would hurt, whether it was possible that it might be wonderful first time around. She knew it rarely was, remembered Caitlin's and Holly's warnings, and yet, if it was with Sam, whatever happened, surely it couldn't be a disappointment?

She pulled open the door of the small single wardrobe and pulled out the dress she was going to wear that she'd found in Notting Hill with Holly, just before she left

London for the last time. A sea green halter-neck dress, the top half fitting close, made from thick stretchy silk which floated out around her legs.

Emily stood at the edge of the crowd at her party, holding a glass of warm champagne, searching through the faces for Sam. She had kept an eye out for him since the beginning, and an hour later he still hadn't arrived. All around her the noise of her party swooped and dived. The doors and windows had long since been thrown open and people spilled out onto the usually quiet street, the lights and noise on that glimmering evening attracting the attention of the few passers-by.

It was going well, if noise and numbers proved anything. Having sat out the first half-hour with Arthur and Jennifer and the girls from London, wondering if anybody was going to show up, suddenly Emily found the room was full and now still more people were arriving. She presumed they would last as long as the drink did.

At seven Arthur took it upon himself to propose a toast to the success of Saltwater. Then Emily stood up and thanked them all, thanked Arthur and Jennifer most of all and all the while scanned the room for Sam. Then, just as she was finishing speaking, she saw him standing in the corner of the room. When she caught his eye he smiled at her, lighting her up so that the grumbling headache she hadn't even been aware of instantly lifted, the panic subsided, and she was transformed from looking decidedly half-hearted about the whole evening to glowing, beautiful, mesmerizing.

When she had finished thanking everybody for coming, Sam moved across the room to her side and told her she was brilliant, kissed her hard and hugged her tightly so that she could feel his heart beating fast against hers with all the promise of what was to come.

Emily glided through the rest of the party. On a high, knowing he was waiting for her, savouring the anticipation, as she circulated and did a perfect job of looking after her guests.

And then, almost abruptly, the party was over, the tail-enders straggling out of the door, talking about restaurants and catching last orders, and Emily was left with just the girls and Arthur and Jennifer, and Sam.

'So,' said Caitlin, draining her glass of champagne, 'who's clearing up?'

'Not me,' said Emily. 'The caterers.'

'That's all I need to know. It's not down to us. So we can go and find something to eat?'

'Good idea,' Emily said, even though she couldn't imagine eating, going along with it even though she was thinking, *no. No, I do not want to do that. Not at all.*

One by one they filed out of the shop. Emily locked up and they set off down the street.

'I've called the Pelican,' Arthur told her. 'We've got a table at ten thirty.'

'Great.' Emily smiled. 'Lovely idea.'

But she and Sam never made it to the Pelican. The others ambled slowly through the streets, and it wasn't until they reached Arthur's and Holly's cars that they realized Emily and Sam weren't with them.

18

In the car Sam and Emily didn't speak, but he kept hold of her hand all the way to Trevissey.

Outside the house Sam stopped the engine and Emily opened the door of the car and stepped out, waiting for Sam to come around and join her, and then together they walked through the archway cut into the wall and into the gardens. Feeling the grass beneath her feet, she stopped, bent down and slipped off her sandals. The grass was spongy and cool between her toes.

Silently Sam slipped his jacket off his shoulders, passed it to her and she pulled it around herself gratefully. Emily could tell that there was a purpose to Sam's stride. He was heading somewhere specific. In the moonlight they passed the huge greenhouses but he led her past them, then cut around the side of the house until finally he stopped and turned to her, and she knew that whatever he was bringing her to see was here.

She looked around but could see nothing different. They were standing beside the old pear tree where Sam had lifted her up and she'd found the platform high in the branches.

'What is it?' she asked, curious.

'Damn it for not being daylight,' he replied, 'but still I had to show you tonight. It wouldn't be the same if you saw it tomorrow. You have to see it tonight, on your birthday, on the night of your party for Saltwater.'

'But what is it?'

He took her hand and led her over to the pear tree, put his hands around her waist and once again lifted her up. This time she found there was an old rope looped around the trunk of the tree and she used it to pull herself up and onto the platform.

She stood in her dress and her bare feet and Sam's jacket, looking out across the grounds, to where one garden ended and another began, and still she could not see what it was he wanted to show her.

Then Sam pulled himself up behind her and slipped his arms around her waist. It felt so indescribably perfect that she found she had no voice to ask him again.

He crossed his arms around her. 'Do you see those arches dividing this garden from the next?' he asked. 'Do you see those seven arches?' She nodded. 'There's a rose growing up each of them. It's the same rose that I brought you this afternoon, only none of those is flowering yet. Not quite yet.'

She nodded again. She could see where he meant now. In the light of the moon she could just make out the shoots twisting and spiralling, and, high up on one arch, a single rose was starting to flower.

'That rose is very special,' Sam told her. 'It's one of the three roses that we're launching at Chelsea this year.'

'It's beautiful.'

'And the reason Dad was so cross about your party being tonight wasn't because he wanted me at Chelsea. It was when I explained that *you* couldn't be there that he was really put out.'

'Why?'

'Because I've taken a leap of faith.'

She leaned back against him, still not sure what he was going to say, yet knowing it was about her.

'It's your rose, Emily,' he told her. 'It's called Emily, after you. And usually, if a rose is being named after someone, and the someone hasn't died, then they turn up at the flower show to celebrate. But then, to be fair, usually the recipient of such an honour knows about it in advance. And I didn't tell you,' he went on. 'I thought it would be nicest if you found out today, on your birthday, on the night of your party. I gave the roses to you this afternoon but I managed not to tell you their name because I wanted you to see them here, now, with me. It's why I had to leave so fast.' He grinned at her. 'I knew if I stayed another second I'd tell you everything that I wanted to save for tonight.'

She turned in his arms. 'Oh, Sam, how can you have done that for me? I think that's the most lovely thing that's ever happened to me.'

And before Sam could stop her, she'd leapt straight out of the pear tree, landing in a heap on the grass below.

'Emily, you are stark raving mad,' Sam called, immediately jumping down after her, relieved to see her getting to her feet, laughing at his concern.

'I knew it was a soft landing,' she told him before she set off again. 'I guessed I'd survive. I want to see Emily close up.'

At the arches he reached up and pulled the single flower down so that she could look at it.

'How beautiful it is,' she said, reaching forward and burying her nose in its soft folds.

'Read the catalogue entry before you thank me too much,' he said with a grin. 'You might change your mind.'

'Thank you, thank you, thank you,' she said, hugging him tightly to her.

He hugged her back, then bent and kissed her gently.

She looked up at him, watching his eyes. 'What do I do now, Sam?' she asked. 'If a girl gets a rose named after her, I don't know but I think there must be some kind of payback due, don't you?'

'Kiss me,' he told her and she stretched up and did what he said.

'And then what do we do?'

'And then you put your arm around the back of my neck, like this,' he murmured against her face, lifting her arm, and she wound it around his neck and clung on to him. 'And then I kiss you again.' She stretched her other arm around his neck. 'And I kiss you again and again and again,' Sam said, 'and I never stop, I just keep kissing you for ever.'

They stood in the moonlit gardens, Emily in bare feet, Sam in his shirt, grass stains on his knees, kissing each other until kissing was no longer enough. Then Emily took his hand and led him underneath the arch of Emily roses to the little summer house.

When they got there, it was Emily rather than Sam

who jumped up the step and tried the handle of the door. It opened, and it seemed natural and inevitable that she should lead him inside. Stacked up along one wall were deckchairs and sun loungers and along the other were the cushions for them. Without waiting for Sam to say or do anything, Emily walked over, picked up an armful of cushions and chucked them on the floor, then sat down and looked up at him. 'Come here,' she said, reaching out for him.

He sat down beside her and she could tell that he was unsure about this moment.

'It's all because of the rose,' she joked. 'Look what happens when you give a girl a rose.'

'Emily, Emily, Emily,' he groaned, burying his face in her neck.

'Yes, Sam,' she said, holding him close, 'I know you're concerned about doing the right thing. And you *are* doing the right thing. We are doing so much the right thing. This is what I've been waiting for. This is how it should be. You don't have to worry, because I know it is. I know what I want to do, and that's to be with you. You're everything I've been waiting for, everything I ever wanted to find.'

He touched his hand to her face and then kissed her again, tenderly, softly, and she could feel herself opening out for him, long slow ripples of lust flowing through her. She slipped her hands under his shirt, feeling his ribs rising and falling, then moved down to the flatness of his belly.

'Don't talk,' she told him. 'You don't need to tell me anything. You don't need to tell me that you love me, you certainly don't need to tell me that you'll marry me. You don't even need to tell me you'll respect me in the morning.'

He said nothing, just reached for the tie at the back of her neck with infinitely gentle hands. He moved his fingers slowly down her back, then around to the soft flesh of her stomach and to the curve of her hips. She pulled her dress over her head and then grabbed him to her, finding she wanted to push against him, be passionate and rough, not gentle or sweet any more.

Later, Sam got up and she heard him rummaging in the corner of the summer house and then felt the delicious warmth of blankets being carefully draped over her, and then, with his arms around her, she fell asleep.

As dawn broke across the gardens she woke up again and beside her, almost to the second, Sam woke up too, saw her there beside him and smiled a smile of such sweet happiness that she felt her eyes burn with tears.

'I can't promise any croissants for breakfast,' he said, kissing her. 'But I can run to the house and get some toast and coffee.'

She snuggled deep under the blankets, keeping her arms around him. She wondered if she was different. If what had happened had changed her. But she knew that it hadn't at all. It wasn't who she was that had changed, it was how she led her life. Because from now on her life had Sam in it. She wasn't alone.

'Everyone told me it's not so good the first time,' she said.

'And what do you think?'

She turned in his arms and kissed him. 'I think that I need something to compare it with.'

Epilogue

Emily King (Heritage rose) – 'Unique Blanche' ×
Hybrid tea 'Monique'
× 'Constance Spry'

There are some roses that one is rather doubtful about introducing to the garden and at first Emily seems such a rose. Truly beautiful, its colour combines a mixture of pale pinks and gold. Emily is capable of considerable climbing feats, especially into trees but has a tendency to ramble in the opposite direction to where you were hoping, especially when exposed to the cold. Hates the snow, which can affect the bloom, but in its favoured habitat richly rewarding, a flawless, perfect rose with a wonderful heady scent. Climber 5′5″.

Acknowledgements

Special thanks to Jill Bevan, Charles Davies, Michelle Scorah, Petra Reitmayerova, Louise Cripps and Louise Voss, Chris Manby, Alex Roads and Miranda Fricker, and to my Barnes and Unicorn friends for all their advice and enthusiasm and to everyone else who came up with great reasons for staying a virgin (but didn't act on them). Also to Caroline Gardner, particularly for pointing me in the direction of the Cockpit Studios and for having a shop as gorgeous as Fig, and to David Austin for showing me around his wonderful nurseries in Albrighton and for taking the trouble to explain the intricacies of cross-breeding roses to me. His excellent books, especially *Old Roses and English Roses* (Antique Collectors' Club), were also very helpful. As was John Armstrong's book *Conditions of Love* (Allen Lane) and *Been There, Haven't Done That – A Virgin's Memoir* by Tara McCarthy (Time Warner International). Huge thanks to everyone at Pan, who once again have made publishing a book such fun, especially to Imogen Tayler and Lucy Henson. Thanks again to Jo Frank for her great editorial eye and such wise words. And lastly

Louise Harwood

thanks to my family, especially Tom and Jack, and, of course, most of all to Ant.

Six Reasons to Stay a Virgin is one of several new novels that include the name Nessa O'Neill following a charity bid at an auction in support of War Child.